Praise for

Summer at

"A great summer beach read."   *—PopSugar*

"A perfect beach read about rediscovering oneself, second chances, and the power of healing."   *—Harlequin Junkie*

It Started with Christmas

"This sweet small-town romance will leave readers feeling warm all the way through."   *—Publishers Weekly*

The Summer House

"Hale's rich and slow-building romance is enhanced by the allure of the North Carolina coast... North Carolina's beautiful Outer Banks are the perfect setting for this sweet, poignant romance, and authentic characters and a riveting story make it a keeper worth savoring."
                              —Publishers Weekly (Starred Review)

"Like a paper and ink version of a chick flick... gives you the butterflies and leaves you happy and hopeful."   *—Due South*

Christmas Wishes and Mistletoe Kisses

"[A] tender treat that can be savored in any season."
                              —Publishers Weekly (Starred Review)

"[Jenny] Hale's impeccably executed contemporary romance is the perfect gift for readers who love sweetly romantic love stories imbued with all the warmth and joy of the holiday season."   *—Booklist*

Christmas
at
silver falls

ALSO BY JENNY HALE

Christmas Wishes and Mistletoe Kisses
The Summer House
It Started with Christmas
Summer at Firefly Beach
A Christmas to Remember
Summer by the Sea

Christmas at silver falls

JENNY HALE

FOREVER

New York   Boston

This book is a work of fiction. Names, characters, places, and incidents are the product of the author's imagination or are used fictitiously. Any resemblance to actual events, locales, or persons, living or dead, is coincidental.

Copyright © 2019 by Jenny Hale

Cover design by Debbie Clement.
Cover images © Shutterstock.
Cover copyright © 2021 by Hachette Book Group, Inc.

Hachette Book Group supports the right to free expression and the value of copyright. The purpose of copyright is to encourage writers and artists to produce the creative works that enrich our culture.

The scanning, uploading, and distribution of this book without permission is a theft of the author's intellectual property. If you would like permission to use material from the book (other than for review purposes), please contact permissions@hbgusa.com. Thank you for your support of the author's rights.

Forever
Hachette Book Group
1290 Avenue of the Americas, New York, NY 10104
read-forever.com
twitter.com/readforeverpub

Originally published in trade paperback in 2019 by Bookouture. An imprint of Storyfire Ltd. Carmelite House 50 Victoria Embankment, London EC4Y 0DZ
First Grand Central Publishing Edition: September 2021

Forever is an imprint of Grand Central Publishing. The Forever name and logo are trademarks of Hachette Book Group, Inc.

The publisher is not responsible for websites (or their content) that are not owned by the publisher.

The Hachette Speakers Bureau provides a wide range of authors for speaking events. To find out more, go to www.hachettespeakersbureau.com or call (866) 376-6591.

Library of Congress Cataloging-in-Publication Data has been applied for.

ISBNs: 978-1-5387-0572-8 (trade paperback)

Printed in the United States of America

LSC-C

Printing 1, 2021

Christmas
at
silver falls

Chapter One

Scarlett Bailey clicked off the string of twinkle lights outside her apartment and clutched her mistletoe-print gift bags tightly as her father pulled up in his old truck, giving her a friendly wave on her way down the steps to greet him. All week, she'd thrown herself into Christmas shopping, focused on seeking out the most personal gifts for each of her family members, finding just the right wrapping paper, and adorning each present with sprigs of holly or little pine cones she'd found at the craft store. But as she stood amidst her pile of gifts now, she had to face the fact that, after this year, the holiday as she knew it would be changing. She may never have another Christmas at White Oaks Inn.

This was huge—she hadn't been able to confront the idea at all until this moment, while she wedged the last of the family Christmas presents into her dad's truck and climbed in. She couldn't even be sure if going through with this plan was the right thing to do. But she'd been outvoted. Over plates of Aunt Alice's maple-pear tarts with eggnog mousse, the Bailey family had made a decision on the matter, and she had to try to make the best of it.

The white puffball on her dad's Santa hat swung back and forth like a stuffed pendulum as he glanced over to her and then back to the road. He'd always worn the ruby-red fur hat with its pearl white trim and matching ball whenever they'd traveled to White Oaks for their annual family holiday gathering. It was a fond memory of Scarlett's. But today, it just didn't feel right.

They drove for five hours with barely a sound between them. Scarlett steadied the large package she'd been holding all the way there. It was something her dad had bought for her uncle Joe, wrapped in red and green plaid paper, a bow of cranberry ribbon securing it. It didn't fit in the back of the truck, so she'd kept it up front, a glaring reminder of the fact that Christmas was only five days away.

Scarlett's body sprang up and down with the movement of her father's truck tires along the unsteady mountain road they were climbing, propelling them deeper into the Great Smoky Mountains and closer to White Oaks Inn. Her anticipation was bittersweet.

She could still conjure up the image of Pappy, with his hands in the pockets of his red and black lumberjack-style coat, his shoulders raised and his elbows tucked near his body to combat the cold as he waited for them on the impressive front porch of the sprawling clapboard hotel. The painted wooden siding, bright white against the vegetation of the mountains surrounding it, looked like a pearl beside the falling snow, the east and west wings reaching out along the mountainside like two arms awaiting a hug.

Every year, when her father would pull up, before he drove around back to park in the inn's private lot for family, he'd roll down his window and wave. Pappy would nod, happiness radiating from his weathered face, and then head inside to let everyone know they'd arrived. Last year, Uncle Joe had taken Pappy's spot on the porch. Her uncle must have missed Pappy's greeting as much as Scarlett had. They'd all been so heartbroken to lose him, but they rallied around Gran that

Christmas and in the two years after. The last thing Pappy would've wanted was for her to be anything other than happy at Christmastime.

She gazed out the window at the blur of white surrounding them. The mountains ascended directly from the edge of the curving road and stretched into the sky, the trees barely visible under the snow-cover. She just couldn't fathom that this might be her last holiday in the magical place that had shaped who she was today; it would most likely be her *final* visit to the inn that her grandparents had run since before her father was even born.

And poor Gran had no idea what they'd all planned to do. She was about to be blindsided. The guilt of that swarmed Scarlett.

"You haven't spoken a word the entire five hours that we've been in the car, except once to say you needed to stop for a restroom break," her father said, gripping the wheel with one hand as he rounded a turn up the mountain easily, despite the deluge of snow, his four-wheel drive working overtime. "I wanted to let this sink in for you, but I'm dying to know how you're feeling." He rested a relaxed hand on the stick shift. For anyone else, the trip up the mountain was treacherous, but her father had made the journey so many times that he knew every bend in the road, every dip in the terrain.

"I know you don't agree with putting the inn on the market, Scarlett," he said, "but Gran can't handle running it without Pappy, and even if she could, White Oaks is struggling. Gran had to drop the room rates this past summer to entice people to choose White Oaks over those new resorts. Yet still she barely hit a third of the revenue she needs to keep it running. It's costing her more to stay open now than she's making. And, as we discussed during the family meeting last month, we don't even—collectively—have the kind of money she needs to keep it going."

In its prime, White Oaks Inn was a summer retreat for those searching for a shaded mountain reprieve from the relentless heat in the south. But with the development of resort-style mountain-living condos and inns popping up in nearby towns, White Oaks was having a difficult time keeping up with the demand for amenities. They didn't have on-site yoga studios, fly-fishing classes, hiking guides, Olympic-size swimming pools—none of the offerings the other locations had. And Gran refused to add those things.

"This is a place for rest," she'd said, when Scarlett had suggested a few upgrades on the phone the last time they'd spoken.

Scarlett knew that making major changes to the inn for it to become profitable would be a full-time job. And she'd have to convince Gran of each and every modification. Scarlett was the only one in the family who could take on this role, as she only had herself to worry about. She'd spent a long couple of years doing a job she hated, but she'd only just been given a new position as Marketing Manager at Electra Media. She was much happier, although the job took up more of her time. She had barely been able to get away for the Christmas holiday, much less run an inn. So while Scarlett didn't want to let the inn go, she knew that she would have to agree with the family's decision to sell it. It was the best financial option for Gran, even though she would certainly be devastated when she found out what they'd been planning. Nevertheless, Gran didn't have a choice. At the speed she was losing money, she'd go broke if she opposed the decision.

When the family had met, they'd decided it would be best to wait until after Christmas to tell her, so as not to spoil her holiday. While they wanted Gran to be part of the family discussion, they had to be very delicate about how to approach it with her. White Oaks Inn was an extremely special place to her. She'd bought it with Pappy and raised all her children there. Selling it wasn't something they could easily drop into conversation, so they'd decided to tell her while they were all present to give her support, *and* after they'd had one more Christmas to add to their wonderful memories over the years.

Scarlett realized she hadn't answered her father's question when he added, "I also know how much you love White Oaks and how hard this must be for you. But it's all we can do now."

"If we have to go through with this, I just hope a new buyer won't want to change it. I wish there was something else we could do…" Scarlett finally said. Christmas was the time when all the people in town rallied around one another, lifting everyone up. This didn't feel like Christmas. They were going to go through the motions of the annual Christmas party—they'd unwrap gifts; the entire family and all their friends in town were joining them—but Scarlett would know the whole time that after Christmas they had to drop that news on Gran, and she didn't think she'd be able to enjoy herself at all. Nor did she feel it was fair to Gran that they all knew this, but she did understand about the holiday—Christmas was Gran's favorite time of year, and it would be terrible to ruin it for her.

Scarlett took in a breath of cold air and let it out slowly to ease the tension in her shoulders. "Can we go the long route through Silver Falls on the way to White Oaks? Maybe it'll help me feel more like Christmas."

"Absolutely," her father said, changing course and taking the right side of the fork in the road, headed for town.

Silver Falls was nestled on the side of the mountain, with sweeping views of the valley below. It was named for the iridescent falls that cascaded down the mountain. The water whooshed past the wild hackberry, cherry, and pine trees that surrounded them. In the summer, Scarlett would swim in the river pools that collected under them, only coming out to have a snack. She'd make a little pile in her lap of wild chestnuts that grew in the area, crack them, and snack on them while sitting at the edge of the waterfalls, dipping her feet in to combat the heat.

Scarlett had always loved how she could see for miles, the river winding like a blue ribbon through the foliage. Silver Falls had a little park with a perfect panorama of the falls that attracted vacationers in the summer, but in the winter, they were just as beautiful: ice crystals clung to the rock behind the falling water, causing it to sparkle as if it were full of gemstones. She couldn't wait to see it again.

In the warmer months, Silver Falls was a bustling tourist spot with shops full of handmade goods, a local watering hole, antiques stalls, a little coffee shop, and a bookstore, but in the winter it was spectacular, and with lower visitor numbers it was always a time to celebrate for the locals. Anyone lucky enough to get up the mountain to visit at Christmastime would find the townspeople decorating to the nines for the holiday, keeping their doors open past closing time, and gathering together to celebrate their tight-knit community.

"Oh, look." Scarlett's dad pointed to the sign outside the only bar in town. It was actually named The Only Bar in Town, but referred to simply as "The Bar" by locals.

Scarlett read the sign and grinned for the first time all day: *Live music all weekend! Preston Meade! He'll be taking requests from everyone but Loretta.*

Even Loretta Fitzpatrick, who ran a local dating service, would laugh at that one. Scarlett and Loretta were the same age, and had spent many summers together. Loretta was a great listener, and she loved to hear all about Scarlett's love life as a teenager. They'd talk by the falls until the evening bugs in the woods were unbearable and they had to go in. Sometimes, they'd just move the conversation to the back garden at the inn until there was barely any light left in the sky. When it got too dark, Scarlett would ask her dad if she could take Loretta home in his old truck. Her favorite memories were driving back to the inn with nothing but the summer wind in her hair and the sound of the radio.

Since starting the agency, Loretta was always trying to find local musician Preston Meade's true love, throwing women his way any chance she got. The problem was that Preston was one of those people who could perform on stage, but in his personal life, he was an extremely private guy, working days at the town bank, where he had a small office in the back.

Everyone joked with him, saying he'd taken the job because he didn't have to speak to anyone. He was a good sport about it. His quiet demeanor never affected Loretta, though; she would bounce over to him, talking a mile a minute about someone she knew was the perfect person for him whenever he came into the bar, and he always respectfully humored her by nodding, when it was clear that he had no interest in whomever she had in mind. She'd step away to powder her nose and he'd disappear—sometimes completely, and other times to go on stage. It only seemed to fuel her determination to set him up. She'd scan the crowd, her eyes sparkling with interest.

"Why don't we stop in for a minute and see Cappy?"

"It would be nice to see him."

Scarlett had to admit that, despite her current conundrum with White Oaks and Gran, she was thrilled to stop in to The Bar to visit its owner, Cappy Bradshaw. She'd known him since she was a little girl. Having grown up with only her father—sadly, her mother had died of cancer when she was eleven—she'd always been her dad's shadow. They spent every summer and holiday in Silver Falls, and when he needed to let off a little steam and grab a beer, he'd taken her with him. Cappy's wife Jess had had a special place in the back room for her, and the two of them would talk while her father and Cappy caught up on the latest in sports or what was going on in town. Scarlett's time with Jess was one of the few opportunities that Scarlett had received the one-on-one attention of another woman she trusted.

Scarlett's dad pulled the truck to a stop in front of the bar and hopped out, Scarlett rounding the vehicle to follow him inside.

Her father tugged open the thick walnut door, cloaked in an enormous Christmas wreath of fresh evergreen and pine cones, with a red ribbon trailing nearly all the way down to the cobbled path that led to the bar. Scarlett tried not to slip on the sheet of ice that had covered the cobbles, despite the layer of what looked like salt that Cappy had probably put down this morning instead of his usual sweeping.

Cappy was behind the bar, which was trimmed in more Christmas greenery. The glistening live tree in the bay window at the front cast little champagne-colored circles onto the shiny surface of the bar top. Cappy's almond beard had grayed a bit more since Scarlett had seen him last, but his smile was just the same.

"Blue!" he called, slapping the small towel he'd been using to shine the bar over his shoulder and walking to the other side to greet them.

Blue was Scarlett's father's nickname and the name that he'd used her entire life. He was born Steven Bailey, but everyone called him Blue—even Gran. The name had stuck after he'd attempted to paint a water tower when he was in high school, only to never make it up the ladder because he spilled the bucket of paint on himself and the young lady walking by. He'd married that very lady ten years later. Her name was Evelyn, Scarlett's mother.

"Seeing you two is getting me excited for the big Christmas party at White Oaks," Cappy said, pulling a chair out from one of the empty tables for Scarlett and kissing her on the cheek. As her father sat down beside her, Cappy turned another chair around backward and straddled it, folding his arms on top. "Your brother was in here earlier," he said to her father. "I'm sure he's at the inn by now. I think you're the last of the Baileys to make it up the mountain."

"Joe's here already?" her father asked, shaking his head, amused. "Always the overachiever."

Cappy chuckled at the sibling rivalry between her father and his older brother, Joe. But then he sobered. "I didn't have time to talk to Joe about it because he was headed out the door, but he mentioned you might be selling White Oaks."

Blue offered a solemn nod. "Yes. We haven't told my mother; we're keeping it very quiet. I think we're going to be forced to sell, though…" He shook his head as if he still couldn't believe the words that were coming out of his mouth. "We need a buyer fast if we want White Oaks to remain in good condition. Know anyone in the market for a thirty-thousand square-foot hotel?" her father asked with a forced laugh.

Cappy looked thoughtful. "Actually…" He stood up and went behind the bar, where he grabbed a small white card, bringing it back over to them. He slid it across the table to Blue. "This guy came in about eight months ago. His name was Charles Bryant. Do you remember him at all?"

"That name sounds a bit familiar," Blue said, clearly searching his memory but coming up short of the connection.

"You might have heard of him. He's the one who built Croft Ridge Resort and Suites down the road."

"The big one with the water slides?"

Cappy sighed. "Yep." He pulled the towel from his shoulder and set it on the table, leaning on the chair again. "But he has quite a story. He came in to drop his card off, and I didn't think anything of it. He went on his way. But last week, he showed up again and dropped a bombshell."

"What was it?" Scarlett asked.

"He asked if I remembered him from his last visit, and, of course, I did. He also told me he was Amos's *son*."

Scarlett had childhood memories of Amos Bryant. He'd often dance into the farmers' market, whistling, and when June, the owner of the market, greeted him, he took her hands and twirled her around, making her laugh before heading over to the dairy section or the vegetables. He seemed to always be cooking something back at his cottage, his shopping list full. But what no one knew until his final days was that he was lonely—he'd admitted it to Gran once. His wife had passed away well before her time, and he'd spent the rest of his days alone, except for his visits to Gran and Pappy's and the mornings he spent at the coffee shop with his book and his favorite mug that he brought with him every day. He'd said that he'd bought his cottage in Silver Falls with the idea that he'd have a family in it one day. But he never did. The story had always stayed with Scarlett. But the thing that she hadn't heard in all those years was that Amos had a son.

"Amos had a child?" Blue asked.

"Apparently. Odd that we never saw him, right?"

"Now that I think of it, I remember seeing Amos with a boy once," Blue said. "He was about thirteen. Amos got him ice cream. But it was only the one time. I just figured he was a nephew or something."

"Weird, isn't it? But I digress," Cappy said. "What I wanted to tell you was that the first time Mr. Bryant came in, he said he was specifically looking for a plot of land in Silver Falls to open one of his resorts." This information pulled Scarlett out of her thoughts about Amos. "He wants to do something completely different, thank God—something more traditional. As he said, he wants 'to represent the fabric of Silver Falls.'"

Scarlett lit up at that news. "If we have to sell, he sounds like a potentially great buyer," she said, taking Charles Bryant's business card off the table and looking it over.

She'd seen the profiles of a few of the people her father had contacted regarding their interest in buying the inn, and none of them had felt right. Their other properties were either too showy or downright tacky. If she could have a conversation with Charles Bryant, she might be able to convince him to keep the integrity of White Oaks Inn—if he was, in fact, Amos's son. Amos was a family friend and a long-time resident of Silver Falls—he'd passed away the same way he'd lived: quietly. Amos's cabin on the hillside, now vacant, was understated, nearly blending in with the terrain. He'd never been ostentatious in any way. So, even though Charles Bryant clearly hadn't grown up in Silver Falls, he must at least be familiar with Amos's way of life.

Blue nodded, clearly considering the prospect as well.

"May I keep this?" Scarlett asked, still holding the card in her hand.

"Absolutely. Y'all want a beer?" Cappy asked.

"Maybe later," Blue said, patting Cappy on the shoulder as he stood up. "We just wanted to stop in on our way to White Oaks to say hello."

"Yeah, you'd better go help Joe with the tree. He just left with the biggest one ol' Farmer Jax had." Cappy nodded toward the view through the window of the Berry Farms Christmas lot, the place where Jax Henderson set up trees from his farm every year. He personally toted each one to the lot himself in his fully restored 1958 pale blue Ford pickup. "Glad you stopped in!" Cappy continued happily. "Jess is home today. She'll be so sorry she missed you. She's already baking for the Christmas party."

"I can't wait to see her," Scarlett said, standing up and pushing her chair back under the table, Charles Bryant's card secured tightly within her fist.

Scarlett was already plotting how to steal a moment away from the rest of the family as soon as she got to the inn, so she could make the call to Mr. Bryant to get a read on him. It would be such a relief to go through Christmas knowing that she had a solid plan that even Gran might approve of. Although, with a new owner, Gran would have to leave the inn, it could lighten the blow if she knew it would be in good hands. This might be Scarlett's chance to save White Oaks. But with Christmas just a few days away, she'd have to work fast.

Chapter Two

The snowfall drifted to the ground like feathers, light and airy, settling on the Christmas garland that was draped along the length of both the upper and lower lacquered railings of the main house of White Oaks Inn. When Scarlett and her father arrived, the ten-foot spruce on the front grounds sparkled in white lights, and wreaths of fresh greenery were already hung from every window by wide ribbons the color of red wine. Local firefighter Wes Warren helped Gran hang them every year. He used his truck ladder to put them up for her.

Blue greeted Uncle Joe, who was standing on the porch again in Pappy's absence, and then gingerly pulled the truck through the unplowed private drive that overlooked the valley below at the back of the main house. The snow clearly wasn't enough to deter Scarlett's seventeen-year-old cousin Heidi from her yearly quest for phone service. She was pacing outside in the cold, alternating between waving her phone in the air and peering down at the screen.

Wi-Fi was one of the amenities that guests needed to have consistently, but Gran just couldn't understand it. Gran had said that there was no need to upgrade the service because her guests were here for the views and the family time. They needed a break from their phones, and she was just giving them permission to take one.

Blue maneuvered the truck to the side of Heidi and put it in park. She stopped momentarily to offer a distracted wave to them when Scarlett got out.

"You'd think I'd have learned from all the times I've been here that there's no service on this mountain," Heidi said to Scarlett without even a greeting, with that brooding teenage version of affection, her annoyance stated in a friendly way to show their camaraderie. White flakes peppered her shiny dark hair as she shook her phone and wiped the screen with her sleeve to clear the water droplets caused by melting snow. "I told Michael I'd call him. Things haven't been great lately."

Scarlett stepped up beside her and Heidi offered a side-hug.

"Your boyfriend?" Scarlett asked.

"Yeah. I'm trying to make things work…" She wiggled her phone again as if the signal could somehow be jostled free. "I'm going away to college next year. I've been accepted to Johns Hopkins."

"That's wonderful," Scarlett told her.

They'd been waiting for that acceptance letter for a while. Uncle Joe had graduated from Johns Hopkins, and he'd dreamed of Heidi following in his footsteps at the university. He'd had lunches with the alumni association, taken her on tours of the campus, and even bought her a T-shirt with the university logo on the front.

Having been Daddy's little girl as a child, Heidi had spent long hours bandaging his arms to see if she could wrap the bandage just right, listening to his heart with a stethoscope, dropping candies in a little paper cup the way he had when giving out meds to patients. As she grew older, her math and science grades soared and a path in medicine could be a real possibility for her. But she was extremely creative as well. Uncle Joe had said her creativity would be her edge when she was under pressure. She'd begun an honors pre-med track this year—her senior year in high school—and she was doing very well.

"I know your dad will be thrilled to bits," Scarlett said.

"Dad's really excited, but Michael's not tickled about the drive he'll have to make to see me."

If only Heidi knew how young she was, how much time she had in front of her. At seventeen, she really didn't need to have to try to make things work with someone. Scarlett had been down that road. The situation with Heidi opened up the fresh wounds of her own recent breakup, and only added to Scarlett's conclusion that this Christmas wouldn't be one of the highlights of her existence. Tonight, Scarlett's ex-boyfriend Daniel would be attending their Christmas work party at Electra, the media company where they'd met, sporting the suit Scarlett had picked out for him. And Bethany from accounts receivable would probably be wearing the heels that Scarlett had urged her to buy when they'd been out shopping on their lunch break a few weeks ago.

Scarlett hadn't wanted to break up with Daniel only weeks before Christmas, but he was moving too fast, and she knew that he wasn't the one for her. Scarlett had a habit of falling for the same types of men: the ones who had baggage or something they were "working on." She wanted to help them all, to make them better in some way, and every time the relationship progressed, she realized that her determination to make things work was more out of her need to support them rather than passion. But this would be the last time she made that mistake. It was time to find someone strong who could take care of *her* for a change. However, any update to Scarlett's relationship status would have to wait, because she had more pressing family matters pulling on her attention.

Heidi lifted the hand that was holding up her phone to greet Scarlett's father as he rounded the truck. He'd been organizing the gifts into bags to get them all inside the house. "Hi, Uncle Blue," she said.

Blue attempted to return the gesture, his arms full of presents, and shut the door of the truck with his foot. Scarlett shuffled up beside him and offered to help, but he shooed her away and told her to go enjoy herself.

She considered offering Heidi her own phone, so she pulled it out of her pocket to see if it worked any better, but hers, too, was struggling to find a connection. The snow must be making the usual spotty service even worse. It reminded her of the business card in her pocket and made her question whether she'd have a working phone to call Mr. Bryant.

"Don't catch pneumonia out here," Blue said, tightening his scarf with his only free finger as he grabbed their bags and headed inside, a suitcase in each hand and the packages wedged against his body with his arms.

"Wanna come inside?" she asked Heidi. "It's freezing."

"Might as well," Heidi said, the words sailing in on a sigh, her phone lowered by her side in defeat.

"You could use the landline," Scarlett offered, holding the door for her. The heat from the fire wafted toward her, instantly warming her.

"And have to talk to Michael while the entire family is in the room with me? *No way.*" Heidi came in and shut the door behind them both. They walked together down the hallway and into the living room. "It's okay. I'll try to text him later. Glad you're here!"

"Me too," Scarlett said.

While the snow fell outside, the main living area that Gran shared with the guests was toasty and warm. And it was beginning to look festive. The central house was original, and included a parlor, a living room, a kitchen, a very large dining room where Gran hosted many wedding receptions every summer—until they'd dwindled as the décor had started to date—and the living quarters for Gran and the family. The living room, parlor, and dining room were open to the public most of the year.

The cedar staircase in the entryway had already been draped in cascading garlands and red ribbons; the small table outside the living room and the accent tables inside were dotted with peppermint candles and poinsettia arrangements sitting on runners that were hand-embroidered by Gran with holly leaves and berries; the grand piano in the corner had its own ring of pine and balsam branches. Scarlett took this moment to commit to memory the rich aroma of pumpkin pie and cranberry sauce that danced its way under the mistletoe from the kitchen into the room, where a roaring fire popped and sizzled for the family and guests.

"Scarlett!" Uncle Joe called her lovingly from the highest rungs of a ladder, while he wobbled an angel onto the top of Jax's enormous Christmas tree. He'd clearly come in and gotten right to work. The lights and garland were in place already, the baubles and ornaments still wrapped in tissue and tucked away in their boxes on the floor. "How's my favorite niece?"

He always said that. And what made it chuckle-worthy was that Scarlett was his only niece. "Wonderful," she said, locking eyes with him, their unspoken words giving away their concern over the weeks to come once Christmas was over. But there was also a sense of unity in his look that gave her strength—the whole family would work together to do the best they could for Gran. She just hoped they could make Gran see their need to move her out of White Oaks. Her grandmother had already been without so much over the last two years since she lost Pappy.

Scarlett stepped over a strand of lights on the floor to get nearer to the tree. Only then did she notice Archie, Gran's hound dog, curled up on the tree skirt between a few presents. "Need any help?" She reached under the tree and scratched the dog's brown and black spotted head.

"I should be asking you that," he said, coming down and then peering up at the angel. "We're all settled in."

Gran's three children, Joe, Beth, and Blue, had grown up at White Oaks, and Gran adored the fact that they still brought their families to visit every Christmas and summer. Joe, his wife, Alice, and their three children—Heidi and the twins, Riley and Mason—had a competition with Blue to see which family would arrive the soonest each year. Joe usually won. He always made sure to point out playfully to Blue that, even though he and Alice had quite a few more people to get in the car, they still managed to beat him. Beth had never married, but she was right there with them, mothering her nieces and nephews as if they were her own.

Joe repositioned an ornament, squinting one eye to inspect its new placement. "Aunt Alice and the kids are putting the Christmas welcome baskets in all the guest rooms, and Aunt Beth just ran out to get us some more wine."

"Doesn't Esther usually do the baskets?" Esther had been working at the inn since Scarlett was a little girl—she was like family. She lived on the premises and she was the one Gran trusted with the tasks of the highest security.

"Gran had to let her go a few months back. Not enough money to pay her." He bit the inside of his lip while telling her silently that this was exactly why they'd had their family meeting. "She took a general manager position at a hotel in Knoxville, making nearly double the pay, so even if we wanted her back, we can't have her."

This loss hit Scarlett hard. Esther had been like a mother to Scarlett, growing up. She was so kind, and whenever Scarlett stayed as a girl, she always made sure to have something waiting for her. Sometimes it was a patchwork doll she'd made of old clothes or a book she'd found at the secondhand store. Esther, Gran, and Aunt Alice, the cooks of the family, would sing together in the kitchen when they prepared their big dinners.

"Esther did everything here," Scarlett said. "Who's doing it all now?"

"Gran."

She couldn't imagine the burden Gran was faced with, having Esther gone. Everything from paperwork to guest relations was now on Gran's shoulders. At eighty-two years old, taking on that amount of work wasn't healthy for her.

"Do you or your dad need help with anything?" Joe nodded hello to a couple of wandering guests—an elderly woman with silver hair and ruby earrings, and her husband, both clearly excited to get an early peek at the decorations.

"We're fine, thanks. We only brought a suitcase each," she answered, giving a friendly wave to the couple. "Where's Gran?"

"Cooking," he said happily.

That was a good sign. When Gran was excited, she expended her extra energy by cooking and baking. The family often said that they could guess the productivity of the New Year by how many hours Gran spent in the kitchen that Christmas. The year after Pappy died, she'd hardly cooked a thing that Christmas; she'd only made a light Christmas dinner and baked a cake. So things were looking up; judging by the smells wafting in from the kitchen, she was in good spirits this season.

"How's the tree looking?" Uncle Joe asked. He hung a bauble and then tweaked a few more ornaments, stepping back to view his work.

"It's gorgeous," Scarlett said.

"Jax outdid himself this year," he said after removing another bauble from the box. He carried on decorating the tree quietly.

As Scarlett's Uncle Joe was a doctor, and with the nearest hospital a good twenty-five-minute drive away, Joe was known to make house calls whenever he was visiting. He always said he didn't mind because he loved helping people. One night Jax's neighbor came running across the field along the edge of the mountain, distraught, telling Uncle Joe that she thought Jax was having a heart attack. Joe had rushed straight over, stabilizing him until the ambulance could reach them. Not having a whole lot of extra money, Jax had to think long and hard about how to repay him. Finally, he came up with a way: every year he offered to give Uncle Joe his best Christmas tree free of charge. And now it was the Bailey family tradition to put it up in the grand living room at White Oaks.

"Call me if you need me," Scarlett said to Uncle Joe. "I'm going to head to the kitchen to say hello to Gran, and then I'll see if I should work the desk for guest checkout so she can keep cooking." She followed the buttery, sugary smells, excited to see her grandmother.

When she got to the doorway, Stitches the cat snaked around her ankles. The calico stray-cat-turned-pet had gotten her name by sneaking out of the cold and nestling in the cushiony fabric of Gran's sewing box last winter. She was thrifty, which was a good trait to have when she was shut in all season with Archie. Gran's hound dog was famous for touring the inn of his own accord and only showing up when he felt like it, or when Stitches got comfortable.

"The trick is," Gran was telling Heidi, the same way she used to tell Scarlett when she was that age, "you need to preheat your sheet pan before putting the pie in the oven, and then place it on the lowest rack. That prevents the bottom of the crust from getting gooey." Heidi looked on intently as Gran held one of her famous apple pies, her bright red Christmas manicure visible from across the room. Scarlett noticed Gran had the house phone in front of her and the booking record open—she was having to take reservations during her family time because Esther wasn't there to do it.

Scarlett hung her coat and handbag on one of the chairs. Her father was at the kitchen table already, his novel sitting beside him, nearly lost in the clutter of cooking utensils and bowls. She doubted he'd have a chance to read today, since they needed to help Gran with the cooking and decorating as well as unpacking.

Reading was how Blue spent most of his vacation time, and Scarlett adored that about him. In the evenings growing up, she'd bundle herself in a blanket on the sofa beside him, tuck her feet under her, and the two of them would read until they couldn't keep their eyes open anymore.

He had his sleeves rolled to his elbows and he was kneading dough, the ball on his Santa hat dangling in front of him, making her smile. Her movement distracted him and he looked up. "Hey there," he said. "Is Uncle Joe doing okay with the tree?"

"Yes." Scarlett went over to Gran and kissed her cheek. "He's almost finished with it. Hi, Gran."

"Oh, my dear Scarlett, I've missed you! Give me a squeeze." Gran wrapped her thin arms around Scarlett, the warmth from the oven making her grandmother's clothes feel like they'd just been pulled from the dryer, her jasmine scent filling Scarlett's lungs and taking her back to a time when her worries were few and her entire future was ahead of her.

"I'm going to go upstairs and unpack," Blue said, standing up and clapping the flour off his hands after placing the well-kneaded dough into a bowl. "Call me if you need me." He gave Gran a hug and headed upstairs.

Heidi used the moment to excuse herself as well and headed to her room, where she would undoubtedly try to call her boyfriend again. Stitches mewed at Blue from her perch on the windowsill as he passed by. That window held a view of the entire valley from the back of the house. Today it was a vast expanse of white, plunging down and then back up, desolate, quiet. Nothing like the cheery, welcoming atmosphere inside.

"All the baskets are done!" Aunt Alice said, entering the room. Scarlett had always looked up to her aunt. She was stylish and she had the heart of an angel. "Scarlett," she said, crossing the room with her arms open wide. "Are you going to bake with me and your gran?"

"Of course," Scarlett said, embracing Aunt Alice. "Tell me you're going to make those chocolate peanut butter cookies you bake every Christmas."

"The twins have been cracking peanuts for days," she said, with a smile that lit up her face and showed off the sparkle in her eyes. She took Scarlett by the upper arms tenderly. "Oh, I'm so happy you're here. I just love it when we can all get together. Was it tough to get away from work?" Her aunt's face dropped in concern. "You've got that new job now. Your dad says it's quite demanding on your time."

Gran eyed her and seemed to hide a disappointed look by wiping down the counter. When she was a child, Scarlett had told Gran that she'd planned to live at White Oaks forever. Back then she'd meant it, but life had carried her away to something different. Gran was supportive of her career, but Scarlett always wondered if Gran had hoped she would make good on her childhood promise.

"It's not too bad." Scarlett didn't mention the fact that she'd left a massive pile of work on her desk, and it would all be waiting for her after the holiday. She hoped she'd be in the right mindset to tackle it after telling Gran the news.

"That can't be possible," Gran said, pulling Scarlett's focus back to her grandmother. Gran was now headfirst in the refrigerator, rummaging around. "How in the world...?" She set a few dishes on the counter and rearranged bottles, clearly searching for something. "I think I'm out of butter." She finally stopped and regarded Scarlett in pure shock. "I've never been out of butter in my entire life. How did I manage to do it when I'm trying to prepare for the holiday season? I can't finish my cookies now."

Scarlett smirked, just the sight of Gran warming her.

"Do you need me to go back out?" Scarlett asked.

"Oh, I'd hate to make anyone go out in this mess. And you just got here," Gran said, peering into the fridge once more, still obviously baffled as to how she could let such an important ingredient run out.

Gran used butter for almost everything. Not only did she cook with it, but Scarlett had seen her grease her snow shovel with butter, convinced it kept the snow from sticking to the metal; she shined her leather shoes with it; she'd even managed to get gum out of Scarlett's hair when she was a child, using butter.

"It's no problem. I'll take Dad's truck." Scarlett reached over and rubbed Stitches, making her purr. She really didn't mind going, and it might also give her an opportunity to be alone to make that call to Charles Bryant. "Is there anything else we need?"

Gran tapped her chin in contemplation. "We could use more milk… But I think that's it for me. Do you need anything, Alice?"

"I don't think so…" Alice said, opening the door of the oven to check the pie, the scent of apples and cinnamon wafting toward her.

Scarlett grabbed her handbag and fished around inside it for the keys to the truck. "Text me if you all think of anything else."

"All right, dear. Be careful."

Scarlett slid her coat on and headed outside, immediately twisting toward the inn to shield herself from a brutal gust of icy air. With few visitors from November to March, the inn's wide-stretching porches were buried in snow all the way down to the valleys below. She was glad that her dad and Uncle Joe were there now to help clear them. The inn sat on the edge of a mountaintop, clinging to its foundation in the harsh weather, most roads incredibly slippery and icy, with the exception of the one route into Silver Falls that was plowed.

Scarlett got into the truck and shut the door, glad that a bit of heat from their original journey still lingered in the vehicle. She pulled the card from her pocket and peered down at the number. A tiny seed of optimism began to sprout as she took out her phone. But then she realized that there still wasn't any service at the moment. She clicked off her phone. She'd try again once she got into town.

With a deep breath, she cranked the engine and then slowly turned toward the main road. This stretch was long and winding, but not terribly hilly, so she felt comfortable driving it. The first time she'd sat in the driver's seat of Blue's truck was when she was sixteen years old. With her driver's license still warm from the printer, Blue had made her get into the truck to learn the way the gearshift worked, right there at the DMV. He'd told her that she'd have to learn the tricky clutch on dry ground before she took it up to White Oaks. He'd spent many days, patient as ever, helping her get used to working the clutch to change gears. She'd lost count of how many times the old truck had stalled in the process. After a few months of practice, she'd made the trek up the mountain. To this day, she couldn't drive a single stick shift except for that truck.

Scarlett clicked on the old radio to Christmas tunes and bumped her way through the snow toward town, happy to have this time to herself. She'd felt a little better seeing Gran. The festive atmosphere would help to keep the worries about losing the inn away for a short while. She wanted to keep them away for good; that business card was her only hope.

While driving the truck in regular weather was something she could do in her sleep, maneuvering it in the snow still didn't come quite as easily for her as it had for her dad. She had to grip the steering wheel with both hands, and the only time she let go was to downshift, her foot reaching as far as it could to press in the clutch. But now, after many years of practice, she was much better.

The old porch lanterns on either side of the door of the general store were draped in fresh greenery with silver bows. A wreath made from spruce with white twinkle lights hung on the glass door, the reflection glimmering like stars in the night sky. In the center of the wreath was a small woven dream catcher. Ato Harris was behind the counter. Ato was short for Atohi, a Cherokee word for "woods." His family had moved here three generations ago from Mississippi. With the exception of Christmas, the store hadn't closed a single day since they'd first opened it.

Ato was ringing up a customer when Scarlett entered. His shiny straight black hair, usually secured at the base of his neck, was left loose tonight. He caught her eye as she walked to the back, his happiness upon seeing her evident in the creases at the edges of his deep brown eyes.

Scarlett pulled a gallon of milk and butter from the refrigerated section at the back and headed up to the counter. She delighted in seeing the table behind Ato. It was still covered in remnants of his craft-making, the wooden top stained darker from the clay he used to make his stone-shaped pots; a bucket of those stones—round and so smooth they felt like glass—beside a decorative basket that was half woven. He'd told her once that crafting was a way to force balance on himself in a world full of noise. She'd often found him weaving in the quiet moments between customers—no music, no other sounds, just the snapping of the rattan as he fed it through the other pieces and broke it off.

"Hello, Miss Scarlett," he said in that husky, deep voice of his. "Glad to see you're in town. I hope you've brought the whole family with you."

"They're all here," she said, his friendliness making her feel nostalgic for the days of her childhood, when she came in barefoot from swimming all day, her hair wet from the falls, holding a handful of change to buy the penny candy that lined the front counter. He'd always given her an extra piece or two.

Ato rang up her items and put them in a bag. He dropped two hand-painted bookmarks made of thin wood into the bag as well. "I hope you get some time this busy season to breathe, read, enjoy your calm." He held the bag out to her.

"Me too," she said, taking the bag. She smiled at him, said good-bye, and then headed out the door.

When Scarlett got into the truck, she set the bag in the passenger seat and started the engine to get the heat running. She contemplated

Ato's comment about calm. There was no way Scarlett could be calm until she knew that she had a solid plan for the inn. She grabbed her phone and the business card for Charles Bryant. When she opened her phone screen, she had two bars of service—it was a sign. With a deep breath, she steadied herself and dialed the number.

Chapter Three

We're sorry. The number you have dialed is no longer in service. Please check the number and try your call again.

Scarlett gazed down at Charles Bryant's card. She'd dialed it twice and both times she'd gotten the automated message that the number wasn't working, so she definitely hadn't dialed it incorrectly. That was disappointing. She scanned the name of his business:

Crestwood Development
Bringing you the finest in upscale comforts.

Scarlett immediately texted her dad. It was her go-to coping strategy whenever she struggled for what to do next. Perhaps it was because, growing up, it had been only the two of them. He was her rock, and he always made her feel better.

I just tried the number for Charles Bryant and it's out of service, she typed.

Right away, a response came through: *Please don't spend your entire Christmas worrying about this. Try to enjoy the holiday. Things have a way of working out. I love you.*

She texted back: *Love you too.*

But for once she didn't believe him. Not this time. She opened the search engine on her phone and typed in "Crestwood Development." Nothing. Wouldn't they have a website? Then she typed in "Charles Bryant" and scrolled through the results, scanning the first three:

Crestwood Development CEO Charles Bryant makes waves…

New resort to be built by Crestwood Development, Charles Bryant says…

Charles Bryant to acquire three blocks for development at…

None of them hit the mark. They all just seemed like news articles rather than contact information. She'd have to find some other way to get in touch with Mr. Bryant, and with the way the Wi-Fi was working at the inn, she wasn't sure if she'd be able to search alternative methods to find him anytime soon. Cappy said he was in town. Perhaps she'd run into him. Except she had no idea what he looked like. Disheartened, she tossed the card on the seat next to her and pulled out onto the main road, headed for White Oaks.

She knew she shouldn't, but she pondered what the moment would be like after Christmas when they broke the news to Gran about selling. Who was going to bring it up first? Would they sit her down formally, maybe make her a cup of coffee before jumping into the discussion? Just the thought soured Scarlett's stomach. Where would Gran go? Would she live with Scarlett's father at his home?

Blue's house was small—a little two-bedroom in East Nashville. Gran loved the yard at the inn that she and Pappy had made by clearing the brush and planting roses and other annuals, often spending hours in the gardens outside. She'd never be happy in the crammed city space. Gran spent her free time gardening, taking long walks, and baking. How would she survive in an urban area? But her father was the best candidate for taking Gran in because Scarlett's little apartment was even smaller, and Uncle Joe and Aunt Alice were too busy. Uncle Joe worked crazy hours, and of course they had three kids. She could live with Aunt Beth, but Beth was always running, never still. Gran would be alone a lot, and when Beth was at home, she was hosting neighborhood card games and wine nights, staying up way past Gran's bedtime. Scarlett contemplated the possibilities most of the way back to White Oaks, but she wasn't any closer to an answer when she rounded the final turn.

As she hugged her side of the bend in the road, bumping over a small bridge that ran across a stream—its water a solid sheet of ice—something caught her eye through the gray haze of snow. She slowed her speed to get a look at the light in the distance. It was a dull yellow, and it appeared to be flickering because the trees she was passing kept obscuring it. It was way out on the edge of the mountain. She'd never noticed any light out there before, and, as she pulled into the drive at White Oaks, she speculated about what it could be. It wasn't a boat out on the river because it was unmoving. The road didn't go that far, so it couldn't be someone's headlights—there was only one light, anyway. A motorcycle? In the dead of winter, during a snowstorm? Definitely not. Maybe Gran would know. Scarlett cut the engine, grabbed the grocery bag, and headed inside.

Riley and Mason, Scarlett's twin eight-year-old cousins, were at the table when Scarlett came into the kitchen. Riley was petite, with ringlets of golden curls that fell along her shoulders, while Mason was stout, tall, and had hair that matched the tiny freckles across his nose. They were both on their knees, nibbling on cookies from a Christmas platter in the center of the table. Stitches was on one side of them and Archie was on the other.

"I think Stitches is after their milk and Archie is hoping for a treat," Gran said, amused, as Scarlett reached into the bag and handed her the butter. While Gran opened it to put some in her batter, Scarlett put the milk into the fridge.

"How are the cookies, kiddos?" she asked while Gran stirred the ingredients together, pressing the large ceramic bowl against her aproned bosom to get leverage, her thin arm straining against the thickness of the dough.

"Me-ish-ish," Mason said, his hand over his mouth, his lips barely able to move while holding in all the cookies.

"Please, no talking with full mouths," Gran said, with a wink, over her bowl.

Scarlett grinned and translated. "Delicious?"

Riley nodded.

"May I?" Scarlett stretched over the table for a Christmas tree sugar cookie that was piped with green icing. Still chewing, Mason slid the plate her way to lessen her reach.

Scarlett took the cookie and walked over to Gran. "What are you making?" she asked, taking a bite and peeking over Gran's shoulder at the batter. It looked to be some sort of gingerbread. The unique sweet yet salty mixture of Gran's sugar cookie recipe was to die for, but her gingerbread was simply outstanding. Scarlett had always wanted the recipe but had never asked for it, for fear she'd make them so often that they'd lose their Christmas charm.

"I'm making the pieces for the mini gingerbread houses for the Christmas games," Gran said, pointing her large wooden spoon at the metal molds on the counter. "How was the road into town?"

"Not bad," Scarlett said. "Oh, that reminds me… There was a strange light on the side of the mountain. I've never seen it there before. It was down the hill from the bridge."

Gran searched the air above Scarlett's head for an answer. "Down the hill? Isn't that Amos's land?"

"It did look like a porch light, now that I think about it."

"That's most likely what it was. No one's lived there since Amos died, so you probably aren't used to seeing any light coming from the house in the dark."

Scarlett felt the excitement wriggle up her spine. Could Charles Bryant have come back to his father's home? The house wasn't in the best shape…

Gran frowned. "I have no idea who it could be. I thought it was still empty."

Scarlett didn't want to let on that she had an idea, both so as not to bring attention to it for Gran's benefit, and also because she didn't want to allow the hope to well up that she could actually get in touch with Charles Bryant. Why would he be there? Surely he couldn't be looking at potential building options in all this snow. And it was nearly Christmas.

It didn't matter why he was there. She'd have to try to get down the mountain to Amos's tomorrow to find out if it was him. It was her best chance at finding a solution to all this.

"I'm going to head upstairs and help Dad…make sure he's got everything unpacked. I need to double-check that all my shirts are hanging in the closet and not folded in a drawer," she said lightly, concealing her need to divulge this new information to her father. "Is there anything you need before I go?"

"No, dear. I'm just fine. The kids and I will finish the baking. You need to slow down for a minute and relax. You've been running since the minute you got here."

"Okay, Gran." Scarlett blew her grandmother a kiss and headed up to talk to her dad.

Since the whole family shared a corridor in the private quarters of the inn, it was quiet. When she got to her dad's room, the door was still open, propped with her suitcase. Blue was folding a sweater; a small pile of clothes that he was sorting was arranged on the bed. She pushed the luggage out of her way, letting the door close behind her as she went in.

"Hey." Scarlett plopped down next to a stack of blue jeans, wobbling it. "Almost finished?"

"Yep. Nearly. Aunt Alice is up here somewhere. Have you seen her?"

Unable to contain herself or manage any more small talk, she waved him closer. Blue leaned in and, her voice quiet, Scarlett got right to the point. "Guess what I saw on the way home from town."

Blue grinned at her and set the sweater down to give her his full attention. "What?"

"There was a light in the distance down the road, where Amos's house is. It was hard to tell with the snow, but it looked like a porch light. *Someone* might be there right now."

He immediately connected the dots and could tell what she was thinking.

"That house is falling apart. We don't know if whoever's there is anyone of significance to us," he said, his gaze darting over to the closed door, his tone skeptical. He resumed folding and then turned away from her to open a dresser drawer.

"We don't know that it's *not*." She stood up and put her face into his line of vision. "You said yourself that things have a way of working out. I'm going to go over there tomorrow to see who it is."

Blue turned around. "I think I preferred it when you weren't talking about this at all," he said, teasing. "How could you go to Amos's anyway? The snow is so deep that you'll never find the road, and it's almost totally downhill. You won't get a vehicle down there."

"There has to be a path if the light was on. Someone had to get to the house, right?"

"At some point, yes. But they might have come before the storm. I can't imagine anything's been plowed in the last few days." He picked up his toiletries bag and fished around inside it, retrieving a few bottles and placing them on the dresser in organized groups. "Given the shape the old house is in, no one should be living there at all. The property's been neglected since Amos passed away years ago. It's probably just someone doing some maintenance. If they're still there at all. They could've just left the light on."

"Well, I'll let you know if that's the case after I've gone tomorrow."

"I'm not going to have you risk your life chasing some ridiculous idea that you can save White Oaks for Gran. You can't control what happens, Scarlett. We'll find a buyer."

"I can't let it go when there's a chance that I could help."

"Stubborn like your mother," he said with a huff.

"Maybe," Scarlett said, standing up. "But I love you like she did too." She hugged him, making him smile, and on her way out the door she turned to him. "I *am* going to Amos's house tomorrow," she stated matter-of-factly for emphasis. "It'll all work out."

Blue shook his head with a playful smile, but trepidation was still lurking around his eyes. He'd always been overprotective. Maybe that was *his* go-to strategy. She understood it, though, and she never complained. They only had each other.

"Love you!" Scarlett bounced out of the room. "Come down and get one of Gran's cookies!" she called from the hallway. "They're delicious!"

Chapter Four

"Oh, my stars!" Loretta's familiar voice sailed over the breakfast chatter at the Wynn Family Diner, originally an old saloon that had been converted to a restaurant by Samuel Wynn and his family in the 1980s. It boasted cooked breakfasts fit for a mountaineer, and in the warmer months it was standing room only in the reception area, the hostess madly scratching down names as visitors waited in the endless stretch of rocking chairs for their turn to sample the local fare. Still the busiest restaurant in the area, even in the off-season, it brimmed with people this morning.

Scarlett had gotten up early, fed Archie and Stitches for Gran, and then headed into town without even a cup of coffee, claiming she needed to get a few last-minute gifts for her dad. But she was going to fuel up and then see how far down the mountain she could get toward Amos's. She had to find out if Charles Bryant was there.

"Fancy seeing you here!" Loretta swished over in her long winter coat and riding boots.

She took it upon herself to pull out the chair across from Scarlett and take a seat, mouthing to the waitress to get her a cup of coffee as she unwrapped her scarf and draped it on the back of the chair. Scarlett was so happy to see her friend. Loretta was like family.

"How have you been?" Loretta asked.

Scarlett had to think quickly about that answer. Anything she said could be used to match her with someone, and Scarlett wasn't really ready to date anyone at the moment. "I'm great," she said, withholding all information until she could determine whether or not Loretta had ulterior motives. "Any new couple match-ups on the horizon?"

The waitress set a mug of coffee in front of Loretta and then topped off Scarlett's.

"I think I may have finally found someone for Preston."

"Oh?" Scarlett was intrigued as she tried not to laugh. Preston couldn't possibly have agreed to anything Loretta had set up.

"My cousin Sarah." Loretta took her stocking cap off and ran her fingers through her soft auburn hair.

It baffled Scarlett that Loretta could help so many people find happiness but she'd never settled down herself. She was stunning and friendly; she could make anyone feel like they'd known her for years. Growing up, Loretta had been a dancer. Scarlett could still remember how she'd exhale when she put her sore toes in the water at the falls after a day of ballet, her toe shoes still in her backpack, which she'd hung on a tree limb when she met Scarlett to swim. Scarlett couldn't remember the day she'd stopped dancing or the moment she'd decided that she would start the agency. It was as if the two parts of Loretta's life were completely separate.

In the age of internet dating, Loretta had managed to make people feel like they were missing out if they didn't have her personal attention, and now Scarlett understood why. Loretta wasn't just putting a set of matching answers together to make a couple. She was invested in their emotions and how they felt about the other person. She advertised online, offering singles a quiet retreat in their mountain town, putting them up in rooms at White Oaks, boasting the romantic locations they'd find in Silver Falls, and hand-picking whom they'd meet on their getaway. Her planning and organization were second to none. She kept numbers small and prices high, but her ratings were so good that people were willing to pay good money for their happiness. Because at the end of the day, happiness was most important.

"Have you introduced them yet?" Scarlett asked, trying to push down the amusement that bubbled up at the thought of Loretta possibly chasing Preston around The Bar last night. But now, with new insight into Loretta's motivations, she wondered if perhaps Preston should give her suggestion a chance.

"Not yet." Her eyebrows bobbed up and down with excitement as she dumped some cream into her coffee and stirred. "How about you? Any love on the horizon?"

Scarlett finally let her smile emerge, knowing this question was coming. "No. I'm fine with my life at the moment. I like being single."

"Nonsense." Loretta lifted her mug to her lips and quietly sipped. "No one likes being alone. They like being *busy*, but never being alone."

Scarlett considered this, only heightening her curiosity about Loretta's relationship status. She seemed so in tune to what others needed; had she considered what *she* might need?

"I thought about you, actually, when we got our newcomer," Loretta said.

"Newcomer?"

"Living at Amos's."

A winter chill snaked through Scarlett at the mention of Amos's name, and she feared that it showed on her face. She focused on her eggs, cutting the omelet in front of her into tiny bite-sized pieces.

"He looks a little older than you—handsome. Got here about a week ago, right before the bottom fell out of the winter bucket. I wonder how he's getting along…I thought for sure we'd see him in town, but I haven't heard a peep from him since he got here, and even then, he'd only stopped to fill up at the service station—that's how I saw him. It's a mystery where he's getting his food from, and with all the snow, no one can bring him a welcome basket or anything. I'm dying to make him some muffins and find out if he's available for matchmaking…"

"Do you know… who he is?" Scarlett asked carefully, trying to be as nonchalant as she could while still prying for any information she could get. It would definitely be worth the danger in getting down the mountain if she could be sure Charles Bryant was there.

"Nope. But I haven't asked too many people."

If Loretta was anything, it was observant. She made a sport of it. Scarlett decided to see if she had any clues that might help the situation. "Did you know that Amos had a son?"

Loretta's gaze flew over her coffee mug, clearly soaking up this new information. "What?"

"That's what I'd heard. But I never saw Amos with a child growing up, and his wife died when they were young—Gran told me once—so where was his child?"

"No idea…" Loretta gaped at her while she let this news settle into the archives of her well-managed brain, as if she were stockpiling classified information. "I've never seen anyone but Amos at that house," she whispered. "Not until a week ago."

"That's so strange."

"Sure is…" Loretta touched the tips of her fingers to her mouth absentmindedly, lost in thought. Then she surfaced, her hands clapping down onto the table. "What if Amos had some kind of secret affair with someone?" She started looking around as if the person could be present, then zeroing back in on Scarlett. "What if it was someone here in Silver Falls?" She clutched her chest, but her eyes glistened with interest.

"I doubt that," Scarlett said, bringing her back down to reality. "If it were someone here, then we'd have seen the child around town when we were kids. And Amos couldn't have had an affair if his wife had passed when they were younger. He'd have just had a regular old relationship, so he wouldn't have been hiding anything."

Loretta nodded, still clearly thinking of scenarios.

"But even if he had a child with another woman in a different town, wouldn't he see the child? Amos was so kind. There's no reason he wouldn't be allowed to see his child," Scarlett said. "He used to visit my grandparents and he told them that he was alone a lot."

"Maybe the mistress ran off with his child!" Loretta leaned forward for emphasis, making Scarlett laugh. Loretta had seen it all in her line of work, Scarlett was certain. "I'm serious!" Loretta said.

"I guess it's possible," Scarlett said, breaking her biscuit in half to butter it.

Loretta looked at the time on her phone and then dropped some cash onto the table for her coffee. "I've got to run. I have a couple coming in at nine, and I need to make the introductions. It's tough getting clients up here in the winter, so when I get one, I have to make it worth their trip. Catch you later!"

"Let me know how things go with Sarah and Preston."

Loretta grabbed her hat and scarf. "I can feel it this time," she said with a sparkle in her eye.

Scarlett wanted to get going too. She finished quickly and paid the bill, so she could head for the edge of the mountain to see if she could find some answers.

*

Scarlett punched the gas again, the tires spinning madly, digging her deeper into the snow. In all the times she'd driven in this truck with her dad, she'd never gotten stuck. But now, as she fumbled around with the stick shift, she had a sinking feeling that there was a first time for everything. She'd made it a considerable way down the mountain. She could see Amos's house from where she was. It definitely looked neglected, run-down. It was missing a couple of shutters and there were areas of the roof that were completely devoid of shingles. One of the windows appeared to be cracked. But smoke billowed from the chimney and there was a light on inside. Scarlett wondered if she could make it the rest of the way on foot in the thick snow. But the house was just far enough away that she didn't think she could without getting frostbite.

Pulling out her phone, it occurred to her that her father could bring out the tractor and clear them a path to get the truck out so they could, at the very least, go back to the inn, but when she checked her screen, she threw her head back in frustration. No service. She wriggled the stick shift into reverse and gunned it. The truck groaned in protest but didn't move an inch. After the trip from Nashville, and all the engine revving she'd done just now trying to get the tires free, she was also getting low on gas. If she didn't stop, she was going to run the gas tank dry.

With a huff, she opened the door, the frigid air slicing through her. The wind rolled down the mountain, nearly knocking her over, her low boots no match for the snow that had piled up on its descent to the valley below. She reached into the back of the truck and retrieved the snow shovel her dad had packed for emergencies. She was hoping not to have to use it, but she was running out of options. Scarlett heaved the rectangular blade into the snow surrounding the front tire and scooped a shovelful. The weight put an extra strain on her arms as she dumped it in a lump beside her. She set in to dig some more.

After she'd worked her pulse into a frenzy, her feet completely numb in her boots, Scarlett evaluated her progress. To her dismay, the tire didn't look like she'd done a thing to it. The snow was falling too quickly, and the shovel was no match for the amount that was already on the ground. She got into the truck and ran the engine, blasting the heat as high as it would go to get warm while she prayed for signal, now very worried she might run out of gas. She turned the radio on and cranked the volume to listen for any advisories through the static, but the only thing playing was Christmas carols. Scarlett checked her phone again, turning it on and off—nothing.

Bang! Bang! Someone rapped loudly on the truck, nearly sending her jumping out of her skin.

She rolled down her window to find a very annoyed man standing at the door to her side. He had a rather large coat on, a scarf, and a winter cap, his cheeks pink from the icy wind—none of it able to hide his attractiveness. She took in his broad cheekbones, the slight space between his lips as he assessed her, air puffing out in the cold around him, his dark amber eyes boring into her.

"Are you trying to freeze to death?" he barked.

"Ummm…" She couldn't form words, still too stunned and relieved at the notion of encountering anyone out here. She looked past him to find a sleek and very modern snowmobile—it wasn't the type of vehicle she was used to seeing in this area. Her gaze followed the glossy lines of it, noticing the tracks under the runners that led down the hill to Amos's.

"Why are you here?" the man demanded.

All coherent thought was sucked out of her the minute he spoke again. Was this Charles Bryant who had been dropped right in front of her, like some sort of Christmas miracle? But Amos had been so friendly; by the clenching of the man's jaw and the irritated look in his eyes as he waited for her to speak, she doubted it. He huffed around, opening her door and looking the truck over, shaking his head.

"Are you Charles Bryant?" she finally managed.

He stopped cold and turned toward her, those eyes so intimidating that she wanted to shrink back into the truck.

"If you want something from me, I don't have anything to give you."

His tone changed slightly with those words, and she noticed something different in his expression, but she couldn't place it. Hurt? Before she could get a handle on it, though, the irritation returned. He was stomping back to the snowmobile. Was he going to leave her there?

"Wait!" she called after him as she marched clumsily over the drifts of snow.

He didn't turn around so Scarlett tried to pick up her pace, but it was like treading water; the hills acted as a wind tunnel, and the air was pushing against her so much that she could barely even hear, the silence chilling.

"Charles!" she said into the howling gusts, praying that was his name.

The large expanse between the truck and the snowmobile made her realize that there was absolutely no way she'd have gotten to Amos's by walking through the snow, and the farther she moved away from the truck, the more nervous she got. She'd lose body heat out there, and she couldn't feel her fingers anymore, so even if she wanted to call for help to get out of there, she couldn't check her phone for service. How had she managed to get herself into this situation?

He stopped at the snowmobile, and her heart raced.

Please don't leave me here, she prayed, exerting herself to catch up to him.

The man lifted a compartment at the back and pulled from it a large wool blanket and a pair of rubber boots. Then he shut it and mounted the snowmobile.

As panic rose in her throat, he started the engine. But relief swept over her as he drove toward her.

"Put these over your shoes," he snapped loudly to be heard above the noise of the engine and the deafening whine of the wind. He held out the boots.

She didn't question it. The wet, icy snow lashed at her face and all she wanted was relief. Once she got the boots on, the man wrapped her in the blanket and pointed to the seat of the snowmobile.

"Get on," he called out to her.

While his demeanor was not very inviting, her only other option was to freeze solid in the truck. She swung her leg over the seat of the snowmobile, pulled the blanket tighter on her shoulders, and put her arms around the handsome stranger.

The ride was as smooth as if they were gliding on a sheet of ice, not a sound around them but the engine. The warmth of his body kept the cold from overwhelming her. Scarlett felt safe holding on to him despite his less-than-welcoming reception.

"So, *are* you Charles?" she shouted into his ear, above the hum of the snowmobile.

He gave no answer, which frustrated her. His response to her didn't make him seem like the kind of guy who would have a conversation over a beer with Cappy and hand him his card. She also knew that shouting over his shoulder wasn't the best way to do business, so she'd have to wait to speak with him properly until they stopped. Scarlett was willing to bet that he had no idea her gran owned an entire hotel that they were ready to sell, if he'd only be cordial enough to allow her to tell him.

But fear crept up her spine as doubt settled in. What if this wasn't Charles Bryant? Then who was it? What if he was some sort of murderer, hiding out in Amos's abandoned house? And she was falling right into it. He knew she'd have no other option than to go with him. No one even knew where she was at this moment, she had no cell service, and the truck was nearly buried in snow off the main road…

The snowmobile came to a stop outside Amos's and the man turned off the engine and dismounted, offering Scarlett a hand. She didn't take it. If he wasn't going to be forthcoming with her, she wasn't going to allow him the satisfaction of thinking he could help her. Even though he had already. No matter, she could get off the thing just fine. But the blanket got tangled around her legs as she tried to step down and all the snow was in her way… The man's arms found her just as she was about to fall, and as their bodies came together, she caught his scent. It was a mixture of the embers from a woodstove and the clean freshness of aftershave. He set her upright. Before she could thank him, he had his back to her, opening the door to the house.

"Come in," he said from inside. Then he turned around and headed to a small coatrack in the corner. He pulled off his thick coat and hung it up, followed by his scarf and cap. He pushed his fingers through his crop of dark hair and then ran his palm down his face, over his light shadow of stubble. With a quick glance her way, he went into the kitchen area that was open to the living room.

Scarlett stepped inside and shut the door behind her. The roaring fire in the stone fireplace sent a shiver racing from her head to her numb, frozen toes. She fumbled with the big boots the man had given her, wriggling until she could get them off. Setting them and the boots she'd put on this morning neatly to the side of the door, she cinched the blanket up around her body and went over to the hearth to get warm, her teeth chattering, her socks soaked.

A mug of coffee hovered in front of her, and she met his eyes. He seemed different now, less angry, more defeated. By what? But then she realized that he may very well be Amos's son, and perhaps he was struggling with being in his father's house without him. She took the coffee with both hands.

"Thank you," she said, holding eye contact.

He nodded, his gaze curious yet guarded. He went back into the kitchen area and got his own mug before he sat down on the sofa.

Scarlett turned sideways, stretching her legs alongside the stone hearth, hoping the heat would dry her socks, as she surveyed her surroundings. The décor seemed as though it had probably been Amos's. From the look of this man's perfect haircut, his designer sweater and stylish jeans, it didn't seem like it would be his style. He appeared to be the kind of guy who would live at the top of some high-rise in the city with glass views of the skyline and trendy, upmarket furniture. Her gaze moved to a bucket on the floor that was catching drips from the ceiling.

When he caught her looking, she quickly turned toward the fire and stretched her fingers out to warm them, glad for the heat to hide the pink that was most likely surfacing in her cheeks. She wasn't judging him; she was just looking around.

"Why are you here?" he asked. This time, his voice was more direct than snappy, less urgent.

Scarlett deliberated over whether or not to tell him about the inn; she felt like she should find some common ground first before suggesting that he drop a few million dollars on a run-down property. Especially when he wouldn't even confirm who he was.

"I saw Amos's light on, and I just wanted to see who was here," she said carefully. "He was a friend of my grandparents'."

There was a shift in his expression, almost relief. She didn't understand it.

"Are you Charles, Amos's son?" she asked again, hoping that perhaps he'd tell her now.

"Yes."

She quietly let his answer settle between them. Something about the way he looked at her made her want to tread lightly. "My name is Scarlett Bailey," she said, and then sipped her coffee to let the warmth spread through her. "I never saw you around here growing up…" The thought came out before she'd had a chance to think through whether to say it aloud. She looked up from her drink and he was staring at her, that curiosity back with a vengeance as if he were trying to place her.

He opened his mouth just slightly as if he were about to say something, but then he looked away, focusing on the liquid in his cup.

"Do you live here?" she asked.

He stood up abruptly, striding over to the kitchen and clanking the mug down in the sink. He hadn't even finished his coffee. "Look," he said. "I didn't want to see you freeze out there, but I'm not really in the mood for small talk. Or guests. Do you have someone who can pick you up?"

There was an undercurrent to his rudeness that made Scarlett feel like he wasn't always this way; he was using his anger to cope with something else, some other emotion. "I didn't mean to impose," she said, wishing she could figure him out so she'd know how to approach him better. She'd never be able to tell him about the hotel if he was this closed-off. "I was just asking to pass the time." When he didn't speak, she added, "I don't have any service on my phone or I would've already called someone."

He walked over to her and pulled out his phone, typing in his code to open the screen. Then he set it on the hearth beside her. "Use mine. I have a hot spot." Then he left the room and a door shut loudly down the hallway.

Scarlett scanned the apps on the screen, trying to get a read on him. What kinds of things did he have on there? Her finger hovered over the call button while she peered down at the apps. He had no social media that she could see, just the standard factory settings and a couple of navigation tools. But surely Charles wouldn't just give her his phone if there were anything important on it that he didn't want her to see. The way he was acting made her wonder what was behind some of those little buttons. She eyed the camera app but thought better of it. He definitely wasn't behaving like Amos had. She couldn't imagine that he was just an angry person. His outward responses didn't seem to match the look in his eyes. The screen on the phone started to go dark, so she hit the call icon to dial her father.

It went straight to voicemail. Scarlett bit her lip. Her father probably wasn't answering because he didn't recognize the caller. He never picked up for people who weren't in his contact list. "Hi, Dad," she said after the beep. "It's Scarlett. I'm with Charles Bryant," she uttered with purpose. "I'm at Amos's because I got stuck in the snow. Call me back on this number."

Still alone in the room, she set the phone on the hearth and examined her environment more closely. The kitchen cabinets were worn, the hinges tarnished. An old farm table sat wedged up next to the wall. It only had one chair. The living room sofa had seen better days, the leather cushions now a patchy shade of tan against the otherwise chestnut color of the rest of it. The braided rug, its fibers threadbare, scarcely hid the weather-beaten wood floor beneath the coffee table. But the space was warm from the fire, the sink empty and clean with the exception of Charles's coffee mug, and the rest of the area was relatively tidy.

Scarlett waited for Charles to come back from wherever he was, but when she considered the fact that he might not be returning, she grabbed his phone and got up to venture down the short hallway, leading presumably to the bedrooms at the back of the cottage.

"Charles?" she called quietly, but didn't get a response.

She pushed open one of the doors, careful not to open it too quickly in case he needed privacy for some reason. But when she saw it was empty, she stopped and took stock of what was in there. The room was sparsely decorated: a single lamp in the corner, a chair next to a battered old dresser, a few stacks of books on an old four-poster bed. Curious, she went over to them and pulled the top one off the closest stack to read the title.

"What are you doing?" The bark was back, startling her and making her drop the book at her feet. She picked it up and returned it to the pile on the bed.

Why did he think he could keep talking to her like that? She'd had about enough of the up-and-down nature of his mood already and she'd only just met him. Scarlett turned around. "I was looking for you," she said, her voice direct and unworried as if she were meant to be there. "You left me in the living room, and this isn't my house, so it was a little strange." She held out his phone in offering. "I called and left a message for my father."

"I got more wood for the fire," he said, pointing toward a pile of wood in the small laundry room that housed the back door to the cottage. He was calmer now, that resigned tone returning. "Why don't you have a seat in the living room? I'll bring it inside and then join you."

He actually said he'd *join* her, which was surprising. Usually when someone joined someone else there was chatting and the sharing of pleasantries. This should be interesting. She realized his unpredictable behavior was making her edgy, which wasn't like her. Well, he wasn't going to put a damper on her Christmas mood. She'd had enough to ruin her holiday already, but she wasn't going to let it crush her spirit. Christmas was her favorite time of year. It was about celebrating with friends and family. Perhaps she could teach Charles a thing or two about hospitality.

When he'd dumped an armful of wood onto the hearth and settled on the sofa beside her, she twisted toward him, but as she did, he regarded her with interest, disorienting her. "You don't have a Christmas tree," she said, her words coming out gentler than she'd originally intended.

He seemed startled by her statement, blinking his eyes unnaturally as if it had stunned him. "No," he said, regaining composure.

But then, out of nowhere, the corners of his mouth turned just slightly upward. Had her comment made him smile? Or was she just imagining it? That curiosity in his eyes bounced around, making her want to talk all day if she had to, just to learn his story. She wondered if she'd been insensitive, mentioning the Christmas tree. It might be a difficult time for him, not having any family around. He may still be grieving the loss of his father... Scarlett couldn't imagine not having her family at Christmas. But he hadn't seemed to mind her observation.

"Why not?" she pressed, her softness beckoning him to take down whatever this wall he'd built around himself was and relax. She swore that a few times she'd seen a glimmer of kindness, but there was something holding him back.

His chest rose with his breath—a long, slow inhalation that seemed laced with unease. He looked into her eyes. "It doesn't feel much like Christmas," he said, and his moment of honesty, the pure vulnerability in his gaze, took her breath away for a minute. It was such a different reaction from what she'd expected, and it nearly confirmed her thought that he was grieving in some way. But as soon as it had happened, he got to his feet. "Are your socks dry?" he asked. He showed less emotion now than he had a second ago, but his manner wasn't as bothered as it had been before.

"Yes," she said, and then silently questioned his redirection. He answered her by turning away, and she knew that whatever the moment had been, it was now gone.

"Great. Text your father the change in plan." He tossed his cell over to her and she caught it. "Then get your boots on. I'll take you into town on the snowmobile."

A tiny flutter swelled in her stomach when she realized that he could've done that from the beginning. But he hadn't. He'd made her coffee, warmed her up, let her in just a tiny bit. Maybe her inclinations about him were correct after all. She decided right then and there that she wanted to find out.

Chapter Five

"My phone's working now," Scarlett said to Charles as she stood by the snowmobile that he'd parked outside the coffee shop. "I'll call my father and wait for him here. We'll get the truck moved from outside your house as soon as we can."

"All right," Charles said, his attention lingering on her for a tick longer than it should've. He started the engine.

"Would you like to have a cup of coffee with me?" she asked over the growl of it, in an act of complete impulsiveness. It was forward, but it just felt right.

If she was ever going to bring up the sale of the inn, she'd have to learn how to talk to him, and she'd have to do it fast. At least that was what she told herself, when really she'd asked because he was maddeningly aloof and she wanted to get to the bottom of it. It seemed to her that if he would open up a little bit, they could be friends.

"You jumped up so fast back at the house that we never really drank our coffees," she added. "Not the way I'm used to drinking them anyway."

"And how are you used to drinking them?" He cut the engine off, so she could answer. A good sign.

"Well, there's usually sugar and milk involved. And with the right person, it might take me an hour to drink a whole cup."

"Who would be the right person?"

"Keep talking like you are and you might be one," she teased him a tiny bit to see how he'd react.

He huffed out a little chuckle, and relief flooded her. Her joke had been a risk, given their rocky beginning, but his energy just now hinted again that deep down there might be a soft underbelly to that hardened outer shell.

"Come on." She nodded toward the shop called Love and Coffee.

He looked down at the icy pavement, clearly considering. The decision seemed to eat at him, his gaze unstill.

"If it's their famous triple-decker caramel drizzle you're scared of, don't be," she said, putting her face in his line of vision. "It's more bark than bite."

She made him smile again, and it sent a fizzle through her chest as those brown eyes swallowed her, his earlier irritation now replaced by hesitation.

"I'm not a fan of caramel drizzle," he admitted, the corner of his mouth turned up just slightly in an adorable way. But his eyes were still full of thought.

"Personally, I never get the caramel drizzle either. I'm usually a peppermint kind of girl."

He didn't respond, his mind elsewhere.

"It's just a coffee," she assured him. "And I'm freezing again, so we'd better get a warm drink before we become ice sculptures out here."

His trepidation waned a little, and he stepped up beside her. "It's my fault you're in the cold," he said. "I'll treat." He opened the door for her and allowed her to enter.

"Well, hellooo!" Loretta's voice floated over to Scarlett as they came through the door. She found Loretta at a table for one with a stack of self-help books and an empty coffee mug, her hand on her heart and her focus like lasers on Charles. "Look who you picked up." Her gaze moved suggestively to Scarlett and then she stood and hurried over to them, jabbing her hand out to Charles. "Remember me? We met at the gas station." She nearly batted her eyelashes at him.

With a sugary smile, she addressed Scarlett. "My couple is having a grand time together right now! I'm going to check on them soon, so I'm killing time with some pleasure reading." Her bracelets jingled as she leaned over to the table where she'd been sitting and held up her book: *Lasting Love: Making it Work.* Loretta turned back to Charles. "Love is my specialty."

Charles eyed Scarlett for an explanation, and she had to hold back her laugh as she imagined what might be going through his head.

"It's good to see you again, Loretta," he said.

Loretta looked like she would faint when he remembered her name.

"I was just getting Scarlett a coffee. Would you like another?"

"Oh, no," she said, flirtier than Scarlett had ever seen her before. "I'm about to leave, but thank you for asking." When he turned away, her eyes widened at Scarlett, and she mouthed, "He's so adorable."

"What do you recommend then?" he asked, peering up at the menu and making Loretta jump.

"I like The Mistletoe with triple caramel drizzle," Loretta said.

"Ah," he said, sharing an unspoken moment of camaraderie with Scarlett at Loretta's suggestion. "Good to know. You can learn a lot about a person by the drink she orders."

This sent Loretta into a full tailspin of excitement. She could hardly pick her books up, fumbling them awkwardly as she headed out the door.

Charles greeted the barista kindly. "I'll have two peppermint lattes, please."

"You like peppermint lattes?" Scarlett asked, her mind in a fog of delight and confusion at his change in behavior. She couldn't decide if she was more baffled now than she had been before when he'd been so cranky.

"I've never had one," he said. "But I figured I'd try it. If you really do plan to talk for an hour, I'll have plenty of time to finish it if I don't like it. Tiny sips…" He allowed his teasing to show on his lips and Scarlett felt a little like Loretta had for a second.

"What are you thinking about?" he asked, as he took their mugs from the barista and gestured for her to find a seat first.

"I can't figure you out," she said truthfully as she found a table. "You're hot and cold."

"I'm sorry." He took off his coat and sat down across from her, wrapping his large hand around the handle of his cup. "Some people aren't very happy with me…" he said in some sort of cryptic explanation, his thoughts obviously heavier than he was able to articulate in that instance. "I'm not very happy with myself either. I was defensive and I'm not usually like that."

"Why?" she asked, indulging in the question. It wasn't any of her business, but he'd been the one to mention it, and she was extremely curious.

"It's nothing to worry about," he said on an exhale, two deep lines forming between his eyes before he straightened out his expression. "Just work. But don't worry. I don't want to talk about work. In fact, I promise not to mention it again."

"Well, I don't mind talking about your work," she said, taking this as her opportunity to say something about the inn. "In fact, I was wondering—"

He cut her off. "I *do* mind. The last thing I want to talk about is my job." He scooted his mug forward and leaned his forearms on the table. "Somehow, you made me think of something other than my work for the first time in a very long time. And I'm not sure how, but you also managed to get me into this coffee shop when I haven't wanted to go out since I got here. I bought a peppermint latte..." His eyes widened, playfully aghast. "So please, don't mention work."

"All right," she said, feeling her chance to have a reasonable option for the inn to present to Gran by Christmas slipping away. "Why haven't you wanted to come into town?" she asked, taking a sip of her latte and letting the smooth, minty flavor of it pull her back into the Christmas spirit.

He rolled his shoulders as if there were tension there. "I don't really want to talk about that either."

"Well, what *do* you want to talk about then?"

"I shouldn't have come," he said under his breath, suddenly looking as though he were annoyed with himself.

"Look, I know you don't know me..."

He visibly regrouped. "I do know you, actually." Oddly, there was a slight affection lingering in his eyes when he said it.

His comment took her by surprise. "You do?" She examined his face for something that she recognized, dissecting his features with this new lens. As she did, a flash of eyes like his flickered in her memory, but it was just fuzzy enough to make it difficult to place what she remembered.

"How do you know me?" she asked.

"I realized it back at the house. We met at the falls. Just the one day. We were young."

For the first time since she'd gotten stuck in the snow, Charles gave her a soft but genuine smile that made her heart beat like a snare drum, and she remembered. Not only the smile, but the way her heart had pattered then too.

"Charlie," she said, trying out his fifteen-year-old nickname on her lips after twenty years.

"Yes."

"Do you still go by Charlie?"

"Only with people who know me well." He fiddled with the edge of his mug.

She remembered that day at the falls. She was swimming in her new pink bikini, her long, wet hair dripping down her back. Charlie had jumped in from a rock above her, splashing her accidentally. He'd rushed over to apologize, meeting her in the water to the hoots of his friends, but he'd shooed them off. She told him it was really fine; she was soaking wet already. She asked his name and he just said, "Charlie." He'd told Scarlett he was on a break from school, and she'd assumed that he was there visiting. So he must have been at Amos's…

That day, they'd struck up a conversation, talking until evening about everything and nothing at the same time. Before they knew it, their friends had gone, and it was just the two of them in the water, the soft swish-washing sound of the falls behind them. As the sun disappeared behind the mountains, it was clear that neither of them wanted to leave, but they both knew they couldn't stay. She asked if he'd be back to the falls tomorrow, and he said he wouldn't—it was his last day there—which had disappointed her. He reached through the water and gently put his hands on her waist, asking her permission with his gaze. She let him. She could still remember the way their skin touched as their bodies bumped against each other with the movement of the water rushing around them.

"Maybe we'll meet again," he'd said.

And then he'd kissed her. She still remembered that kiss because it had always seemed so much more mature and tender than the other boys her age. It hadn't lasted long, however—the whooping of his friends on the bank tearing them apart. They'd come back to get him.

"So here we are again," he said, breaking her from her moment of nostalgia.

He smiled at her and she tried not to focus on his lips, now wondering if the feel of them would be the same as they were in her memory.

"I'm going to call you Charlie," she decided right then and there, and his smile widened.

Then he sobered. "I should never have treated you the way I did when I met you by the truck; I shouldn't have treated anyone that way... I really just wanted to be alone and your showing up disrupted that. But I'm glad for it now."

"Yeah, you definitely didn't seem like the same person I met that day so long ago," she said, wishing he would divulge whatever it was that was bothering him.

He looked into her eyes. "We were just kids," he said, but it was almost as if he were stating that to see if she agreed, or if she felt the vibe of familiarity that seemed to float around them. Did he notice it too?

She didn't know how to read him well enough to tell for sure, so, tentatively, she nodded.

"There you are!" Her father's voice sliced through the moment. "I got your text, and I went out to Amos's to get the truck unstuck, but

I couldn't get close enough, so I decided to see if I could get ahold of the snow plow." His gaze fluttered to Charlie and then to Scarlett.

Charlie stood up. "Charles Bryant," he introduced himself, causing Scarlett to shoot out of her chair just as her father's eyebrows rose in interest, his mouth opening to speak.

"Blue Bailey," he said before she could interject, reaching out a hand eagerly to shake Charlie's. "I'm sure Scarlett has—"

"Dad!" she nearly screeched, not wanting him to mention the inn. She'd do it in her own way when she felt like it was right. Something was upsetting Charlie, and she had a strong feeling that it was why he was at Amos's. Getting to the bottom of that was more important right at this minute because the boy she'd met all those years ago had had so much life in him, so much ahead of him—which was very different from the man he seemed to be at the moment. She just needed more time.

"I got stuck at Charlie's and he gave me a ride into town," she said, "but we'll need to get the truck out of the snow, and he and I haven't really had a chance to catch up too much…" Scarlett was babbling, none of her thoughts coming through in their entirety. She widened her eyes at her dad to let him know something was up, but he didn't seem to catch it, so she kept going. "How about we get you a coffee to go? You can order it and sit with me, and then we can let Charlie get back home. I've bothered him quite enough…" She tugged on Blue's arm.

"Scarlett," her father laughed. "You're talking a mile a minute." He slowly pulled free from her grasp. "I'm able to order my own coffee, and I'm sure if Charlie needs to get back, he'll let us know—you will, won't you, Charlie?"

Scarlett's exchange with her father was clearly affecting Charlie. He was perceptive enough to sense her tension. He was visibly withdrawing right in front of her, his shoulders tensing as he eyed them both warily, clearly realizing Scarlett was attempting to cut her father's visit short.

"If you're able to get home safely, Scarlett, then I really should get going," Charlie said, taking his coat from the back of his chair and slipping it on.

This wasn't how she wanted things to go, but she couldn't ask him to stay for fear her father would say something too soon. The last thing she wanted was for Charlie to think that she was being kind to him in an effort to convince him to buy the inn. He'd said that he didn't want to talk about his work. She liked Charlie. It was Christmas, and the one thing she'd learned over the years was that the residents of Silver Falls came together at Christmastime. More so than any other time of the year. He didn't need to be sitting out there all alone in that run-down cottage. Once she'd gotten him talking, being with him had been nice.

"Thank you for the coffee suggestion," he said, nodding toward the cup on the table.

Scarlett picked it up. "It's still full," she said, remembering his comment about tiny sips. "Oh well, at least you gave it a chance. Every now and again, trying something new will surprise you."

His eyes found hers. "Yes. Yes, it will." But caution flooded him again as he regarded her father, noticeably recalling how Scarlett had tried to rush Blue away. "Enjoy your coffees," he said. Then he headed for the door.

"Bye," she called after him. He looked over his shoulder at her and raised his hand in farewell.

If they met up again, she was willing to bet that he would have questions for her about this moment, and she wasn't quite sure how she would answer. But there was a lot that he hadn't told her either—that was pretty clear.

None of that mattered, however, if she didn't see him again. But she was going to make it her own Christmas mission to make sure she did.

Chapter Six

"Why did you hurry Charles off like that?" her father said after he'd gotten his coffee and sat down. He'd opted for black, no sugar, in a house mug—simple, the way he enjoyed his life.

The snow must have kept people away, because the coffee shop sat empty except for the barista behind the counter and Sue, the owner, who was in the corner, wiring fresh greenery to the windowsills and tugging on her pashmina between bouts of shivering. Scarlett hadn't looked around to notice until now, her focus having been entirely on Charlie.

"Dad, there's something going on with Charlie; I can tell," she started. Then she launched into the last few hours she'd spent with him.

After her explanation, Blue clasped his fingers together, resting his chin on them, mulling it all over. "Do you think it has anything to do with Amos?" he speculated.

Scarlett shrugged. "I don't know. He wouldn't talk about work, though. That was so strange, since he'd openly given Cappy his business card."

"Could he be in some kind of financial trouble?"

"Maybe, but by the look of that snowmobile, I think he's probably doing just fine."

"Sorry to eavesdrop," Sue said, poking her head into the conversation, her hands full of holly. "But if you're referring to Charles Bryant, he's definitely not in financial trouble. I head up the girls' and boys' home, you know, and he just donated twenty thousand dollars to it for Christmas gifts. But that wasn't all. He gave me another fifteen thousand to give to any charity or Christmas need of my choice." She waited dramatically for their reactions, her eyebrows raised.

"Wow," Blue said, his interest satisfying Sue enough for her to resume decorating.

"That was incredibly generous of him," Scarlett said, as she pondered their first meeting. "You know, he doesn't have a Christmas tree."

"Maybe he hasn't had a chance to get one yet."

Sue set a vanilla votive with a ring of red berries in the center of their table.

"When can we get the truck out from in front of his house?"

"It's supposed to warm up slightly tomorrow. Maybe we can let the temperature do some work for us and try to get it out then."

"Okay," she said, eyeing Charlie's cup, which still sat, full, on the other side of the table. "When we get the truck out tomorrow, I want to run down and check on him."

"Sure."

"I thought you were shopping," Gran said from her chair next to the Christmas tree when Scarlett and Blue came in. Her pen stilled on the crossword puzzle in her lap.

"I was, but I got stuck in the snow."

Gran allowed a knowing smile. "You were doing some shopping at Amos's?"

Scarlett felt the heat in her cheeks. Gran must have heard about her visit to Charlie when Scarlett had called her father to come get her. She went over and sat down next to the fire, her mind whirring with what to tell Gran as a reason for going over there. Scarlett hated that she'd put herself in the position of keeping things from Gran. It made her want to sit her grandmother down right now and tell her what was going on, but she knew her family would never forgive her.

"Amos always wanted to fix that place up," Gran said. "He'd be happy to know someone was in the old cottage. I've wondered about the state of it over the last few years. How bad is it?"

"It's pretty beat up," Scarlett said, the fire popping, causing it to dance, sending a small burst of heat toward her.

"I hear his son Charles is easy on the eye."

Scarlett let out a laugh, despite herself. "How do you know this kind of stuff?" she said, Gran's comment surprising her. Gran always knew the gossip around town. She was never one to spread it herself, but she would definitely listen when someone had something to say.

"I spoke to Loretta today when she called to get the time for the Christmas party."

"Of course." Scarlett scooted a basket of glitter-covered pine cones to the side to give herself more legroom, and twisted toward Gran. "Did Amos ever mention having a son to you?"

"Only once," she said, more seriously. "He said they were estranged. It was in passing; he didn't elaborate, as if it were just a regular piece of his history, and I didn't want to pry..."

"Estranged. Wow. So why do you think he's here now when Amos is gone?"

Gran shook her head sadly. "I don't know, dear. Did you speak to him?"

"Yeah. He seemed like something was bothering him."

"I can imagine."

Gran could always see some sort of bigger picture, making connections before anyone else. "What can you imagine?"

"He's alone. At Christmas. And his father is gone. I'd imagine that he would, indeed, seem bothered." She cleared her throat. "Not to mention he built that monstrosity down the road. That's enough to bother anyone." She rolled her eyes, folding her crossword around the back of the book to keep it open and setting it on the side table.

Scarlett reached down to stroke Stitches, who'd sauntered up to her from her perch on the piano bench to be nearer to the fire. "You mean Croft Ridge Resort and Suites?" she said.

"I suppose I do. That's certainly a mouthful, which is fitting. The name is as big as the amount of countryside it ate up." She pursed her lips in disapproval.

"Would you approve of it if it weren't so large?" Scarlett said, being careful not to give away her motive for asking the question by keeping her gaze neutral. She didn't like the way the conversation was going, considering Charlie Bryant was Scarlett's only option for viable purchasers. She'd been hoping to get a better reaction from Gran when she finally mentioned his name.

"Any time our gorgeous views are obstructed by concrete of any size, it's a tragedy."

"The inn has concrete parking," she challenged. "At one point, White Oaks was as new as these resorts popping up… It was a simple house before it was expanded to the size it is now."

"True. But White Oaks feels like part of the mountains themselves. The resorts don't have history," Gran said, leaning forward and placing her hands on her knees for emphasis. "They don't tell the stories that White Oaks does. The original family who owned the main house built the corridor leading to the west wing of the inn. Do you know why? Because it hid tunnels underneath that were part of the Underground Railroad. They led slaves to freedom. The back garden where we have the benches—that was originally planted when this was an orphanage. I cleared the area with your pappy and restored it, and would you know that some of the original annuals returned? Every single flower blooms for a child who lived here. I count them, and make sure that we always have exactly fifty-two flowers. No child is ever left behind. During the Civil War, this home was a hospital. The dining area still has deep grooves in the wooden floor, a reminder of the rows of iron beds that lined the walls. Those are only a few of the inn's many stories. This house has always been about love, about helping others, and about togetherness, and it is in that spirit that I house my guests."

Scarlett studied the room with new eyes and an appreciation for the type of businesswoman her grandmother was, feeling a loss because she knew she probably wouldn't be able to find another owner to live up to that type of hospitality and loyalty to preserving the feeling and the history of the inn. No wonder she didn't like the resorts. It all made sense now. Scarlett knew how much Gran enjoyed running White Oaks, but she'd never asked her why. In all those years, she'd just assumed that the only reason was that the place had a lot of memories from her life with Pappy.

"Gran, that's incredible. I've been coming here my whole life and I haven't heard those stories. Why?"

Gran looked thoughtful, her eyes on the Christmas tree, the reflection of the lights dancing in the glass of a nearby window. "The stories are buried within this house where they belong. I've let them rest here peacefully without stirring them up, to keep them the way they were meant to be—in the hearts of those who lived them."

"But, Gran, people would love to know these things when they stay here. The inn could offer a tour; it might bring in more guests."

Gran's chest rose with a slow, irritated breath. "I will not capitalize on nor exploit the histories of those who came before me, for monetary gain. It is my duty to maintain this home and to use it how I see fit as the owner. I couldn't live with myself if I made a profit on the hardships of others."

Sometimes Gran could be so frustrating. Scarlett felt that her grandmother's kindness could occasionally have a negative effect on things. She missed important opportunities because she was stubborn in her beliefs.

"Hello, you two!" Aunt Beth said as she walked in. "What were we talking about?" she asked, happily oblivious to the conversation at hand. She gingerly lowered herself down onto the sofa so as not to spill the brimming cup of hot apple cider in her hand, which wobbled with her movements.

"We were talking about Loretta," Gran said, effectively shutting down the conversation they'd been having.

"Oh." Aunt Beth rolled her eyes in jest. "I didn't even get in the door of Love and Coffee in town without Loretta dashing over to me to find out if I'm still single. Yes. For God's sake, I'm single. Of course I am. It's a holiday, and we all know that I somehow manage to spend every holiday alone." She huffed as Aunt Alice entered the room and plopped down beside her.

Aunt Alice put her arm around Beth. "You're not alone! You have us," she said, having caught the tail end of the conversation.

"I'm getting too old for dating anyway," Beth said. "I'm over sixty! The word 'boyfriend' doesn't even sound right coming off my lips. And the whole thing is exhausting."

"There's nothing wrong with dating at any time in your life. Anyway, you're young at heart," Alice said with a grin.

"You're all young to me," Gran interjected, picking her crossword back up and setting it in her lap. "So I don't know what you're going on about. Beth, you ought to let Loretta set you up with someone. She wouldn't have been in business for all these years if she weren't any good at finding people who fit with each other. She's surprisingly amazing at it."

Beth was fashionable and sophisticated, and Scarlett always thought she was perfectly capable of having a solid, wonderful relationship with someone; she just hadn't found that special someone yet. "I don't know..." Beth said, running her hand through her graying hair, the style bouncing back to perfection.

"Why not?" Alice asked.

"It seems so... forced," she answered before sipping from her mug.

Scarlett caught the scent of Aunt Beth's cider all the way across the room; it smelled of nutmeg and cinnamon. That particular fragrance took her back to her childhood when this room was closed to guests and the family was all gathered together on Christmas morning, opening gifts in their bathrobes and slippers, the fire going in the fireplace, the sun barely peeking over the mountaintops, bits of ribbon and wrapping paper strewn around the room. She would miss those times. What about the twins, Riley and Mason? They'd grow up with only fuzzy memories of this place. She wouldn't think about it right now, or she'd start to tear up.

"I could mention something to Loretta in passing when I see her again, and just feel out the situation to see what she might think…" Scarlett offered.

"No," Aunt Beth said kindly, "if I'm meant to find Mr. Right, it will happen."

"Would you date a friend of a friend?" Scarlett challenged. "Say I introduced you to someone I knew?"

"Of course."

"I don't see where it's much different from Loretta then. She'd be introducing you to someone new. Same thing."

Aunt Beth sipped her cider thoughtfully. Then she wriggled her back straighter, the way she always did before she made a point. "Being by myself doesn't bother me on a daily basis. Besides, I don't want to waste my Christmas running around with a stranger. I'd much rather spend it here. My dating life isn't our number one concern." She gazed meaningfully at Scarlett, and Scarlett knew that Beth was referring to Gran. But when Gran eyed her, Beth added, "Our number one concern is to have an amazing Christmas at White Oaks, am I right?"

Gran settled back in her chair with a smile and resumed her crossword puzzle. Just then, Scarlett realized that she'd been holding her breath during the exchange. Truck or no truck, first thing tomorrow she was heading over to Charlie's, and this time she was going to make sure she didn't leave until she'd talked about the sale of White Oaks.

Chapter Seven

Scarlett was finally close enough to make out Charlie's features, as he stood on the small porch at Amos's house. He was in the same coat as yesterday and what looked like pajama bottoms and boots, his hair disheveled in an amazingly attractive way, that guarded look on his face as she trudged toward him. She'd used her dad's phone to get Charlie's number to text this morning, telling him she'd like to stop by, but when Charlie hadn't responded she'd decided to come anyway, worried about his well-being out here on the edge of the mountain.

"Good morning," she said, when she reached him across the side yard by foot.

He stared at her. Yesterday's irritation was replaced by a quiet in-difference, that wall of his built strong today. A new pile of wood sat next to the door.

"I did text…" she said, trying not to let his gaze rob her of her purpose. She didn't want to admit that, even though they'd shared a nice moment together over their peppermint lattes, she was just as cautious about him as he seemed to be about her. She worried that he didn't trust her after her exchange in front of him with her father yesterday, and she wondered how obvious it was, now, that she had something on her mind that she had yet to say.

But then a slight crack formed in his stoic demeanor, a hint of an upward turn of his lips, and a sense of relief washed over her. Until he cleared it with a breath of icy air. "Can I help you?" he asked, looking over her shoulder at her dad's truck, which was still stuck in the snow. He didn't let her answer, his curiosity clearly getting the better of him. "How did you get here?"

Scarlett pointed to Pappy's tractor, which sat at the end of a side road that had been completely hidden by the storm, the plow on the front of the machine full of snow. She'd taken it through the field and along the lane that had been impassable until she'd cleared it just now.

"You drove a tractor?" He allowed a grin then, those eyes glittering with interest before he could turn away. He opened the door. "I suppose we should go inside."

He pushed the door open further, allowing her to enter, and then he followed her in and shut them into the damp, warm space of Amos's little house. The rich aroma of freshly brewed coffee hit her the moment she got inside. It was mixed with the unique scent of Charlie and the age of the house. She inhaled it, appreciating the complexity of it.

"Did you just get up?" she asked. She'd left the house at ten o'clock, so it was probably close to ten thirty by now, and by the look of him as he shrugged off his coat, he hadn't done much to improve his appearance this morning.

He poured her a cup of coffee as she sat on the hearth, their little moment becoming a ritual of sorts. He handed the mug to her just like he had yesterday. "I was up late," he said.

Right as he said it, she noticed the ceiling above the spot where the bucket had been before. A tarp was nailed to it, the bottom bulging slightly with water from melted snow. "Oh my gosh!" she said, standing up and walking over to it.

"I think the old wood's giving out," he said, filling himself a cup and joining her. "The weight of the snow was too much for it and bits of the ceiling were falling into the room." He took a sip from his mug and swallowed. "It was quite a project to get the tarp up and keep the place heated last night. Kept me awake until after two in the morning."

Scarlett felt the sting of guilt, concerned now that she'd imposed on his sleep. She should've thought better of coming when he hadn't texted back. "May I ask you something?" She turned to him, allowing his moment of candidness to give her an opening for a personal question, as she tried to make sense of why he was devoting all his time to this house when there was no one there but him and when there were plenty of better accommodation options in town. "What brought you here?"

He closed up right in front of her, the tension shooting back into his shoulders, the dark eyes as he looked at her returning, and she wasn't sure what she'd asked, but clearly it wasn't something he was ready to answer. He went to the counter and slowly placed his mug down, his gaze not leaving his still hands as they continued to grip his mug.

Scarlett walked over to him, pulling his attention toward her. "I just wondered, that's all," she said gently. "I'm sure Amos would've been thrilled to know you were back."

The comment seemed to slice through him, the pain evident.

All of a sudden there was a loud crack, and the tarp that had been holding the bits of ceiling and water came crashing down, along with part of the roofing, sending fragments of wood and snow sliding across the hardwood floor. Scarlett let out a yelp in surprise and fear, jumping backward. With what seemed to be an instinctive action, Charlie grabbed her, wrapping his arms around her and leaning over her body to protect her face from the falling debris. His embrace was comforting in a way, and made her feel safe, slowing her racing heart.

When all the commotion had settled, he slowly let go of her, and the two of them peered up at the gaping hole in the ceiling.

"Damn," he said under his breath, as he stepped onto the crumpled tarp and over a chunk of wood on the floor to peer straight up to the gray sky that was now above them. "Well," he said on an exhale, "that's my day taken care of. Looks like I'll be fixing this." He ran his hand over the scruff on his tired face.

"How will you fix it in all this snow?" Scarlett said. "It needs to be repaired from the outside in. You'll freeze out there. And how will you get the supplies you need? I doubt they'll fit on the snowmobile." Her worries tumbled out one after another, her distress getting the better of her.

Charlie seemed to process her questions, glancing toward the window.

Scarlett could see Pappy's tractor through the glass.

"No way," she said. "Even if we get what you need to repair the damage, you're not climbing up on a rooftop in the dead of winter. I can't allow you to be that ridiculously unsafe. It's icy! And it would be nearly impossible to get medical help out here if you hurt yourself." Even Uncle Joe didn't have the kind of resources required for someone who fell off a house.

"What's my other option?" he said, quietly exasperated. "I'll freeze to death if I don't fix it. I had to keep the fire going all night long just to battle the cold that seeped in through the break in the ceiling last night. I'll never be able to properly secure it unless I repair that hole." He went over and grabbed his coat, evidently planning to get started right then.

"I have another option," she said, attempting to stop him.

He kept moving, sliding on his snow boots.

"My gran owns White Oaks Inn. We have plenty of rooms available. You can stay with us until the snow clears."

She hadn't planned for it, but the perfect opportunity might have just fallen into her lap. At the very least, it would give Scarlett an opportunity to get to know him more, to see if her hunch was correct about him, if he was the right fit to be their buyer. And if he was, she could show Charlie how gorgeous and wonderful the inn could be, get Gran to share more about its history, and really sell him on it. Then, when the time was right, she could ask him if he was interested. She'd talk to Gran about letting him stay, later. Once Gran had heard about his generous donations to charity, she'd certainly change her opinion of him. And maybe she'd even like him, which would make selling a whole lot easier on Gran.

"Tomorrow night's the town Christmas party at our place. It might be fun," she added, trying to sway him.

"I hadn't planned on being anywhere but here…"

He trailed off in thought and scrutinized the giant hole in the ceiling, frustration flashing across his face. But then his expression softened when he looked back at Scarlett, making her wonder if he could read her silent encouragement. At the heart of her request was the basic need to get him somewhere safe, where she wouldn't spend all night worrying about him being exposed to the elements.

"You can't stay here," she said gently.

Charlie deliberated only a moment more and then his shoulders slumped in defeat. "Thank you," he said, offering a genuine smile. "I suppose I should try to get this hole secured and then pack. Mind giving me a lift in the tractor?"

"Not at all."

Scarlett felt anticipation bubble up for the first time since she'd heard about selling the inn. Amos's crumbling house might have just saved Christmas for her.

Scarlett's father loped over to her happily as she came through the main door of the inn with Charlie. His arms were full of wood for the fire—something Gran's staff usually took care of. Scarlett wondered how many people Gran had let go this year.

"Where have you been?" he asked, lumping the logs onto the small cart they used to carry wood around to the various fireplaces in the inn. He grabbed one of Gran's Christmas table runners that she always spread along the sideboard for the holiday.

Scarlett had spent the last few hours working together with Charlie to shield the interior from the elements as best they could before leaving. She couldn't just sit back and not help. They'd nailed three tarps to the ceiling and lined the floor underneath with any dishpan or bucket they could find, then scooted the furniture out of the way so it wouldn't get damaged.

It was strange to be working so close to him, but she didn't mind at all. In fact, it felt very natural to be by his side. Perhaps it was because of their one memorable day together so long ago, but she enjoyed helping him, and she realized that if she hadn't, she truly would've worried about how he'd get along with the repairs.

Charlie's head swiveled slowly as he took in the interior of the inn. "This structure is incredible," he said, running his finger along the woodwork that encased the door. "This wood is as old as the house—I can tell by the craftsmanship. Is that the original staircase?"

"Probably," Scarlett said, excitement welling up. He liked what he saw. "My gran would know."

"The main building seems like it's in great shape considering its age. Is it part of a historical preservation program?"

"You'd have to ask Gran."

Charlie and Gran would have so much to talk about; she could hardly wait. What if Gran fell in love with Charlie's vision for running the inn and retired happily without a care in the world? With Charlie running it, they could probably visit anytime they liked. As he was single like Gran, all but the main bedroom in the private quarters would be empty, just like it was now when all the family visited. This could be the perfect scenario… Scarlett knew she was getting carried away with her daydreams, but she could hope.

"Hello again," Blue said, offering a warm handshake, but then he shot a questioning look over to Scarlett after noticing Charlie's suitcase.

"Charlie will be staying at White Oaks," she explained. "The snow damaged the roof of his house."

"Oh no," Blue said, his face creasing in concern. His serious expression didn't fit with the rest of him, given what he was wearing. He was still holding Gran's Christmas table runner, and he had his Santa hat on, as well as the Christmas sweater that Scarlett had bought him last year.

"I'll have it looked at by a professional once the snow clears a bit more," Charlie said. "We got it as secure as we could for now."

"Glad to hear that." Blue turned to Scarlett. "Why don't you check him into room 1B? That way he won't have to walk too far in the cold every day to get to the main house. You'll have to grab the key from reception since Esther's gone. I'll let Gran know the room will be occupied."

"Thanks, Dad," Scarlett said.

"You two should get rested up so you can come with us! We're all going to watch Preston at The Bar tonight. It's Christmas carol night…" His eagerness was evident in the wide grin that spread across his face.

"Christmas carol night is tonight?" Scarlett said, knowing exactly why her father was so excited.

"You can't miss it," Blue said as he headed toward the kitchen. "Everyone's getting ready now. We're all leaving at six o'clock."

"What's Christmas carol night?" Charlie asked, picking up his suitcase and following Scarlett to the reception desk.

"It's a super fun night at The Bar," she said, going behind the desk and rummaging on the wall of keys for 1B. "It happens once a year, and Cappy keeps it a secret until the very day. He changes out all the taps to locally brewed Christmas ales and lagers, and he has a scavenger hunt that's a little like a grown-up Easter egg hunt, except he uses Christmas carols." Scarlett took the key to 1B off the hook.

"Sounds like fun," he said.

"It's a blast. All year, people donate things as prizes, and the prizes can be pretty substantial. Gran's giving away a free one-week stay at White Oaks. The merchants in town have donated things like boating trips, spa days, a year's worth of free cakes, and even a pair of diamond earrings once." She opened the door leading outside to the west wing where Charlie would be staying. He tipped his head up toward the ceilings, paying attention to the summer paddle fans that were stilled in the winter weather.

"And who's Preston—your father mentioned him."

"Preston Meade. He's a banker, but he can play the guitar like no one I've ever heard before, and his voice is amazing."

"A musical banker," Charlie said, the corners of his mouth turning up ever so slightly, like they had when he was on Amos's porch. It was as if he wanted to enjoy himself but he wouldn't allow himself to for some reason.

"Yes," she said, as they walked along the covered porch. She hardly noticed the cold, or the fact that Uncle Joe must have shoveled it. She was too busy wondering what was going through his head. He was so perplexing. She observed the creases at his eyes, evidence that there used to be laughter in them, and the kind look he allowed every now and again when he caught her eye... Who was that boy she'd met so long ago now? What kind of man had he become? "Would you like to come with us?"

"Ah, I don't know..." he said, coming to a stop outside 1B. "I was up late with the repairs, and it's your family time..."

"It's not just our family. The whole town is there. But if you're tired, I understand." Scarlett couldn't help her disappointment. She couldn't stand the fact that he was alone all the time, and, while she wasn't thrilled with the circumstances under which it had happened, she was glad that Charlie was staying at White Oaks now. Maybe if she could get him in a more festive atmosphere, he'd open up like he started to at the coffee shop.

She slid the key in the lock and pushed open the door, remaining on the porch as the buttery radiance of lamplight shone out from the room. Gran always turned on the lamps in the empty rooms at dusk, giving the inn a warm glow. Charlie walked in and looked around, leaving the door open, so Scarlett waited to see what he wanted her to do next. He lifted out one of the chocolate bars from the Christmas basket that Aunt Alice had been helping to deliver to each room when Scarlett and her father had arrived.

"Is there anything I can get you?" she asked.

He shook his head, running his hand along the crisp duvet. "No…" He turned toward the doorway where she stood. "I have more than I need, thank you."

Hopefully *more than he needed* was a good thing. She prayed that it meant he immediately felt comfortable and cozy in the space. Against the soft, delicate décor of the inn, he looked more haggard than he had at Amos's. He seemed exhausted.

"Are you sure you won't join us? I'd like you to come," she offered.

Her last statement had stopped him in his tracks, his hands now still by his sides, interest all over his face. But then it disappeared. "Why?"

"What?" His question took her by surprise, but from what she knew of him so far, it probably shouldn't have.

"Why do you want me to go? You don't know me." He was defensive.

She thought they'd gotten past that. "I might get to know you if you'd go out with us tonight."

"I doubt that," he said quietly. He broke eye contact and pulled his suitcase over to the bed, unzipping it.

"You doubt it?"

Freezing now as she stood on the open porch, she came into the room and shut the door behind her. It was forward of her to come into his personal space, but they'd spent enough time alone at Amos's that she didn't feel uncomfortable. Two could play at this being-blunt game. "If you doubt that I won't be able to know you better after a night out with us, that's your fault."

The wall he was so good at erecting came sliding back up. He opened a drawer and started unpacking his clothes from the suitcase.

"Please don't do that," she said, pulling back, her tone more sensitive. She didn't want to be snappy with him. She wanted the exact opposite.

He shut the drawer. "Do what exactly?"

"Shut down."

He spun around and the intensity from their first meeting flashed in his eyes. "Maybe you don't *need* to know me because I might not be the person you want me to be."

Scarlett felt the confusion slither across her face and she couldn't straighten it out. "I don't want you to be anyone. It's Christmas and you're all by yourself. I just thought you might like to have a little fun, that's all." She put herself between Charlie and his suitcase, demanding his attention. "You deserve to have a nice Christmas."

He withdrew right in front of her, making her scramble to figure out what she'd said wrong.

"No, I don't." Charlie ran his hands down his face and then back up to his temples as if a headache were forming.

"You don't deserve a Christmas?" she asked, completely baffled.

"No."

Scarlett had no idea what had happened to Charlie to make him think that, but she had to believe her gut feeling, and the memory of that one day so long ago. He was a good person; she knew it deep down. Nobody should feel like they don't deserve Christmas. He was hurting and clearly masking that hurt with abrupt behavior. He was pushing her away when he so clearly needed someone around him. He wouldn't keep letting her in unless that was the case. It was pretty clear to her that he was fighting it.

"Look," she said, allowing her affection to show, "I won't pressure you. Get some rest. I'll be waiting at six o'clock in the main living room. I'll stay five minutes and then leave for The Bar. How your holiday goes this year will be your decision. You can't move forward from whatever it is that's eating at you unless you take a step. And I'm giving you an opportunity right now to take that step. Your call."

He didn't say anything, but she could see thoughts crossing his mind.

With a little wave, she let herself out to give him some time alone. She headed back into the main house with more questions than before, feeling even farther from her original purpose for going to Amos's this morning.

Chapter Eight

"Do you like the red boot or the black one?" Heidi asked, alternating from one foot to the other, wearing two different boots, and bending her thin legs at the knee to get Scarlett's opinion.

Scarlett and Heidi had gotten ready to go to Christmas carol night together. Scarlett enjoyed having family around. Heidi had gone down to Scarlett's room and tried on everything in Scarlett's suitcase, convinced she had nothing to wear despite the fact that Heidi's suitcase looked as if she'd packed for a small army.

Scarlett squinted one eye to imagine both feet in the same shoe. Heidi was youthfully stunning with her dewy skin blushed just slightly, her long dark curls cascading down her back to her tiny waist, her form-fitting jeans showing off the womanly curves she'd developed in the last year.

"I like the black one," Scarlett said.

Heidi pursed her lips. "I should probably wear different jeans then." She dove into her suitcase, rifling through the mass of clothing. "I'll be a few minutes after you," she said. "When you go downstairs, will you tell everyone that I'll be down in a second? I need to call Michael."

"Are you sure you need to call him right now?" Scarlett asked, brushing her hair one last time and checking her reflection in the mirror before she went downstairs.

"Yes, I'm breaking up with him."

Scarlett stopped brushing her hair in surprise. "Oh, Heidi, are you okay about it?" She set the brush down and walked over to her cousin.

"Being here is helping me get clarity about our relationship, and I don't think it's going anywhere. With college next year, I don't know where I'll be… Yesss!" Heidi said, yanking a pair of jeans from under her pile of clothes.

"Just go with your gut," Scarlett offered. "Trust your gut in everything you do, and it won't lead you the wrong way."

Heidi looked up. "You're so right…" She stood up with the second pair of jeans in her hand, staring into the distance. "I *do* need to go with my gut." She came to and slipped her boots off for her wardrobe change.

"Come get me if you need me," Scarlett said. "I'll be downstairs."

The main living room was empty, with the exception of three guests who'd taken photos in front of the Christmas tree. Scarlett offered to snap one of all of them, to their obvious delight, and then they'd left, headed for dinner, they'd said.

It was 6:04. Heidi had managed to get herself together in time to catch the group as they left for The Bar, and they'd all piled into cars, leaving Scarlett to drive Gran's car. Scarlett sat on the edge of the large sofa with her coat and scarf draped across her lap, the last one to leave.

Gran always let Scarlett use her car when she visited, and since Gran had gone with Uncle Joe, Scarlett would use it tonight. She was hoping that Charlie would show up so she wouldn't have to drive it on the dark roads alone, but he hadn't come through the door. Not yet. She waited, her eyes darting between both entrances to the room.

6:05. She'd said she'd only wait until then.

Her shoulders slumped in disappointment. She didn't know why she thought Charlie would come. He hadn't done anything to make her think he would. She remembered what he'd said about not deserving Christmas, which seemed so preposterous that she couldn't even understand what he meant. What decent person shouldn't have a Christmas? She considered going down to his room, but thought better of it. She'd told him where to meet her and given him the choice. There was no need to try to convince him now. It was too late. With a deep breath, she got up and slid her coat on, tying her scarf around her neck.

Scarlett turned around to leave and stopped still, happiness warming her like a cup of Christmas hot cocoa.

"I'm late," Charlie said, standing in the doorway. He was clean-shaven, his hair combed, and he had on a navy sweater and jeans. He'd never looked quite like that before; he was jaw-droppingly handsome. "I slept a little longer than I'd meant to. I'm sorry."

"It's fine. I'm glad you're here." She had to work not to show the enormous smile that wanted to crawl across her face.

"I'm happy you waited. And that you invited me."

"I'd hoped you'd come," she admitted. His presence tonight caused her honesty to slip out even though she was trying to play it cool.

That kind look that Charlie had allowed a few times surfaced.

"We have to take Gran's car. It's either that or the tractor. They're about equal in size," she said with a laugh, making him smile in return.

Charlie looked down at her, his expression softer. "Show me the way."

*

The crowd was already rowdy when Scarlett and Charlie arrived at The Bar. Preston was on the small stage at the back, the edge of it lined with poinsettias and a glittering Christmas tree full of gifts to the side. He sat on a stool, his guitar in hand, singing an original tune. The song was bluesy with a great beat that made her want to forgo her chair and dance between the tables.

"He's talented," Charlie said into her ear so she could hear him over the music. "And you say he's a banker?"

By the look of Preston's frayed jeans, the worn condition of his square-toed boots, and the tattoo peeking out from his rolled sleeve, it probably did seem odd. "Yep," she answered, watching him perform. "He's in the loans department."

Preston's gaze flickered over to Loretta and then away, warming Scarlett. Preston and Loretta's friendship had a unique harmony. Even though Preston avoided her, there was an unsaid connection between the two of them that was undeniable. It was as if he accepted the fact that she could be pushy and overly open, and he didn't mind. There was a sort of rhythm to their cat-and-mouse game.

Loretta was sitting next to another woman, presumably her cousin Sarah, at a table by the stage, right in the center of the front row, and Scarlett's family had pulled two tables together next to them. Her dad had caught sight of Scarlett and was waving them over.

"Glad to see you two made it! The Christmas carols are about to start," Blue said when Scarlett and Charlie reached the table. She waved to Preston and he nodded hello as he strummed his guitar. Charlie pulled out a chair for Scarlett and then sat down beside her.

Even with all the sound in the room, Riley and Mason were playing checkers with Aunt Alice coaching loudly, while Uncle Joe listened to Heidi, who was animatedly talking over the music, and Aunt

Beth was helping Gran scoot her chair up to the table. Scarlett took it all in. This was one of her favorite nights. They ate pub food, sang until their throats hurt, and spent loads of time together, all while enjoying the Christmas carol hunt.

"Hey, y'all." Preston's deep voice echoed from the speakers on the stage when he'd finished his last song. "All the prizes are hidden somewhere in this room, and we're about to begin the Christmas caroling. Everyone ready?"

"Yes!" cried Loretta, the loudest of all, before tipping her head toward Sarah.

Preston grinned at Loretta but then quickly looked back out at the rest of the crowd, and Scarlett wondered how much he actually enjoyed her attention. "Here's your first carol," he said. "It's appropriate for the weather tonight." He strummed slowly on his guitar and began singing the song "Walking in a Winter Wonderland."

The crowd was silent as they listened for clues. Blue frantically scratched the words onto a pad of paper at the table: sleigh bells, lane, bluebird... Scarlett knew the lyrics by heart so she wasn't taking notes. Instead, she was busy scanning the room for possible hiding places. Cappy was excellent at coming up with the most inconspicuous locations to hide the prizes, but he was no match for Scarlett, who had managed to win something every year. She wasn't about to let her winning streak end. She zeroed in on a few places, gauging the fastest route to reach each one of them.

"Start your hunt!" Preston said when he'd finished the song, setting his guitar down to watch as everyone began looking for the prize. Loretta and Sarah stood up, Loretta leading her cousin to the stage. The fondness in Preston's eyes became more restrained when he regarded Sarah. He shook her hand, however, and offered her a warm smile.

Amusement wiggled through Scarlett as she watched the exchange—Preston had nowhere to escape this time. Loretta had cornered him.

A few people roamed the bar, following their ideas for leads from the lines of the song, looking under beer mats, behind doors, and beneath chairs.

"What do we do?" Charlie asked, leaning over to Scarlett, his soft, shaven face in her line of vision, those dark eyes inquisitive, filling her with nervous energy.

"Something in the song tells us where the prize is," she explained. "We have to see if we can figure it out before anyone else does."

Scarlett's dad got up and inspected a blue concert poster on the wall but came up empty. Aunt Alice was looking under her menu. Heidi and Joe had raced over to the door, and were now peering up at the frame of it.

"I might know. Come with me," Scarlett said to Charlie.

The two of them got up from their chairs and Scarlett led them to the old jukebox in the corner. She glanced all around it and then looked inside at the records. Excited, she tugged on Charlie's sleeve and pointed to the record single of "I Will Always Love You" by Dolly Parton—taped to it was something.

Charlie peered down at it. "What does it say?"

"Do you have fifty cents by chance?"

Charlie rummaged around in his pocket and pulled out a few coins, opening his hand to offer them to Scarlett. She plucked two quarters from his palm and put them into the jukebox. Then she hit the button for Dolly Parton. "The bird sang a love song, remember?" she said. "That was the clue in 'Walking in a Winter Wonderland,' I'm nearly sure of it."

The record slid along the steel shaft and fell flat into its position. As it started to spin, the first Christmas carol card was visible. "I think we found it!" she said, tugging on Charlie's arm. He leaned in closer to view it, putting his arm around her as he did, and suddenly Scarlett needed a glass of water, her mouth drying out. Even though she wanted to stand close to him like that for a little longer, the prize was on the line. "Go get Cappy!" she said. Charlie pulled away from her, making her immediately wish he hadn't. She liked how he felt against her.

Charlie strode over to Cappy and brought him to the jukebox.

"Lucky lady!" he said, patting her on the shoulder and then motioning to Preston. "You two can head up on stage! You've just won the first prize!"

Scarlett clapped her hand over her mouth, but she didn't have a lot of time to consider her luck because Preston was calling her to the microphone. She grabbed Charlie by the arm, taking him with her.

"We have a winner!" Preston said, just before he took one of the gifts from under the tree behind him. It was wrapped in silver paper and tied with what seemed like hundreds of thin dark green ribbons, their tails trailing down past his hands as he passed her the gift. It was light in weight and felt almost empty.

Scarlett offered it to Charlie to unwrap, but he insisted she do the honors. She tugged on the ends until the ribbon fell free in her hand and then tore the paper from the box, lifting the lid to find a single document nestled in tissue paper inside.

"Tell us what you've won," Preston said, his voice coming through the speakers loudly before he scooted the microphone stand toward her so her answer could be heard.

The crowd buzzed with excited chatter, eager to hear the first prize of the night.

Scarlett read the paper. "Oh my!" She read the paper again. "I won a trip for two to the Bahamas!"

Sue from the coffee shop called from the back corner, "You can thank our generous donor for that one! I used the money I mentioned earlier to donate the trip."

Scarlett didn't have to guess because Charlie was already putting two and two together. He huffed out a surprised laugh as he looked at Scarlett, clearly happy that she'd won something so lovely from his donation.

"To the anonymous donor, Scarlett thanks you, I'm sure," Preston said. "Now, let's take a little dinner break and I'll tell you the next clue after I play a few original songs. But before I do, I'm getting a drink." Preston slipped the mic back into its stand and hopped down the stairs over to the bar, slowing down as he passed Loretta. Sarah had stepped away and Loretta was talking a mile a minute to Preston, but he was politely listening to her. Scarlett saw him motion to the bar and then head that way, leaving Loretta looking around the room for Sarah.

"I can't believe our little Scarlett won!" Gran said when Scarlett and Charlie joined them back at the table.

Scarlett set the box between her and Charlie. "I can't believe it either," she said, still in shock that she'd actually figured it out so quickly. What were the odds that she'd win the trip bought with his donated money?

"You haven't taken a trip in years," Blue said. "You deserve to have a great time."

"Want to go with me?" she asked her father, hoping he'd say yes.

Truthfully, Blue was the closest person to her, and he also deserved a trip like this as much as anyone. He'd worked so hard for Gran when Pappy passed away, driving up every weekend the first year, and then making sure White Oaks ran as smoothly as it could in Pappy's absence until Gran had a handle on things.

"I don't fly, remember?" Blue had never flown in his life. He was terrified of being in the air. As much as Scarlett had tried to convince him that he was completely safe, he never would. He said God didn't make people with wings for a reason.

"You're going to make me go by myself?" she teased. One day she'd get him on a plane. She wasn't sure how, but she wasn't going to give up until he faced his fears.

"Take Gran. She could do with a week of cocktails and sun loungers more than I could."

"For the love of Pete," Gran said. "I'm too old to be jet-setting around. I'm lucky if I get to the farmers' market and back on a good day."

Blue interrupted their banter, standing up and eyeing the line that was forming at the bar. "I'll go put in the orders for dinner. Are we getting pizza or did you want to do a couple of baskets of wings and fries?"

"Pizza!" Riley called, twirling her little fingers around a curl with one hand and holding the red crayon she'd used on her word-find with the other.

"Sounds like a good choice to me," Blue said, giving her the thumbs-up. "I'll get a couple of pizzas. And I'll grab us a pitcher of beer too."

"Let's go up to see what Cappy has on tap," Scarlett said to Charlie. "He always feels generous on this night and he'll let you try them all before you get a beer." Charlie seemed relaxed, and she was glad for that. He was smiling, his shoulders down, playfulness in his eyes. She couldn't help but notice the effect it had on her: it made her happy. Perhaps she'd been able to take his mind off his troubles for a while.

Charlie went with her to the bar, where they found a couple of stools next to Preston. Loretta had already found him, pushing through the crowd to get to him, Sarah in step behind her.

"Preston!" Loretta said, as if it were a surprise to see him there.

"Hello," he said, and in less than a second his stage presence, which had been bigger than life, shrank back into him, and his shoulders rose just slightly as he offered Loretta a thought-filled smile. He was probably trying to mentally draw up his exit route.

"I thought you'd like to chat with my cousin Sarah," Loretta said, nearly pushing Sarah forward.

Preston's eyes lingered on Loretta for a brief moment before he turned to greet the blonde in front of him. Sarah had a gentle manner as she moved, and a shy sort of elegance to her. Loretta hadn't done too badly with this match. Maybe she'd finally succeeded in finding the right person for Preston. Only time would tell.

"I'm glad you talked me into coming tonight," Charlie said into Scarlett's ear, giving her a shiver. She turned away from her view of Preston to find that Charlie had a line of tasting cups in front of them. "I got two of each kind, so we can try them all," he said.

Scarlett counted them. "Cappy has nine beers on tap. That's eighteen glasses!" She laughed loudly, covering her mouth. "I hope you and I don't freeze when we have to walk home, because neither of us will be able to drive after this. That's more beer than it seems."

"You said Cappy might let us try them all, so I figured you'd want them. And I wasn't sure what you liked."

"You know what?" she said, delighted he had done something like this, considering the state he'd been in lately. "I *do* want to try them all. Tell me which one is your favorite."

He pushed the glass with the lightest-colored beer toward her. "This one is a local cinnamon wheat. We'll start with that first and work our way darker."

Scarlett tipped hers back and the fragrance of the spices mixed with the wheat exploded on her taste buds. "Oh, I like this one."

Charlie leaned across the bar to view the tap. "That's the Smoky Mountain Cinnamon Bomb." He raised his glass to his nose and then swirled it around a few times before taking a drink. "Not bad," he said once he'd tried it.

"What's this one?" She grabbed another.

Preston tapped her shoulder and Charlie excused himself to the restroom, telling her he'd be right back.

"Hey, Preston," she said.

"Can you do me a favor?" he asked quietly while Loretta and Sarah were chatting to each other. "Will you distract Loretta so I can make a break for it?"

"Why?" Scarlett chuckled, the familiar scenario amusing her. "Sarah seems nice, doesn't she?"

Preston gritted his teeth, thinking, but clearly not about how nice Sarah was. He looked like he had a million other things on his mind but he didn't want to say them out loud. She wouldn't press him on whatever it was that was bothering him. The last thing she wanted to do was to upset Preston on such a festive night.

"Okay, I'll distract them," Scarlett said.

"Thank you."

She leaned in closer. "Why do you always run from the people Loretta finds for you? Why don't you give them a chance?"

"I'm not running from them," he said, looking back at Loretta nervously. He didn't need to worry, however, because Loretta was deep in conversation with Sarah about some sort of decorating idea she had for her living room. "I just don't want to be put in a situation where I have to say something to Loretta that I don't want to say."

"I'm sure she'd understand if you explained that you aren't comfortable with her setting you up. Just be honest."

"I don't think she'd understand," he said, glancing over to her again, but this time, there was something different on his face. Suddenly, in that one look, it all became clear.

"Oh my gosh," Scarlett said, and when he turned back to her, it was evident by the fear in his eyes that she'd guessed correctly: Preston didn't want to be set up with anyone because it wasn't Loretta's dates that he wanted. It was Loretta. "Tell her," Scarlett urged him.

With his cover blown, Preston struggled for his footing. "Look… If she tries to catch me when I leave, just distract her, okay?"

Scarlett wished he'd say something to Loretta, but it wasn't her place to get involved. "Okay."

Preston took his beer from the bar and slipped away into the crowd. He was back on the stage before Loretta even knew he'd gone. As he tuned his guitar and readjusted the microphone, Loretta stopped talking and focused on him. She smiled his way, knowing he'd made another one of his escape moves. Preston smirked back at her, his affection for her now so clear that Scarlett couldn't believe she'd ever missed it. He had stars in his eyes for her.

"I'm back," Charlie said, as he settled on the stool beside Scarlett again. "Did I miss anything?"

"Oh yes," Scarlett said. "Yes, you certainly did."

"What is it?" Charlie's smile reached his eyes and gave her a flutter.

"Maybe I'll tell you later," she said, grabbing the next beer. "What's this one?"

Scarlett felt something magic in the air right then, and she couldn't wait to see what the night would hold.

Chapter Nine

Blue had generously offered to drive everyone home in shifts. When the bar closed, he was the only one still fit to drive. Due to Esther's absence, Gran had asked one of the few remaining staff members to be on call for the hours she was gone, but she didn't have enough funds to pay him overtime, so she had to get back as soon as possible.

Scarlett's prize had been the biggest of anyone's in the family, although Gran got to go home with a new coffee maker and six months' supply of gourmet coffee, which she was pleased about.

Scarlett and Charlie hung back while Blue took Gran and the kids home first. They waited at the bar for Blue to return. Cappy had poured them each a hot cocoa from his personal warmer in the back, promising them that the cinnamon and willow bark in it would combat any dehydration. With all the music and commotion, this was really the first time she and Charlie had had a chance to talk. Scarlett's ears were ringing and her eyes were heavy from the beers.

"I had a good time tonight," Charlie said.

He looked quite different from the man she'd met out in the snow yesterday, and a tiny resemblance to the boy he'd been so many years ago had emerged in his features. He was even more relaxed now that everyone had gone, one arm resting on the bar, his strong hand holding his mug as it sat in front of him.

"Me too," she said.

The lights were still dimmed, and Cappy and the staff had moved all the tables and chairs to the side so they could mop the floor, but they were all in the back now, leaving just Scarlett and Charlie at the bar. The room was warm and smelled of their cocoa, and one of the staff members had set a radio playing soft tunes on the stage. The quiet music coming from it was a welcome change from tonight's loud atmosphere.

"May I ask you something?" Scarlett said, her elbow on the bar, leaning on her hand, the slight buzz from the beer giving her courage.

Charlie smiled at her, clearly enjoying the stress-free conversation. "Sure."

"You can't clam up," she warned him, and to her relief, he didn't move a muscle, his gaze on her, that smile remaining on his lips.

"Okay," he said.

"What brought you to town?"

His smile faded into a look of contemplation, and he studied his mug for a moment before blowing a quiet breath of frustration through his lips. "I needed a fresh start," he said.

Scarlett leaned forward. "That doesn't explain a whole lot." She locked eyes with him. "Tell me." When he didn't say anything more, she sipped her cocoa, allowing the music from the stage to filter between them. "Okay, you don't have to tell me if you don't want to, but will you at least answer this: Amos was your dad, yes? So how come I never saw you around? I only saw you that one day at the falls."

His knee bounced up and down as if he needed to expel pent-up energy while he formulated his answer. Then his leg stilled. "My mom passed away when I was eight. It was just my dad and me, like you and Blue."

There was so much in that one statement. Scarlett knew firsthand what it was like to have lost her mother: the eerie silence that hung in the air for months while she and her dad tried to move on with life, their grief weighing their every move like bags of wet sand, every little moment meaning something because the most important person in their lives wasn't there anymore to share it. Even at the tender age of eleven, she remembered the jarring weeks right after when it felt like she and her father had lost their compass, neither of them able to navigate the stormy sea of life without her mother. She'd suffered through the sleepless nights, her usual childhood fears of monsters under the bed replaced by the very real panic that her beloved mother wasn't ever going to be there to wrap her arms around her again. It was a burden too large for any young girl.

Because of that experience, Scarlett immediately felt a bond with Charlie.

A couple of the staff members had returned and were running large brooms over the floor, but Scarlett barely noticed, all her focus on Charlie as he continued.

"In preschool the teachers noticed that I learned faster than the other children, and they had to work really hard to keep me interested because I mastered the curriculum incredibly fast. My dad got me tutors, and I loved every minute of it. Schoolwork was my playground." He took a drink of his cocoa, fondness for that time showing on his lips. "When I'd finished the entire middle school curriculum in one year, and they were scrambling for something to teach me, it became apparent to my dad that I needed something more, so when he moved here—I was about ten years old—he made what he said was the hardest decision of his life. He sent me away to Heritage Boarding School for Boys. It was the only option to meet my academic needs."

Scarlett couldn't have left her father at such a young age, when the grief was still so fresh, the nights she woke in fear and had to run to her dad's room to curl up with him still frequent. "I can't imagine how hard that was, to leave Amos."

Charlie frowned, nodding in agreement. "I struggled at first. Dad came to visit every single weekend, and he spent every holiday at school with me so that I could associate good memories with the school itself. He called me every night. I cried a lot and told him I wanted to go home, and he said he'd come pick me up, but then I'd meet with the counselors and they'd get me through another week. It went on like that for quite a while."

Gran's comment about Charlie and Amos being estranged came back to her. This didn't sound like two people who could drift apart. Charlie's story was heartbreaking, and unimaginable.

"After a while, I began to trust the people around me. I made friends, and living there started to feel normal. By the time I was about thirteen, I didn't ever want to leave."

"Thirteen is still so young," Scarlett said, her heart aching for Amos and Charlie. What must Amos's nights have been like, having lost his wife and then sending his son so far away?

"Yes," Charlie said gravely.

"My gran said that you and your dad weren't speaking when she knew Amos. What happened?"

Charlie's eyes glistened. Instinctively, Scarlett's throat contracted with her emotion and she hadn't even heard the explanation, but his sadness was palpable.

"The kids who went to Heritage came from wealthy backgrounds. My friends drove sports cars and spent holidays in the Hamptons. Most of them came from a long line of Heritage alumni, and they were raised in privilege. From the age of ten, that was what I was exposed to, and I grew up in this little bubble of wealth, the only line to the life I had being my dad. When I was older, in my late teenage years, I got caught up in all the social aspects of school, my interests and view of life growing further away from my father's. I chose a week in the Cayman Islands with my best friend over a week at home with my dad. The older I got, the vaster our differences, until I struggled for conversation and opted for other ventures on school holidays."

Charlie pressed his hands together and put them to his lips, the guilt visibly flooding him. "He still phoned me every night. Even when I'd stopped answering his calls." His eyes filled with tears.

Scarlett swallowed to try to clear the lump in her throat, her own tears welling up. She thought about Amos dancing with June, the smile he carried every day, and it all felt different knowing what sadness must have been underneath it.

"I wish I could go back and change it," Charlie said in nearly a whisper. "When you're that age, you feel like you have forever. You'd think I'd have learned from losing Mom that that's not the case. But now I know the hard truth: that there are some things you won't get to do again. I wish I could tell him how much I appreciate him, how much I love him. I ache now to have known him." He tipped his head back and stared at the ceiling, his chest rising as his lungs filled with air. His pain looked as though it would eat him alive.

Scarlett felt helpless, struggling for a way to comfort him. Then it hit her. "Do you know what your dad used to do every time I saw him?"

Charlie turned toward her, the shame clearly exhausting him.

Scarlett took Charlie's hands and stood up, walking toward the empty floor where the tables had been. Charlie let her lead him. "He used to take the hands of a woman named June—she runs the farmers' market." Scarlett placed one of Charlie's hands on her back, holding the other. "And he used to dance." With the music playing softly around them, Scarlett began to sway back and forth, her eyes locked with his.

Then, unexpectedly, she felt his arm tighten gently around her as if he were holding on for dear life. He pulled her close until her head was under his chin as they moved to the music. And there, in the empty barroom, they danced. They danced for Amos, for the little boy who'd been lost, and for the man that Charlie had become.

Scarlett didn't know a lot about Charlie, or what had finally made him return to Silver Falls, but the one thing she did know was that tonight, she didn't want to let him go. And as she considered the promise she'd made to herself about not getting involved with guys who needed fixing, that feeling was certainly a problem.

Chapter Ten

Scarlett awoke to the buzz of her family moving around as they began final preparations for tonight's big Christmas party, but her mind was still on Charlie. Even a night's sleep couldn't keep the memory of his story from bubbling to the surface of her consciousness. She'd carried Charlie's pain to bed with her and stayed up way too late after they'd gotten home last night, thinking about him and Amos.

Gran, who was slicing fruit to garnish the new batch of cider she'd been steeping since yesterday, eyed her silently from the kitchen table when she padded into the room. The scent of cloves along with the warm, buttery smell of their earlier breakfast made Scarlett's tummy grumble.

"Morning, Gran," Scarlett said, as she opened the fridge to see if there was any pancake mix left. When Gran still didn't say anything, she turned around to find an indecipherable look on her face. "What?"

Gran got up and washed her hands silently at the sink. Stitches wound around her leg and then stretched upward and pawed at her knee. Scarlett scooped the cat up into her arms and stroked her head, the cat purring loudly as she pressed herself against Scarlett's hand. After a few more strokes, she set the cat on the deep windowsill where the light was coming in at a slant.

"Your dad cleaned my new coffeepot for me this morning before he headed across town to dig the truck out of the snow," Gran said, wiping her hands on a towel.

"I could've gone to help," Scarlett said, locating the bowl of pancake mix in the fridge and setting it onto the counter. She knew how difficult it was to move the tires in all that snow, and she wondered how her dad was going to get them free alone.

Gran didn't answer her. Instead, she suggested, "Let me heat us each a piece of the coffee cake I made for breakfast." She took a cake server from the drawer and began slicing two large wedges from a cake in the glass-domed stand on the counter.

Scarlett turned the knob on one of the old gas burners to heat the pan for her pancakes, the blue flame clicking in protest before it caught. The two of them worked side by side without another word.

When Scarlett had a pile of mini pancakes in the shape of hearts, the way her dad had taught her, they finished making up their plates and went over to the table. Gran set hers down in front of where she'd been sitting. Scarlett pulled out a chair so she could sit across from her. It was clear that Gran had something on her mind and they needed to be calmly settled before she went into it. That was how she worked. Whenever anything bothered her, she made a point to have everything else around her still, her focus entirely on the topic at hand.

"What is it?" Scarlett asked again.

Gran gave her an affectionate but worried look. In nearly a whisper, she said, "You are certainly getting cozy with Mr. Resort-and-Suites." She peered over Scarlett's head toward the doorway to ensure that they were alone for this conversation.

"Gran—" Scarlett started but Gran cut her off.

"I don't like him," she snapped quietly.

When something worried her, Gran got irritable, as if her body went into fight-or-flight to protect her loved ones. Like the time that Gran found out Heidi was dating a boy from her high school who was three years older than her. He was a rodeo star, hotheaded, and full of testosterone. Gran's lips were pursed so tightly they turned white. But this time, there was no need to feel that way.

"You don't know Charlie," she said, keeping her tone polite. Gran was only being protective of her well-being.

Gran didn't touch her plate as it sat next to the sliced oranges that she'd been cutting. "Neither do you."

"He's good, Gran," she challenged, but it was clear that Gran had already made up her mind about him.

"If he's hanging around because he wants this property, then he can go back to where he came from."

A stab of panic pinged through Scarlett. "What do you mean?" Had Gran heard something?

"Loretta mentioned that he was looking around for a place to build in the area," she said, her voice so low that Scarlett had to come closer to hear. "She heard him talking to Cappy one day. Make sure your head is in reality and not the stars, my dear. He may have ulterior motives."

Gran's comment stung. It made Scarlett's plan for the inn feel like the wrong one. But she reminded herself that Gran didn't have the whole picture. Scarlett needed Gran to get to know Charlie, to understand his damaged heart, and to see that Charlie wasn't pursuing the inn at all. It had been Scarlett who had shown up at *his* house with a plan for the inn in mind.

"Gran, I'm wondering if he's back in town to be closer to his dad," she said seriously, eyeing the doorway as Gran had done to make sure no one was able to overhear them. "He told me how he and Amos drifted apart, and it's eating him up inside." Scarlett picked at her pancakes, stabbing a bite with her fork, but she didn't eat it. "He's been helping people. He donated large sums to charities in town…" she explained, but Gran's expression didn't soften, so she kept going. "He wasn't bothering anyone. His presence at White Oaks is my doing. I was the one who approached him. He didn't want to see anyone, but I talked him into staying at White Oaks and then going to Cappy's with us."

Gran eyed her thoughtfully, but her distrust was strong. "I think there's more to it than what he's told you," Gran said, still clearly very skeptical. "I can feel it."

"I'm sure there is, Gran. I've only known him for two days." Scarlett relaxed, finally taking a bite of her breakfast and letting the sweet, buttery taste of it settle on her tongue. "But I think if I give him time, he'll let me in."

"Loretta did an online search. There isn't much, but she found an article that mentioned something interesting about him," Gran said, getting up and going to the drawer in the kitchen where she kept an old phone book and a basket of pens and pencils. She retrieved a piece of paper and brought it back over, handing it to Scarlett. "I asked her to print it out for me and bring it last night, but it wasn't the place to share this sort of news."

The piece of paper was blank with the exception of a few cut-and-paste sentences on Charlie: *Charles Bryant's tactics have been criticized by many for the fact that the company's success is reliant on claiming land at any cost. The upscale expansions Crestwood Development brings to the area communities are causing concerns among residents in many of his locations.*

"I just don't trust him. I have to be honest," Gran said.

"Do you trust me?" Scarlett asked, trying not to let what she'd just read taint her view of him. Something wasn't adding up with what he'd told Cappy and the tiny snippet of information Loretta had found online, compared to the person he was last night.

"Of course I trust you," Gran laughed. "But I don't always trust your *judgment*." She gave her a knowing smile. Scarlett had confided in Gran on the phone when she'd broken off her relationship with Daniel. Gran assured her that wanting to help people wasn't always a bad thing, but being with someone she didn't love wholeheartedly just out of courtesy to keep from hurting them *was* a bad thing. Gran was obviously worrying that this might be a similar situation.

"It's not like that, Gran," she said, not wanting to state the obvious. Scarlett grinned at her. "And if you trust me, then believe me when I say that Charlie is clearly dealing with something, but I have a good feeling about him."

Gran cleared her throat and leaned back in her chair, unable to be swayed. "Eat your breakfast before it gets cold, dear. And then leave the truck business to your dad today." She took another orange from the bowl in the center of the table and placed it on the cutting board where she'd been slicing. "We've a lot of preparations to get done before the party tonight, and I'm shorthanded. I'm going to need your help."

After Scarlett had helped Gran clean up the kitchen, she entered the living area and found Charlie behind his laptop, in one of the side chairs by the fireplace. "Good morning," he said as she crossed the room.

"Morning." She sat down on the hearth beside him, the article Gran mentioned still on her mind. "Are you working?"

"No. But I *was* searching my old work database for the contact of a contractor I know in the area, so I can get my roof fixed. I'd hoped to get through the winter and then do a few renovations on the old place, but it looks like I'll have to get started sooner rather than later."

"It'll probably be tough to get someone out there until after Christmas, right?"

"Usually, but I have some connections—a group of guys that work off hours doing extra jobs. They charge a little more, but a team will be there today to patch the roof. I'll tell them where the spare key is so they can let themselves in and out of the cottage as needed. I'll work on aesthetics later." His smile was laced with something else, but she couldn't read it. Disappointment? Frustration? He finished whatever it was he was typing and closed his laptop, setting it on the side table to give Scarlett his full attention.

"White Oaks is having its annual Christmas party tonight, if you'd like to join us. It's usually a great time," she said, hoping he'd say yes. When he seemed to deliberate, she decided not to push him.

His candor at the bar had been such a pleasant surprise, and Scarlett would have loved to learn more about him. She wouldn't let his vulnerability last night become anything more for her than what it was, however. It was simply an answer to her question about why he hadn't seen Amos. She ignored the fact that just being beside him gave her a rush of happiness, and that his smile sent her stomach into somersaults. She refocused. It would be important to have him around Gran so that she could get to know him. "I've got a list from Gran of some odds and ends to get done before tonight. Wanna help me?"

"Of course."

"Great. Grab your coat. We have to go into town."

They bundled up and drove to Constantine's Bakery first to pick up the pumpkin pies Gran had ordered. Gran could never keep up with all the baking so Constantine filled in the gaps every year, and no one was upset about that. While Gran was as skilled as any baker, Constantine's pies were to die for. Gran had ordered six of them, along with an assortment of Christmas cookies for a couple of the party games. Scarlett parked Gran's car and shut off the engine.

The bakery had a bright white storefront with Christmas trees on either side of the double glass-paned doors. The bay window at the front was lined with greenery and holiday lights, boasting an array of yuletide treats: cakes decorated with coconut to look like snowballs, cookies with holly so perfectly shaded that the foliage looked real, cupcakes with red ribbons iced on and powdered in confectioner's sugar, and chocolates in the shape of little gifts tied with real ribbon.

"I want to show you something before we go inside," she said, excited to share one of her favorite spots with him. As a girl, she'd spent many summer days here, reading books or having one of the bakery's famous lemon ice cream cones—vanilla ice cream infused with freshly made lemonade and topped with lemon zest and dark chocolate—the whooshing of the falls and the heat of summer lulling her into a kind of peace that was unparalleled by anything else in her life.

They got out of the car, and Scarlett led Charlie to the iron fence that lined the bakery. It overlooked the falls and the sweeping valley below. Cascading water was frozen in place, sparkling even in the dim light allowed by the cloud cover. The mountains were covered in snow; the only color was the deep shade of the evergreens that peeked out from under their blanket of white. The view resembled a real-life snow globe.

"That's incredible," Charlie said, as he peered over the railing to the valley below.

Scarlett pointed to the snow-covered bench beside them. "I like to sit there and read when the weather's good. The sound of the falls calms me, and I can read for hours."

"I'll bet. I'd like to read here sometime."

Scarlett wished they could someday.

"So are you planning on staying in Silver Falls?" she asked, walking with him toward the bakery.

"For now. I don't really know what's next for me, but I think I'll stay a while. It's nice here. And it's far away from the kind of life I've been living." He tugged the bakery door open and allowed her to enter.

"Would it be difficult to work in such a rural area?" she ventured, trying to coax out of him something about his job.

"I'd be fine," he said.

Scarlett couldn't help but notice Charlie's obvious avoidance of the topic of work again. He dismissed it anytime she brought it up. She wanted to ask about his business card, if he realized he was handing out a number that was out of service, but she wasn't quite sure how to weave it into conversation. He'd wonder why she had the card in the first place, and then why she'd tried to call, and she didn't feel comfortable yet telling him about the situation at the inn.

"Mornin'!" Constantine, the bakery's owner, said as they approached the long glass counter stocked with every confection imaginable. She was a stout woman, short, with a smile that could melt butter. Ever since Scarlett could remember, she'd worn that burlap apron with the little embroidered strawberries on it. "You here to pick up your gran's pies?"

"Yes, ma'am!"

"They came out of the oven about an hour ago and they're cooling in the back. Let me pack 'em up for you. I've put the assortment of cookies in a bag for her, too. She was very specific about which kinds she wanted and how many—you know how she is, bless her heart." Constantine winked at Scarlett. "From the looks of this order, I'm guessing she's got a few games up her sleeve."

"I think so," Scarlett said, fondly remembering all the Christmas games they'd played over the years. Gran had held sack races around Christmas trees, pie-labeling contests, and charity stocking-filling competitions to name a few. Every year, Gran added to her games, keeping some old favorites but mixing them up with twists or new games that were enjoyed in the central parlor of the main house.

"Are there any special cookies you want me to throw in for you?" Constantine asked.

"Oh, may we have a few of the caramel chocolate wonders? Those are my favorites."

"Absolutely! I'll get two out for you right now. Who's our handsome sidekick?" Constantine turned her attention toward Charlie.

"Charlie Bryant," he said, introducing himself. "Amos's son."

"Oh, my goodness!" Constantine said, slipping her readers onto her nose from their perch on top of her head where they were nested in her thick crop of gray hair. "I had no idea…"

Charlie studied her face as if he were searching it for her opinion of him, but Constantine was all smiles, her eyes doting, and he visibly relaxed. She grabbed a square of waxy tissue and pinched one of the caramel cookies from the glass case, handing it to him.

"Thank you," Charlie said, holding the cookie.

"You're more than welcome! I hope you'll be coming to the Christmas party tonight." She handed Scarlett a cookie and then dropped a handful of them into a bag. "We'd love to have you."

"You might see me there," he said. Then he glanced over at Scarlett, a half-smile forming at his lips. He seemed to like being welcomed here. After his story about his father and the guilt he'd carried over it, Scarlett felt protective of him, hoping Gran wouldn't show her true thoughts about him when he walked into the party. He needed reassurance that this town would support him.

"You'll never believe what I did," Aunt Beth said, dropping into the last empty chair around the kitchen table. Archie, who'd strolled in when Beth had entered, set his head in Beth's lap. She stroked his ears as her face filled with excitement.

The whole family had assembled in the kitchen that evening for a quick bite to eat and a bottle of wine to share before they got ready for the party. It was something they did every year, the moment of calm before the storm of people dancing, champagne, laughter, and talking into the night.

Aunt Beth reached across the table and snatched a candy cane–shaped Christmas cookie from the array that Gran had set out for them. She broke off the end of it and popped it into her mouth, everyone waiting for her to finish chewing so she could explain. She swallowed. "Stress eating. Sorry." Beth let out a nervous laugh. "I allowed Loretta to set me up with someone. His name is Sean, and he lives in Chattanooga. She's bringing him to the party tonight."

They all burst into a flurry of questions. Scarlett's won out. "Is he driving from Chattanooga now, or is he already here?"

"Apparently, he's on his way," Beth said, her face showing a manic uncertainty about the situation. She ate the rest of her cookie in quick, successive bites. "Loretta's got him in room 3C here at the inn and we haven't had a check-in yet…" She grabbed another cookie, fiddling with it. "Which means that if it doesn't go well, I'm probably stuck with him for twenty-four hours minimum."

"What does he do for a living?" Blue asked.

"Loretta tells me he's an accountant." Beth grabbed the bottle of wine from the center of the table and poured herself a glass. "Given the way I like to shop, we're already on rocky ground if we ever hit it off. He'll cringe when he sees the state of my finances." Beth laughed and tipped her glass up, taking a drink.

"That might be good for you," Gran said with a grin. "Give you some accountability."

"It'll be fun, right?" Beth asked.

"Absolutely," Blue said. "It's great to have someone new coming to share our wonderful tradition. I think it's a good thing."

"You think dating a random person at Christmas is a good thing?" Beth asked. "Not a sad-I'm-alone-on-another-holiday-loser kind of thing?"

"Not at all," Blue said with a laugh. "Dating can happen at any time. Christmas just gives you a festive atmosphere for it."

"Says my brother who hasn't dated in his adult life," she teased him lightheartedly. Then something occurred to her. "Why haven't you dated anyone, Blue?"

He offered a tentative smile. "I'm married," he said, twisting the band on his left ring finger.

Beth frowned sympathetically. "Evelyn would've wanted you to have someone wonderful in your life, I'm sure of it. She was hopelessly in love with you. I'll bet she's sitting in heaven thinking what a waste it is that some lucky woman doesn't have you as a husband."

Blue stared down at the cookie he'd put on a napkin a few minutes prior, but he said nothing. In his silence, it was clear that Beth's idea about Evelyn's point of view hadn't occurred to him before. Beth was absolutely right. Blue's happiness had always been Scarlett's mother's number one concern.

"Sometimes I wonder if I actually want a partner," Beth said seriously, leaning on her forearms, her face crinkled as she pondered the idea. "Is it really all that it's cracked up to be?"

"It is if you find the right person," Gran told her. "And by the right person, I mean the one human being on the planet who knows all your thoughts, and who tells you all of his, under no judgment at all. I understand why Blue is slow to find someone because when you find that person, it's as if you've found the other part of yourself that you hadn't realized, until that moment, had been missing your whole life. An opportunity to find someone like that doesn't come around every day."

"I'm already doubting the accountant. This method just isn't romantic to me."

Gran pinched a cookie from the plate, her amusement clear. "Romance can sneak up on you. Pappy was a small-parts salesman at the local hardware store when I met him. I'm so glad I didn't judge his ability to be interesting by his job choice." She chuckled.

"What *did* make you fall in love with him, Gran?" Scarlett asked. "Was there one thing?"

"Mmm." She closed her eyes briefly and set her cookie down on the small plate in front of her. "We were so young… I worked at the bookshop across from the hardware store. It was pouring rain, the sky growling and angry. I stepped outside to move the welcome mat that always got slippery whenever it was wet, and the door slammed shut with a swirling gust of wind and locked behind me, shutting me out of the shop."

Stitches jumped into Gran's lap and Scarlett noticed the trembling in the old woman's hands as she stroked the cat, giving away the grief that still lingered whenever she mentioned Pappy. Even the day of the funeral, however, all she'd wanted to do was to talk about him, to tell happy stories about their life together.

"Your pappy came jogging across the street with an umbrella. I recognized him immediately because he shopped at our store all the time, always looking for a new book. I wondered quite often how slow business was at the hardware store if he was able to read so many books so quickly," she said with a nostalgic smile. "He offered to get me a cup of tea to warm me up, and then suggested we could use the phone at the café to call the manager to let me back in.

"He locked up the hardware store and turned over the hanging sign that said he was out to lunch, and we walked together under his umbrella all the way to the café where he bought us sandwiches and tea. We talked for far longer than we should have before we both decided it was time to give my manager a call and open the stores back up. I thanked him and told him that I'd buy him a book to show my appreciation." She laughed at the memory, an untold humor registering for her.

"He refused, and I couldn't understand why. It was only the cost of a book, and he read so much. I started to think that perhaps I was being too forward, that my absolute enjoyment of our lunch was one-sided, and he was just being a Good Samaritan. Later, he told me that he'd continuously bought reading material from the shop, trying to work up the nerve to speak to me. You know all those old books on the built-in bookshelf in my office? Your pappy put that bookshelf in.

It's the exact size necessary to hold every single book he bought from me when I worked at the bookshop. He saved them because he said that each book represented one day more he could've had with me if he'd just mustered the courage to say hello. As we moved through life together, anytime he faced a big decision, he always went to the chair next to the bookshelf to think. It was his way of telling himself to go for it. Our destiny comes from the chances we take."

Scarlett couldn't think of a single time when she'd been faced with a major decision like that. Definitely never with a significant other, and never with work either. She had a great job, but she'd taken it because it was a step above the last one she had. That had been the only deciding factor. She'd played it safe her entire life, never shooting for anything grander than the status quo. But what should she be shooting for? She hadn't found her passion yet. Hearing Gran's story inspired her to keep her eyes open for it.

Chapter Eleven

Christmas music played softly over the speakers throughout White Oaks. Fires roared in both fireplaces—one in the grand living room and another in the central parlor.

The tables had been set up along the walls of the parlor, their crisp white tablecloths nearly hidden by a Christmas spread fit for a king: plates of gingerbread cookies, peppermint bark, and assorted sugar cookies lined the edges, and in the center a golden turkey, sliced and garnished on a silver platter, anchored the other plates and bowls surrounding it. Cranberry sauce, sweet potatoes, green beans and ham, dressing, buttered biscuits and cornbread, bowls of chestnuts, and pecan and pumpkin pies with silver Christmas servers already placed under the first slice, were mouthwateringly ready for the crowds. Gran had outdone herself this time.

Outside, the trees were alight in a dazzling spectacle of white sparkles against the black sky, and Blue had just set out the final luminaries, all of them creating a mass of dancing lights that snaked along the hills all the way up to the inn. The Christmas trees sparkled from inside, making it look like a holiday postcard.

Cappy and his wife Jess had already arrived, bringing kegs of beer to set up in the kitchen, each oak barrel wrapped in fresh cypress greenery. The sight of the foliage along with the spread of food and beer was uniquely reminiscent of all the Smoky Mountain Christmases Scarlett had enjoyed over the years.

June had also come with the paper products that she donated every year from the market. Ato surprised them all this year with individually whittled wooden ornaments of the various types of trees in the area. He'd meticulously researched them, each tree ornately carved and tied with a red ribbon, displayed in a wooden bowl to match, that Gran happily placed on the small table at the door with a sign that said: "Thank you for coming."

Preston was setting up a small display on a nearby table as well. Every year, he made singles of different Christmas songs and put them on CDs for anyone who wanted them. Most everyone took one each year, and Loretta would scarf up the remaining ones so that she could pass them out to potential female suitors.

"How do I look?" Aunt Beth said, fiddling with her hair as she tried to view her reflection in the framed artwork on the wall in the living room.

"You look great, Aunt Beth," Heidi said. She was cross-legged on the sofa, her phone in hand, as if this were any other night.

"You really do," Scarlett said, putting her arm around Beth.

"So do you," Beth told her.

Scarlett had her jeans and red sweater on, and her hair was curled in large waves and tied back loosely, the way she liked to do on festive occasions.

"Dressing up for anyone in particular?" Beth asked with a wink.

"Aunt Beth…" Scarlett said, feeling her face flush, betraying her. She had no reason to get ready for anyone other than herself. But she'd be lying if she said she didn't want him to be there tonight. "Charlie hasn't even said for certain that he's coming."

"I'm here," Charlie said from behind her.

Scarlett's knees went weak with the thought that he'd just over-heard their conversation. She'd only mentioned Charlie's name because Aunt Beth had insinuated that she'd fixed her hair for his benefit. She turned around slowly, trying to quiet her hammering heart.

"I'm so glad," Scarlett said, proud of her composure. "I'd love to have Gran answer some of the questions you had about White Oaks. She has so many wonderful stories about this inn." Perhaps if she could get Gran talking about the inn, Charlie could charm Gran before she had a chance to say something that might jeopardize any possible interest he might have.

"Cappy told me that people in town all bring things to the party," he said. "So I brought something for the people I know."

"Oh," she said, surprised. "What did you bring?"

He pointed to a small pile of red and navy velvet boxes tied with bows. "I got everyone silver Christmas ornaments today. The women's boxes are the red ones. They're getting a glass Christmas tree. The men will receive silver bells."

"My goodness," she said, trying to process the fact that Charlie had spent quite a bit on gifts for acquaintances. "Those are really nice gifts."

"I wasn't sure what everyone was bringing after those huge prizes at The Bar, and I had a little bit saved up for…Christmas gifts."

"For Christmas gifts," she repeated, knowing that was a lie. He didn't even have a tree, nor had he planned to do anything other than sit in that empty cottage for the holiday.

He stared at her, and the look on his face told her that he knew she didn't buy it for a second.

"You saved up for Christmas gifts when you weren't planning to celebrate Christmas?"

"Yes," he said, the "s" coming out in almost a hiss as he clearly decided his next move.

Why was he lying? He was certainly careful about what he told her and what he didn't, Scarlett could tell that much. Gran's warning came back to her. Scarlett didn't really know him, did she? There were glimpses of a wonderful man, but he was so secretive that she doubted her gut feeling about him.

"And let me guess, you don't want to tell me about it."

He shook his head, that vulnerability she'd seen before rushing back into his eyes.

Gran, who could read people so well, had decided that Charlie might not be the person Scarlett thought he was. And Scarlett couldn't stand behind him if he wasn't going to be honest with her. The situation made her head start to pound. Maybe this idea that Charlie would come in and make White Oaks great again, become its charismatic spokesperson, and help the inn to thrive—perhaps it was all just wishful thinking. He might not be the one for the job. Which left Scarlett feeling lost again, the way she had at Aunt Alice's that night when they'd all decided to sell.

But as she remembered Gran's advice—*Our destiny comes from the chances we take*—she realized she hadn't given this her all. "Come with me," she said, grabbing Charlie by the elbow and leading him to the hallway. "We need to talk."

Scarlett stopped outside of the back sunroom, an entire room of paned windows at the rear of the house glistening with starlight, the sky having cleared for the moment. The stars and the twinkle lights outside made it feel as if magic surrounded them. Christmas music played softly above them. She dropped down onto the white wicker sofa, the soft navy cushions giving way to her bodyweight. Charlie sat beside her, intrigued, waiting for an explanation.

"I just want to tell you that I'm an amazing secret keeper," she said. "My best friend told me a secret in middle school and I still haven't told anyone."

The corner of his mouth turned up in amusement, like it did whenever he was truly enjoying what she was saying. "What was the secret?"

She laughed. "I'm not telling you! I've kept that secret for two decades. There's no way I'm letting it out now."

"Do you still know her?" he asked.

"No. We lost touch our eighth-grade year when she moved to upstate New York."

"Then why wouldn't you tell me? I don't know her. Why does it matter if you keep the secret?"

She looked him dead in the eyes. "Because she asked me to." Scarlett scooted closer to Charlie. "You can tell me whatever it is that you're holding in. I won't tell anyone, and I won't judge you."

He leaned back, his fingers spread out on his knees.

"You said yourself that there are some things you don't get to do again. You're stuck in this moment—whatever it is. It's got a hold of you. This is a perfect time to get it off your chest."

He didn't move.

"What was that money for?" she pressed. "And why did you decide to spend it on ornaments for near strangers? It doesn't make any sense to me."

He sat up. "I can't do something nice for people?"

"Yes, you can, but you've done so much already. All that money for the girls' and boys' home—Sue told me—the enormous donation to the charity of her choice, and now the ornaments… That's a lot of giving in one season, don't you think?"

"It's my money to give."

"I understand that, but there's some reason for your extravagant giving, and you aren't telling me what it is."

"I just want to make people happy."

She wondered if it was because he hadn't been able to make Amos happy, so she asked, "Does this have anything to do with your dad?"

He seemed disoriented by her question. "No. It has nothing to do with him at all."

"Then what could be so bad that you can't tell me?" Charlie had opened up about his strained relationship with his father in painstaking detail. But this was something he *couldn't* tell her, for whatever reason. What had he possibly done that was worse than deserting his father?

"Look, I was saving that money and the money I put toward donations to repay someone, but it never worked out, and I can't bear to hold on to it anymore. It's not the fact that what I've done is so bad that I can't tell you. It's that the money is from a time I'd rather forget because of the pain it causes me every time I'm reminded of it. The money shouldn't go to me; it needs to go toward some kind of good. Now please, let it go."

"Why won't you talk about it?"

His eyes glistened with emotion before he cleared it by clenching his jaw and breathing in deeply through his nose. He swallowed, clearly struggling to get the statement out. "I've done a lot of things I'm not proud of. And every time I think about it, it tears me apart inside, and I'm *trying* to move on." He stood up. "Let's go back to the party. I want to immerse myself in light conversation, laugh, and eat Christmas cookies."

Scarlett had given it everything she had, and Charlie wasn't budging. Maybe she'd never know his secret, but until she did, she couldn't be clear on the future of White Oaks. And there were no other options for the inn at the moment. What was she going to do?

Everyone was gathered around tables in the main hall at the front of the house, a different one of Gran's Christmas games going on at each one. Every year, Gran worked tirelessly to create around fifteen games—it took her all season to come up with new ones that she added to old favorites. Each game allowed about six people to play, and most of the games were already full, so Scarlett looked around the room for any two empty seats she could find that were together. She pointed to the table full of tiny sample cookies from Constantine's Bakery. Loretta and Sarah were at that table, along with Ato.

"You wanted to eat Christmas cookies, right?" Scarlett asked Charlie as he stepped up beside her.

"Yes." He looked down at her quizzically. "What are they doing?"

"It's kind of like bingo but you play with a partner. You and I will be against the other pairs. Under each cookie is a token for your game board. The goal of the game is to see if you can find the cookie that matches the description on the card. But you have to do it faster than the other teams and get four in a row." She grabbed his arm, leading him to the table. "They're just starting."

"Hi!" Loretta said as they sat down, her gaze bouncing between the two of them. "Glad you could join us." She tipped her head up to scan the crowd. "We need one more player so we can make even teams. Oh! There's Preston! He played this with me last year." She started waving her hand madly in the air, calling his name.

He made his way over to them through the crowd, a wary look hiding under his polite smile.

"Sit with us," Loretta offered. "We need one more. I can pair up with Ato and you can be with Sarah," she said, scooting over one chair and patting the now empty seat between her and her cousin. He sat down, evidently unable to find an excuse.

"I'm so happy to see you," Loretta said to him as she passed the team their game cards.

A tiny spark of contentment showed on Preston's face. He leaned just slightly toward her, his hand on the table, their fingers mere inches from one another. There was so much feeling in his eyes that Scarlett couldn't believe no one had noticed before. "You are?"

"Yes," she said. "You haven't had a real chance to talk to Sarah yet and I'm thinking that tonight you'll finally get some one-on-one time."

Preston slowly withdrew his hand and set it in his lap. "I'm playing songs tonight," he said, feigning regret. "Not much time to talk."

His gaze fluttered over to Sarah only briefly before landing back on Loretta with full force. Sarah seemed to notice that there was something going on with Preston, but she didn't say anything. Instead, she picked up the card that she and Preston would be sharing. Preston leaned over to view it as well.

"Wait," he said, peering down at it. "Loretta and Ato should trade cards with us."

"Why?" Sarah asked.

He tapped two of the clues. "This card has both macaroons and ladyfingers on it. Those are Loretta's two favorite cookies." He regarded Loretta with unspoken words, and Scarlett was delighted to see him putting his feelings out there just a little bit. She hoped Loretta would notice.

"You just gave them the answers!" Sarah said, amused. She had a youthful innocence to her, but she seemed quite perceptive as she took in Preston's energy toward Loretta.

"It's fine. She'll need all the help she can get playing against me," he teased.

Loretta's entire demeanor seemed to lift in response to his lighthearted comment. "Oh, please," she said, playfully rolling her eyes. "My team won this game last year."

Preston let out a loud laugh. "That's because I helped you!"

"You did not. You ate the wrong cookie on purpose."

"I ate the other team's cookie by accident! But it meant the other team had to start over, didn't it? Which put them behind, and you and Cappy won."

"Let's see how we do tonight!" Sarah said, interjecting and quieting their banter. Loretta was still smiling at Preston, shaking her head.

Loretta seemed to have to work to pull her gaze from Preston to refocus. "All right, let's regroup," Loretta said. "Everyone, spend a moment with your teammates; let's all devise our strategies…"

Charlie was taking in the array of cookies, each one in its own little paper cupcake dish. "How do you know if you got the right cookie?" he asked Scarlett.

"On the bottom of the cup is the answer. You have to eat the cookie and take the token before you know if you got it right. There are a couple with the same answer, but if the other teams eat them all before you can get one, then you'll have to find a different four in a row to solve."

"Oh, that's tricky," Charlie said, scanning the cookies again.

Sarah and Preston settled in together at the table, scanning the descriptions.

"Is everyone ready?" Loretta asked, excitement written on her face. "On your mark, get set, go!"

Quietly, Scarlett leaned over to Charlie so no one else could hear. "I know all the cookie names. I'll say them from top to bottom, left to right." She scooted a little closer to Charlie. "Shortbread," she whispered into his ear.

Charlie studied the card and read the clue he had his finger on. "Laughing while drawing small pictures... Probably not."

"Haystack. Truffle. Chocolate Chip..." Nothing seemed to match the description. Loretta grabbed a cookie and ate it, covering up one of her spaces. Scarlett continued, "Snickerdoodle." Then it hit her. "Snickerdoodle!" She nearly squeaked trying to keep it quiet. "Laughing while drawing!" She grabbed the cookie and popped it into her mouth.

"That's definitely it." He took the marker and put it on the square. "I'll just read the next one," he said. "They hide in their shells."

"Oh!" Scarlett pointed to the third one from the left on the bottom row. Charlie picked it up and took a bite of it, the caramel stringing from his fingers to his mouth. Scarlett handed him a napkin. "Turtle," she said, as he ate the other bite.

Once he'd swallowed it, he leaned over the card while Scarlett took in the rest of the table's progress: Loretta and Ato had three covered. Sarah and Preston had two.

"Little Girl Scouts," he whispered.

"Easy." Scarlett went to grab the brownie but Preston got to it first, giving their team three.

Charlie and Scarlett were behind the others with two. She searched for another brownie but was struggling to find any more. Then, at the same time, she and Charlie both spotted another brownie on the other side of the table, and stretched to get it, their fingers landing on it together, their faces inches apart. The proximity stunned her, and before she recovered, Charlie pulled away, grabbing the brownie before Loretta could get it and shoving it into his mouth, making Scarlett laugh—both at the sight of him cramming one of Gran's brownies into his mouth, and the nervous energy that zinged through her. He covered up their third box with a token.

It was tied at three across the table. Whoever could find the next one would win the game.

Charlie read out the clue. "Don't leave this behind at a burglary."

Scarlett jumped up from her seat and scanned the table for her favorite jam-filled cookie.

"You know it?" Charlie asked.

"Yes," she said hurriedly, unable to find the cookie in question. "It's called a thumbprint."

"What does it look like?" he asked her, his rushed question illustrating his competitive side, making her laugh.

"It's a soft vanilla cookie with a circle in the middle that's filled with jam. Do you see one anywhere?"

Ato ate a cookie and checked the bottom of his paper cup, but by the look on his face, he'd chosen the wrong answer. Scarlett scanned the massive array of cookies on the table.

"Ha!" Charlie said, drawing her attention over to the right-hand side of the cookie spread. He pointed to one of the paper cups. "Is that it?"

Scarlett grabbed it and stuffed it into her mouth, as Charlie snatched up the token and placed it on their grid.

"Four in a row!" he called to the others.

"That was the best teamwork I think I've ever seen," Loretta said, interest showing in her eyes as she took in the two of them. "Amazing job." Then she snickered at Scarlett. "Do you need something to wash that down?"

Scarlett, who was still chewing her cookie, nodded, trying to smile with her lips tightly closed around all the cookie bits.

"I'll get us both something," Charlie said, standing up. "Is a glass of wine okay?"

She nodded, grateful for his offer, and happy to have the chance to share a drink with him.

"White?"

She'd finally swallowed it all. "I don't remember my gran's thumbprint cookies being that big before," she said. "She must have gotten excited for the party this year and decided we all needed a bit more sugar."

"Growing up, I didn't get a whole lot of treats at school. I've been making up for that ever since." He reached over, grabbed one more cookie from the table, and popped it into his mouth. "Let's get some wine."

Chapter Twelve

When Scarlett and Charlie entered the grand living area, Aunt Beth waved from behind a mass of people in the corner of the room by the fireplace, its mantel dripping with greenery and dotted with candles. The room was buzzing now, everyone talking and laughing, relaxing into that festive atmosphere that could only be had on this day every year. Jess waved to her excitedly as she stood next to Cappy. Preston was playing music on his guitar, and some guests were dancing while others held little plates of food and Gran's special holiday cups full of eggnog.

Loretta brushed Scarlett's arm to get her attention as they passed by. "I've been dying to set your aunt up with Sean," she said into Scarlett's ear as Charlie took their glasses of wine, walked over to a nearby table full of Christmas hors d'oeuvres, and browsed the options. "He's really great. I hope it works out."

"How'd things go with Preston and your cousin Sarah?" Scarlett was very curious to know.

"It was strange. Sarah said he wasn't her type. I tried to give them another chance, but Sarah wasn't feeling it." Then Loretta eyed Charlie, who was now refilling their glasses. "Looks like you two didn't need my help," she said with a wink.

"Oh, no, we're not—" Scarlett started, but Charlie was back at her side, holding her topped-off wine in front of her.

"For you," he said.

"Mm-hmm," Loretta hummed into Scarlett's ear suggestively. "I'll leave you two alone." Then she walked off into the crowd.

"Thank you." Scarlett took the glass, and they made their way over to Aunt Beth.

"I'd like you to meet Sean Mathis," Beth said to Scarlett, with a discreet he's-not-so-bad-and-I-kind-of-like-him-already look when they walked up.

Sean shook Charlie's hand and then Scarlett's, introducing himself formally. He had a firm but friendly handshake and a nice smile that was accentuated by his light eyes and tanned skin.

"So you live in Chattanooga?" Scarlett asked, making conversation while trying to figure out how he got that bronzed tan in the dead of winter.

"He's *from* Chattanooga," Aunt Beth clarified. Gran walked over with a plate of canapés she'd been so excited to share with everyone that she hadn't waited for the staff to offer them. Aunt Beth snatched one, held it between two fingers, and took a bite. Then Gran swished off to another group.

"I'm only home visiting family for the holidays. This was my mother's doing," Sean said, shaking his head fondly at the mention of his mother. "She says I'm not grounded enough. That I need a good woman. I'm humoring her, since it's Christmas, but I must say, I am enjoying this party and talking with Beth." He gave her a smile.

"So where do you live now?" Scarlett asked.

"San Francisco. I moved out there to work for a company called Worsham Enterprises and I stayed. Been there twelve years."

Charlie's eyebrows rose in interest. "Worsham Enterprises," he said, breaking into the conversation. "Aren't they a world leader in luxury food service?"

"Yes, that's right," Sean said, lighting up at the fact that Charlie recognized the company. "How do you know them?"

Charlie paused, as if he were deciding how to answer. Finally, he said, "My company dabbled in luxury services research in an effort to compete within the resort market."

"Ah," Sean said. "What's your company?"

Scarlett could see the anxiety in his eyes as the topic moved toward work. "Crestwood Development—but the corporation has been dissolved."

Dissolved. Wait, what? Scarlett rolled the word around in her mind. Crestwood Development was no longer a corporation? It was in existence eight months ago when Charlie had passed the card along to Cappy. Had something changed in those eight months? The pieces began to slide together: the nonworking company number on his business card, Charlie's sudden move to Silver Falls, even earlier, when he said "searching my *old* work database" for contractors to get his roof fixed. Had all that extra cash he'd used for donations come from liquidating his business assets? Was Charlie no longer in the resort market at all? Scarlett's heart fell into the pit of her stomach, her hope melting like a snowball in summer.

Charlie seemed to notice her shift in mood, her obvious distress puzzling him. He studied her for a second. Scarlett forced her face into a more neutral position. Perhaps she was wrong. Companies changed all the time. He may have been bought out and he could still have connections.

"Well, I suppose I should get this lovely lady a drink," Sean said, with a polite nod to Beth. "Would anyone else like anything?"

"I'm fine, thank you," Scarlett said, holding up the wine that Charlie had brought her. She couldn't even drink what she had. Any more alcohol would only intensify the throbbing that had started at her temples. She set the glass on a nearby table, unable to drink it.

Charlie also declined Sean's offer, and Sean and Beth went together to get her a drink, which was a good sign. Maybe Beth was enjoying Sean's company.

"You okay?" Charlie asked.

Scarlett opened her mouth to ask directly about the card he'd left with Cappy, but then she thought maybe she shouldn't. Charlie had told her he didn't want to talk about work, and this was a Christmas party. They weren't going to change anything tonight, and she was so worked up that she was in danger of missing the fun. She was trying too hard to fix things again, when she needed to be in the moment and enjoy herself.

"I'm fine," she said, producing a giant smile. "Let's dance." She grabbed Charlie's arm and pulled him through the crowd.

As they danced slowly together, Scarlett didn't want it to end. She wanted to hold on to the feel of Charlie's embrace, as well as the sensation of his lips at her cheek. Her breathing was in sync with his, their feet moving in perfect time as if they'd danced together for years. His grip on her was different from the moment she remembered so long ago. The fearless bravado that he possessed as a young man had changed. It was still there but more settled now, as if he were sure of himself now as a man holding a woman.

Preston finished the song he was playing and Scarlett had to force herself to pull back from Charlie. "That was fun," she said, wishing they could've stayed out on that dance floor all night.

"Yes, it was." There was a kind of serenity she hadn't seen before that had settled over him, and she wondered if being with her had the same effect on him as he had on her.

"Dancing makes everything better," she said, the Christmas spirit whirling around her.

"I'm with you on that," Charlie said. "I haven't felt this good in a while." His gaze lingered on her, and it looked as though he wanted to tell her something, but he didn't. Instead, Charlie nodded toward Loretta, sitting in a chair next to Sarah, and then his attention moved to Preston. "I think Preston should ask Loretta to dance."

"That's kind of hard to do when he has to play the music as well," she said.

"You agree they should dance, though, right?" He had a glint of something in his eye.

'Yes," she said, wondering what he was up to. She liked this playful side of him.

"You work your magic and get them together," he said, walking away.

"Where's he going?" Gran said as she came up behind Scarlett, taking the words right out of Scarlett's mouth. Gran handed her a glass of champagne, and Scarlett was feeling so good after that dance that she hadn't had another thought about the inn, so she didn't object.

"I have no idea what he's doing," Scarlett said, as Charlie made his way across the room.

Charlie said something to Preston and then shook his hand. *What was he doing?* Preston set his guitar down, leaning it against the stand he'd brought with him, and Charlie pointed to Scarlett. Preston looked her way while Charlie walked over to the piano and sat down. He gently rested his fingers against the keys, and then, as skilled as any concert pianist, he started to play "Silent Night," and everyone stopped talking. The notes were intricate and soft, sailing through the air and settling on the crowd like perfect snowflakes.

Gran clapped a hand over her mouth in surprise. "That's incredible," she said from behind her fingers.

Charlie caught Scarlett's eye and nodded toward Preston, who was heading her way.

"Charlie said you wanted to tell me something?" Preston asked, now standing in front of her.

She had to think fast. "Well… I know someone who works really hard for everyone else, and I thought it might be nice to do a little something for her. Could you help me? You know, spread a little Christmas spirit."

"I'd be happy to help," he said, his curiosity clear. He slipped his hands into the pockets of his faded jeans.

"Dance with Loretta."

Preston's eyes grew round, his shoulders rising.

"Sometimes you have to gamble to win big."

He looked around and shook his head, disagreeing. "It's not that easy."

"Why not?"

"This is a really small town. You know that. If things don't go the way I hope, or if they do and then end badly, we're stuck together in close proximity." He checked around him before saying in a whisper,

"Plus, she keeps trying to set me up with people. Why would she do that if she had any interest whatsoever in me?"

Charlie went on to his second song, "What Are You Doing New Year's Eve?" Gran had made her way to the front, evidently interested in this talent he'd only just now shared. She was sitting on a chair next to the piano, her glass in both hands, her feet crossed at the ankles. Pappy used to play that piano every now and again, and Scarlett wondered if it brought back fond memories for Gran. By the unwavering attention she was giving Charlie, Scarlett guessed so. She couldn't help the elation that filled her at the sight of Gran's smile.

"Just a friendly dance," Scarlett urged him, feeling very Christmassy.

Preston pulled his hands from his pockets and rolled his shoulders around as if he were warming up for a sporting event, amusing Scarlett. "I'll get her to have one dance with me. But the condition is that you let me handle the rest in my own way."

"Done."

"Okay." Preston turned around and walked across the room with purpose. Sarah had gone to fix a plate of food and Loretta was sitting by herself.

Scarlett grinned when she saw the bewilderment on Loretta's face, but then, as Preston spoke more, Loretta nodded and stood up, the two of them moving toward the piano together.

Scarlett squeezed past Gran and sat next to Charlie on the piano bench as he played, so she could hear the conversation between Preston and Loretta.

"You're always alone," Preston pointed out, looking down at Loretta. "You should go out sometime with someone yourself. Like a...date."

"I'm too busy with everyone else."

"You shouldn't be…"

"My work here is done," Scarlett said to Charlie, the two of them watching Preston put his arms around Loretta.

Charlie chuckled, his fingers moving effortlessly along the keys.

"You play beautifully," she said.

"One of the perks of boarding school," he said, shooting her a fond look. "We had music lessons every day. I play piano…and tuba."

Scarlett burst out laughing. "Tuba? I need to see this."

"Christmas carols don't sound quite as nice on a tuba." He worked his fingers to produce a dramatic run of notes.

The crowd clapped. This was turning out to be a great party, and Christmas was feeling more festive than she could ever have imagined.

Charlie had taken a break from the piano and was chatting again with Sean. Scarlett was sharing Christmas cider recipes with June and Aunt Beth by the window, when a flash of light through the inky darkness outside caught her eye. She hadn't even had time to process it before she heard a heart-stopping squeal of tires and what sounded like a tree breaking in two. It was enough to halt others' conversations too, people beginning to look at one another for answers, the noise pulling them away from their festive banter.

Uncle Joe was the first to act. "That didn't sound good," he said, already holding his coat, shrugging it on and zipping it up with precision and speed, his life-saving instincts moving his limbs as if he were on autopilot. He jogged through the entryway purposefully, swung open the main door, and disappeared into the night.

"Here," Charlie said, following Joe's lead and handing Scarlett her coat.

As he slipped on his own, the look in his eyes finally registered through her denial that something awful had just happened. The look was fear. It was as if she'd known something horrible had just occurred but hadn't been able to make herself believe it could happen on this festive night until that minute. Charlie put his hand on the small of her back and hurried her outside into the frigid air along with everyone from the party, the smell of burning rubber and exhaust immediately assaulting her senses.

The others followed as she and Charlie moved toward two lone beams of light shining from somewhere down the mountain onto a tree at the edge of the bent and tangled guardrail, the crowd of people enveloping Scarlett. Charlie took her hand and started to pick up speed, headed toward the pitch-black edge of the mountain.

"From the look of that guardrail, we all need to be ready to help," he said, not breaking his stride. Scarlett was losing her breath to keep up with his lengthy steps, panic bubbling up from the pit of her stomach.

When they got to the edge, Scarlett was able to assess the wreckage. A car sat on a small plateau on the side of the cliff, its nose pointed downward, the only thing stopping it from plummeting to the valley below, the tree that its front end was wedged against. The radio inside the vehicle was still playing Christmas songs, and coupled with the sizzle of the engine, it gave her an unnerving feeling. Unable to see the driver at the angle she was standing, Scarlett's gaze roamed the car while she struggled for something she could do to help. Then her words escaped her completely when she took in the view of the back window. She pulled on Charlie's sleeve, her whole body beginning to shake.

"What?" he said, with an intensity that she'd not seen.

She pointed a trembling finger and heard his breath catch when he, too, saw the small boy with sandy blond hair and bright blue eyes, tears streaming down his face, looking directly at him from the backseat inside the vehicle. In an instant, Charlie was at the edge of the guardrail, one leg over it, all his focus on the little boy.

"There's loose rock to your left! Be careful!" Uncle Joe's unruffled voice sailed up to Charlie from below, and Scarlett realized then that her uncle had already made it down to the car and was busy working in the shadows on the driver's-side door to get whoever was stuck in the front seat out of the vehicle.

A few others from the party had gone back to the main house and returned with rope from the groundsmen's shed. They lowered it down, the thick line dangling into the valley as they attempted to swing it into place near the small plateau.

Scarlett's strength wasn't sufficient to help in that way, but she had utmost faith in the two men who were there, and she knew that when they got the little boy to safety, he would need comforting. Her heart slamming around in her chest, she sprinted back up to the inn and threw open the front door.

"How many are hurt?" Gran said from the middle of the entryway, wringing her hands, worry like Scarlett had never seen before etched on her weathered face.

"We don't know," she said, her voice not sounding like her own due to the terror that was coursing through her veins. "It's a single car. Went off the side of the mountain." She struggled to get enough breath to speak full sentences. "There's a child. A little boy…" Scarlett was momentarily frozen after she said those words, the sound of them hitting her like a shard of ice to the chest.

Gran covered her mouth as the two of them locked eyes for a second, in fear for the safety of the child and whoever was with him.

Scarlett was the first to break their stare, a deluge of urgency knocking its way through her once more. "Uncle Joe and Charlie are down at the site now."

"My God," Gran said with a gasp.

"I'm going to get some blankets," Scarlett told her. "And the first aid kit. Anything else I should take?"

"Joe will make sure they're safe," Gran said, nodding as if to convince herself.

"Yes. He will." She couldn't bear to think of any other scenario.

"Charlie's helping?" Gran asked, clearly taking in that fact.

"Yes."

Gran offered her a look of solidarity, and Scarlett knew that Gran was learning to see a different side of Charlie. She definitely had her opinions of people, but she always admitted when she was wrong.

"At the very least, the boy will be scared," Gran said. "I'll wrap up some cookies. Put them in your pocket. If he's well enough, you might need to distract him."

"Okay," Scarlett said as she dashed into the hallway, headed toward the linen closet while Gran got the cookies. She yanked two quilts from the pile and rolled them up, putting one under each arm. Then she ran to the cabinet in the kitchen where they kept the first aid box, grabbing it.

"Here," Gran said, holding out the bag with a few cookies.

"Thank you." Scarlett jammed them into the pocket of her coat and ran as fast as she could back to the wreckage.

When she returned, the crowd had formed a line, all of them anchoring the rope, walking backward in slow, meticulous steps, working in tandem. Cappy nodded to her as she stopped beside him. "You'll need those in just a second," he said, his eyes on the quilts. "The boy is on his way up."

Scarlett ran to the edge to find Charlie very close to the top with both feet on the dirt wall of the mountain, his hands gripping the rope to assist his climb up, the small boy wrapped around the front of him, sobbing, his tiny hands clasped tightly around Charlie's neck and his legs squeezed against Charlie's sides. "I've got you," he assured the boy in the sweetest voice Scarlett had heard from him. Just the sound of it calmed her.

Down at the wreck, the back door was open and the child seat now empty. Uncle Joe had the driver's-side door of the car open as well, his top half inside the car. Scarlett couldn't hear him or see who he was working on, but she knew if anyone could save the driver, it was Uncle Joe. He'd give it everything he had.

Someone must have called a friend with a truck, because a man was busy hooking a cable to the back of the car to keep it from breaking free and plummeting down the mountain.

Cappy and the other men stayed with the rope to keep it anchored as Charlie got nearer the top. Scarlett was right at the edge, waiting. Carefully, she dropped the blankets onto the guardrail and let the kit she'd been holding fall to the ground. She leaned over to grab the child once Charlie got his footing, slipping his ankle through the guardrail to keep him in place. He pushed the child toward her, and she grasped the little boy, immediately stepping back away from the side with giant strides and picking up one of the blankets, while June and a few others helped Charlie over the edge to safety.

Scarlett wrapped the boy in the quilt. He was probably only four years old, curling around her as she held him firmly in her arms. She brushed his hair away from his forehead. He had a scrape near his eyebrow. "My name is Scarlett," she said. "I'm here to help you."

He didn't lift his head from her shoulder, exhaustion clearly overwhelming him. "My mama." His lip wobbled and tears welled up in his eyes as he tried to look over her shoulder at the car.

"My uncle Joe is getting her right now," she said, trudging through the snow up to the inn to get him out of the cold, where she could evaluate any injuries. "We can wait for her inside, okay?"

"I'll help you," Charlie said, stepping up beside her, and immediately the boy reached out for him, nearly pulling Scarlett off balance as he leaned toward Charlie.

Charlie, surprised, took him, the boy wrapping himself so tightly around Charlie that his face was buried completely in Charlie's chest. Charlie put a dirty hand on the quilt at the boy's back while he held him and looked over at Scarlett for an explanation.

"You saved him," she said, feeling an overwhelming sense of gratitude for Charlie's quick work and selfless act. "He trusts you."

They moved swiftly to the house and inside to the living room, where Gran had been pacing.

"Oh my," she said on a gasp of air, her hand at her heart, the Christmas tree glimmering behind her, accentuating her frail silhouette. "Is he all right?" she asked, turning on a nearby lamp for more light.

"I think so." Charlie put his face near the little boy's ear and spoke in that sweet voice Scarlett had heard on the mountain. "I'm going to set you down on the floor so I can make sure you're okay."

The boy looked up at him with trusting eyes.

Gran sat on the edge of a nearby chair, clearly ready to help at a moment's notice.

Charlie gently lowered him onto the rug with his scraped and dirt-caked hands, the quilt underneath the boy cushioning his body. "Can you turn your head toward the Christmas tree?"

The boy moved his head, his eyes red and drooping from fatigue.

"How about the other way? Can you look over at Scarlett?" The boy complied. "How about your belly? How does it feel?"

"Good," the boy said, before he was overcome by a yawn, his eyes closing and then opening again.

Charlie inspected the back of the boy's neck to be sure nothing seemed out of the ordinary. "I'm Charlie. What's your name?" he asked, sitting back on his heels.

"Trevor." He opened his eyes wider, battling sleep. "I'm hungry."

"Do you think you can stand up?" Charlie asked gently.

Trevor wriggled to a standing position.

"Does anything hurt at all?"

"No." Trevor looked around, just noticing Gran. "Does Santa live here?" he asked.

Gran smiled at him, obviously relieved. "No, dear. He doesn't."

Trevor yawned again, turning to the Christmas tree. "It looks like he does. And Mama said we would find Santa Claus this year. We were looking for him. He couldn't find us last year so he didn't come."

Scarlett blinked away her surprise at Trevor's admission. What had happened to him that Santa Claus hadn't visited his house on Christmas Eve? She reached into her pocket and pulled from it the bag of cookies Gran had given her, handing them to him.

His eyes lit up as he opened the bag. "Thank you," he said, eating one quickly and then going for the next.

"Have you had dinner?" Gran asked him.

"No." He finished off the second cookie.

"Why don't we walk together into the kitchen and I'll make you something warm to eat?" Gran offered.

"I want Charlie to take me," he said.

Charlie stood up. "Sure," he said, holding out his hand to take Trevor's. They walked together down the hallway, and Scarlett couldn't help but feel a warm sense of affection for Charlie tonight. She hoped he'd changed Gran's opinion of him as well.

Chapter Thirteen

"How is he?" Uncle Joe said, with no introductions as he entered the kitchen. He dropped a duffel bag onto the floor.

Her uncle's clothes showed his struggle on the mountain; the knees of his trousers were wet and muddy, his pressed Oxford shirt disheveled and wrinkled, untucked from his belt. His nose and cheeks were crimson from the frigid conditions outside, but he was as alert and focused as if he were working in an operating room.

Trevor, now with a small bandage on the scratch on his forehead, was sitting on a pile of cushions at the kitchen table, with Charlie on one side of him and Scarlett on the other. Gran had heated up some of the party food and made him a little plate with a cup of milk.

"He seems to be completely fine," Charlie said. "Just hungry."

Uncle Joe squatted down beside him. "Your mama's just fine too. She's on her way inside."

Trevor's eyes lit up. "She is?"

"Yep. She asked for a minute to get herself together. She was still a little shaky from the big fall you all had, so I brought your bag in for her. I came in ahead of her to check on you. Can you wiggle your legs for me?"

Trevor kicked his legs back and forth, and only then did Scarlett notice the holes in the toes of his sneakers. One of them had a broken lace, the two ends knotted together. Unlike her uncle's appearance, the wear on Trevor's clothing had less to do with the events of tonight and more with the passage of time. His shoes also looked a bit tight on him, and Scarlett wondered when he'd last gotten a new pair. She considered how hungry he'd been when they'd come inside.

"Can you reach way up over your head like this?" Uncle Joe raised his hands into the air and Trevor mimicked him. "Good." He looked carefully into Trevor's eyes for any sign of injury. "Can you tell me your whole name?"

"Trevor Winston Farmer."

"That's a very nice name," Uncle Joe said enthusiastically, scooting Trevor's chair away from the table. "Can you hop down so we can play a quick game, and then you can eat again?"

"I like games," Trevor said, his bright white teeth fanning across his face with his grin as he climbed off his chair. A few partygoers filtered into the doorway. June put her hand to her chest, an adoring breath leaving her.

"Great. Let's play Simon Says. Simon says, 'Walk across the room to the door.'"

Trevor walked across the room, Uncle Joe checking his movements as more people entered the room, all peeking in to see the little boy.

"Simon says, 'Wave.' Simon says, 'Stop waving.' Get up in your chair."

Trevor didn't comply with the last request and everyone in the room smiled. He was focused, happy to be able to play.

"Simon says, 'Stand on one leg.'"

Trevor balanced on one leg, wobbling slightly.

"Great," Uncle Joe said. "Simon says, 'You're all done with this game.' You can eat now."

"That was fun!" Trevor said, crawling back up into his chair.

Scarlett's eyes were still on Trevor, but when the small crowd that had gathered in the entry of the kitchen parted and a woman walked through, the quiet reaction from Charlie made her shift her attention away from the boy. By Charlie's sharp breath, Scarlett had wondered what he'd seen—if the woman had noticeable injuries that caused him to gasp—but when she looked at the woman, everything seemed fine. Trevor began to cry, his arms stretched out for the woman, his brave facade finally crumbling. He'd been holding it together for all of them. Scarlett was captivated.

"Mama," he sobbed, suddenly unable to catch his breath.

The woman—thin, her clothes hanging on her like they were a size too big, dirty-blond hair, tired features, a weary smile—grabbed Trevor and held him tightly, her entire body trembling as she cried. She took out an inhaler for asthma and handed it to him. The sharp sound of air shot from it into his mouth, and his short breaths subsided. She wiped his tears, laughter surfacing through her sobs, as it was clear to her that he was okay.

"Thank you for taking care of my boy," she said to Scarlett, her voice breaking. "I don't know how to repay you."

"Oh, it was nothing at all. I couldn't imagine not helping." Scarlett picked the cushions up from the chair Trevor had been using and offered the seat to the woman. "My name is Scarlett," she said, introducing herself.

"Janie." The woman sat down, Trevor still wrapped around her, his head on her shoulder. "Janie Farmer." She stroked Trevor's hair.

"Let me make you a cup of coffee," Gran said, moving past the onlookers as they all began to disperse into the other rooms to give this woman some space to relax.

"I'm so sorry..." Janie began, shaking her head, clearly still in disbelief at what had happened. "I looked away for a second to change the radio station and we hit black ice." Tears welled up in her eyes.

Gran set a mug in front of her, along with cream and sugar.

Trevor was already almost asleep in her arms.

"My mama always told me we have a guardian angel," Janie said, her voice unsteady. "I never believed her because nothing has ever saved me from anything terrible." She sniffled, using her free hand to pour cream into her cup. Gran stirred it for her and slid the spoon from the liquid, setting it onto the table. "But when the wheels of my car left the pavement, I cried out for my angel. That was when I felt the impact of the tree on the front of the car, saving us. The only tree in that spot." She pulled her other hand free from under Trevor and lifted the coffee to her lips with shaking hands.

"You two were very lucky," Gran agreed.

"Do you live nearby?" Scarlett asked. "Trevor said you were looking for Santa Claus."

The woman swallowed her emotion, her face looking more haggard all of a sudden. "We're very far from home," she said.

"Well, your angel is still working then," Gran said. "You've just arrived at my inn. I have a room ready for you and Trevor if you need somewhere to stay tonight."

Relief flooded Janie's face and she looked up at the ceiling as if her angel would be there, her lip wobbling with emotion, but then her face dropped. "I can't pay you," she said, blinking away tears.

"Oh good Lord, no," Gran said. "I would never expect payment after what you've been through. The room is yours as long as you need it."

"Thank you," she said.

"Scarlett, you can help Janie and Trevor to one of the open rooms—3A is probably good. It's got an extra twin bed. I'll go and get the key," Gran said, turning to Janie, "and then we can bring some food down for you if you're hungry. Will you need anything else?"

"No, you've done so much for us already," she said, her hands a bit steadier now as she held her cup and took another sip. "I'm so grateful."

Gran was totally in her element. Helping people was her specialty. "You've had a big night, but if you feel lonesome, we have a Christmas party going on in the main living room. We'd be happy to have you with us. Otherwise, there's a big bathtub with an array of bath salts and lotions. Perhaps you can tuck Trevor into bed and unwind."

Scarlett turned to introduce Charlie as the man who'd saved her son and ask him if he'd go with her to take Janie to her room, but he wasn't there. She peered into the hallway where a few people had gathered, but he wasn't there either. He must have gone back to the living room with the others. "Let's get you to your room," Scarlett said. She picked up the small duffel bag that Uncle Joe had brought in.

Gran had gotten the key to 3A. She handed it to Scarlett. Then Scarlett led the way, Janie following closely behind her with Trevor in her arms.

When they arrived at Janie's room, Scarlett opened the door for her, and Janie laid Trevor in the small bed. His clothes looked even more soiled and old against the white comforter. Janie's eyes moved around the room. "This is amazing," she said. "I've never stayed anywhere like this before."

Scarlett surveyed the small bag that she'd dropped inside the door. "Do you have clothes for yourself? You're about my size. If you need anything, I'd be happy to loan you something."

"I'm fine in what I've got on," she said, shame in her downcast eyes.

"I know you probably just want to rest, but give me five minutes," Scarlett said. "I'll be back in a flash."

Scarlett stopped by the kitchen and asked Gran if she'd make up some plates and put them in the warmers and refrigerated bags they used for room service. She told Gran she'd be back for them in a second. As fast as she could, she ran into her room and opened her suitcase, retrieving the brand new and freshly washed pair of pajamas she'd planned on wearing tomorrow night on Christmas Eve, and placed them in the empty gift bag she'd brought the presents in. Then she pulled two shirts and a pair of jeans from her pile of clothes, setting them on top of the pajamas inside the bag. She found Aunt Alice and got a few of Mason's clothes and a pair of pajamas for Trevor from the twins' suitcases, and headed out the door with it all.

Bag in hand, she stopped by the kitchen and grabbed a pad of paper, scribbling her number, picked up the food Gran had made, and kissed her on the cheek as she headed for Janie's room. It only took one knock and Janie was at the door. "I brought you food for tonight. There's a little refrigerator and microwave in the corner by Trevor's bed."

Trevor's shoes were neatly lined up against the wall, and he was nearly buried in blankets, sleeping soundly. Scarlett handed the bags to Janie. "And I grabbed you and Trevor some pajamas and a change of clothes."

"You didn't have to do that," Janie said.

"I know I didn't, but I wanted to. If you need anything else, the front desk number is seven, two on the room phone. If no one answers, my cell phone number is on a pad of paper inside the clothes bag."

"Thank you so much," Janie said, her tired eyes glistening from the sentiment.

"It's no problem. Gran makes breakfast at seven o'clock. You're welcome to join us down there. We meet in the kitchen."

"I can't tell you how thankful I am for all you've done for us. If you only knew what we've gone through… This is a Christmas miracle."

"Maybe you can tell me about it over coffee tomorrow morning," Scarlett said with a friendly smile.

"Okay. I'll see you tomorrow."

Her heart full, Scarlett went to find Charlie to tell him what he'd missed.

Chapter Fourteen

Scarlett stopped by Charlie's room again on her way to breakfast. She'd looked everywhere for him last night and he was nowhere to be found. None of the party guests had seen him either. She'd knocked on his door, but no one answered, and she'd even tried to text him. She wondered if he'd gone back to his room to get something and fallen asleep. He'd had an eventful night, after all.

She turned around at the sound of the wrecker that was pulling Janie's car from the side of the mountain. Even with the loud beeping from the truck as it reversed, there was nothing but silence on the other side of Charlie's door. She deliberated—maybe she shouldn't wake him up. He might want to sleep in. Perhaps she should just save a bit of breakfast for him so he could have it whenever he woke up. Deciding that was probably a better idea, she headed down to see her family.

The kitchen was bustling when she got there. The twins were making waffles on the iron skillet mold with Gran, every burner filled with breakfast foods—eggs, bacon, sausage, and potatoes. Heidi was sitting casually by Aunt Alice, braiding her hair, her foot on the chair, one knee against the table. Aunt Alice and Aunt Beth were drinking their coffees and chatting to Sean, who'd stayed last night, and Uncle

Joe had his finger on something in the local paper, showing her father. All of it was lovely to see, but it was Janie and Trevor that made her smile the most. Trevor was in the middle of the kitchen floor, stroking Archie, who'd made himself at home in Trevor's lap, the dog's limbs sprawled across Trevor's tiny legs. Janie was wearing the outfit Scarlett had left her. She sat with the others at the table.

"Morning," Scarlett said to the group, taking a seat next to Janie.

Breakfast was another of Scarlett's favorite things to do with the family at White Oaks. It was the only time when everyone was together, enjoying each other. The main house was closed to guests this morning—she'd seen the sign. She was willing to bet there was a lot of cleaning to be done after the party last night, and the cleaning staff was less than half its normal size. Even though the staff would be working to clear it all, the family usually lent a hand, boxing cookies and bagging up gifts and things brought by people in town. The good news was that they were all so tired after the events last night that they'd all probably want to avoid it for as long as possible, opting to stay together just a little longer.

Gran pulled a tray of biscuits out of the oven, the warm buttermilk aroma filling the room and making Scarlett's tummy rumble. By the look of the spread, Gran had been up for quite some time. But she always went all out for Christmas Eve.

"How did you sleep?" Scarlett asked Janie.

Gran brought the pot of coffee over and set it on a trivet, then handed Scarlett a mug with dancing candy canes on the front.

"Really well, thank you," Janie said. "All the bath salts and lotions—I feel like a queen." She ran her fingers through her shiny hair, the sides pulled back into a clip. "And the bedding is so comfortable," she added. "Trevor said he thought Santa had brought him this inn."

The fact that Trevor noticed the type of bed he was sleeping in at the age of four made Scarlett wonder what their usual accommodations were like. And she'd said they were a long way from home. Why were they so far from where they lived on the night before Christmas Eve? "I'm so happy to hear you had a comfortable night." She poured some coffee and stirred in the cream, and Gran's special peppermint sugar. She made it every year at this time, just for coffee. "If you don't mind me asking, where were you headed last night?"

"We were actually headed to Silver Falls. I was trying to find the address but with all the road closures from the snow, we got lost and then I couldn't see where the road was at all. I tried to lighten the mood since we'd been driving so long, and that was when I switched the radio station and we went over the side." She gave Uncle Joe an appreciative look.

Scarlett's heart lurched at the memory. She didn't even want to think about what this morning could've been like if anything had gone wrong last night.

"Thank you again, Joe," Janie said. "I don't know how to repay you."

"You don't have to," he said, taking a plate from Gran, who was passing them out to everyone before placing the serving dishes in the center of the table. Blue and Aunt Alice both got up and tried to help her, but Gran shooed them away. "Your lives are payment enough for me."

"I didn't get to thank the man who saved Trevor," she said. "Where can I find him?"

"He's staying at the inn as well," Scarlett said. "His name is Charlie. He must be still sleeping."

"Charlie." The name came off Janie's lips kindly, her gratitude showing in her tone. "Funny. We were on our way to find someone named Charles. But I'm willing to guess that he isn't the same one.

The Charles we were going to see probably isn't the type of man who would climb down a mountain and save someone. He isn't a very nice person…" Misery slid across her face, but then she cleared it again, reaching for her coffee. "Sorry. I didn't mean to say that. The name Charlie just took me by surprise. Trevor, wash your hands, please, and come to the table. The food is ready."

Gran sat down and began dishing herself some scrambled eggs, while Trevor left Archie and climbed the small stool by the sink to wash his hands. Gran passed the bowl of eggs to Scarlett.

Silver Falls was a small community. Scarlett didn't know of any other Charles in the area. "This Charles you're looking for, what's his last name? Maybe I can help you find him."

Janie frowned. "Charles Bryant," she said, nearly spitting out his last name.

Gran shot a look of warning over to Scarlett.

"Do you know him?" Janie asked.

Scarlett passed the eggs to Heidi, her mind going a hundred miles an hour. Had Charlie done something that affected Janie and Trevor? Janie seemed really upset by Charlie. Should she tell her that Charlie was the one who'd gotten Trevor to safety? Maybe Charlie should tell her. After all, whatever disagreement they had was between the two of them. She realized she hadn't answered Janie's question. "Uh, yes, I do know him actually. Why don't I call him and ask him to come see you?"

"Thank you. I'd like to have a word with him," Janie said, surrender in her eyes.

"Let's all eat and enjoy our breakfast first," Gran said. There was a look in her eyes as she said it, and Scarlett remembered when Gran had alluded to the fact that she didn't really know Charlie. That was true, but she just couldn't believe Charlie could be the person Janie described. However, his reaction at seeing Janie last night and his sudden absence shook Scarlett. Was he hiding something?

The others, who had evidently been stunned to silence by the turn in conversation, fell into quiet chatter at Gran's suggestion.

Beth was the first to speak up. "Sean is spending the week," she said, offering a bashful look at Sean and drawing everyone's attention away from Scarlett and Janie. "He's staying in town. I'm going to show him around." Sean and Beth shared a happy glance at one another.

"Oh, that's wonderful," Scarlett said, and she meant it, but her mind was elsewhere. Where was Charlie?

"I have some news," Heidi said, speaking up. When she had the attention of everyone at the table, she announced, "I've decided to attend the Rhode Island School of Design in the fall."

Scarlett could've heard a pin drop. She immediately looked at her uncle to see his reaction. He was shocked, clearly, Heidi's decision obviously news to him.

"I have to follow my gut," Heidi said with a wink to Scarlett.

Whoa. That wasn't what Scarlett had meant. When she'd told Heidi to trust her gut, she'd been talking about long-distance college relationships, not which university to attend. This was a big deal. Heidi had built herself quite a portfolio of coursework for the medical track, having taken enough advanced classes to equal her freshman year at Johns Hopkins. She'd have to start over. None of her courses would transfer to a totally different program.

"Would you like to think about this a little bit more, honey, before making a final decision?" Aunt Alice asked.

"I don't think so." Heidi shook her head. "I don't want to be a doctor."

"But for so long you've expressed an interest," Joe said. Even though Scarlett knew he'd want only what made Heidi happy, he was visibly trying to hide his disappointment, but he wasn't doing a very convincing job. "What's changed?"

"I just don't *feel* it anymore, Dad," she said honestly.

He huffed out a chuckle of disbelief. "Heidi, this isn't just where you'll live for the next three to five years; this is the location where you will receive the training that will direct the rest of your working life. Both schools are fantastic. But you have to make sure that your decision is one you can live with forever. If you don't want to be a doctor, what *do* you want to do for a living?"

"I don't know." She twisted her braid around her finger. "Let's talk about it more later, though," she said, grabbing a biscuit and buttering it.

"Yes, you're right," Uncle Joe said, offering an apologetic glance over to Janie. "Trevor, are you excited for Christmas Eve tonight?" he asked.

"Yes, sir! I'm very excited to sleep in the comfy bed. It's the best Christmas ever!"

Joe nodded fondly. "What do you have on your Christmas list?"

Scarlett inwardly cringed, knowing what Trevor had said about Santa Claus not coming last year. Uncle Joe had still been outside. Janie seemed uncomfortable, and Scarlett wished she could help them somehow.

"I don't make a Christmas list," Trevor said. "Santa will find me when he's finished helping all the people who need things." He ate his last bite of bacon. "May I get down and play with Archie, Mama?"

"Yes, you may," she said, as she slid his cup of milk away from the edge of the table to allow him to get down without spilling it.

Trevor ran over to Archie, who dropped his ball, inviting Trevor to throw it. He picked it up and rolled it down the hallway, following the dog chasing after it as Riley and Mason climbed down to join in.

"We don't have a lot for Christmas," Janie informed the table quietly once the kids were out of earshot. "I tell him that Santa helps people by bringing what they need, but he's getting older... His friends were all sharing stories about their favorite Christmas gifts at preschool. He asked why they were getting toys when they didn't need them." The stress of the situation was etched across her forehead. "And now with the baby on the way..." She shook her head.

Joe perked up. "Baby? Are you expecting a child?"

Janie nodded.

"I should've asked," he said, noticeably frustrated with himself. "We need to get you to a clinic for an ultrasound right away. We have to make sure all is well with the baby after the crash."

Alarm filled her face, and then fear. "I can't," she said, tears springing to her eyes.

"Why not?" Joe asked.

"I don't have any insurance. Even if I did, I don't have the co-pay for the visit. I lost my job a year ago, and I can't find one. That's why I came looking for Charles..."

The table had hushed after her admission. Gran tilted her head, compassion filling her features. "We'll help you, dear. Don't worry. We'll figure it out together." She got up and grabbed a tissue from the box on the counter, and handed it to Janie.

"Yes, don't worry about that," Joe said. "I can fill out a few forms and have a chat with some folks, get you into a program that can provide assistance—but we'll have to take you to Gatlinburg—that's the closest medical center. It's about an hour away, however, so we'll need to move now to get you seen today."

"Okay," Janie said.

"That poor girl," Gran said to Scarlett while she helped to clean up the breakfast dishes.

Scarlett had stayed back at her request. The others offered to help, but Gran told them she and Scarlett would be fine taking care of the mess on their own. Scarlett knew by the way she looked at her when she told them that Gran had a specific reason for keeping Scarlett with her.

"I hope everything is okay," Scarlett worried aloud.

"So do I." Gran rinsed a plate and placed it in the dishwasher. "She's such a lovely girl. Something has made her incredibly sad…" She grabbed a bowl and ran it under the water. "I do hope it has nothing to do with Charles. Did you hear how she spoke about him?"

"Yes," Scarlett said, already guarded. Just as she'd thought, all of Charlie's good deeds were wiped clean from Gran's memory with that one moment at the table. "But we don't know the story behind her opinion of Charlie. We need to hear what's going on before we make any assumptions."

Gran shook her head, her hands gripped around a pile of silverware. "I can get a pretty good feel for people, Scarlett, and I'm telling you"—Gran shook the silverware at her to make her point—"there's something amiss here. Be careful with that man."

"I think he might be misunderstood," Scarlett ventured.

"I think you have a tendency to enjoy saving complicated men. It hasn't proven helpful to you yet," she said, her voice calm and kind, but direct.

Scarlett wondered if Gran was right. She'd hit a nerve. The one thing that Scarlett struggled with was trying to find the good in everyone, even when it meant getting hurt. Sometimes, there wasn't a whole lot of good to be had. Was she missing a huge red flag just because she wanted to believe that Charlie was something that he wasn't? She remembered Charlie's own words: *Maybe you don't need to know me because I might not be the person you want me to be.* The only way she'd find out was to talk to him.

"I'm going to call him, Gran," she said. "I need to find out what's going on. I'll be careful, I promise."

"Go right now." Gran took the plate from Scarlett's hands. "But prepare yourself for what you might find out. Not everyone has your heart, Scarlett."

Scarlett nodded, her mind feeling heavy. She'd wanted to trust Charlie, but she wondered now if her need to have him be the answer to her prayers was overriding her judgment. Just because he'd shared a few heartfelt feelings with her, didn't mean that he was the person she was hoping he'd be. She took her phone from the back pocket of her jeans and stepped out into the hallway.

Scarlett dialed his number and waited. Voicemail. "Charlie, this is Scarlett. I need to speak to you." *Where was he?* She hadn't heard a peep from him since he disappeared from the kitchen last night without a word. She started to worry. "I'm coming down to your room right now." She hung up and immediately headed out to room 1B. No matter how exhausted he'd been last night, he should be up by now.

When she reached Charlie's door, she knocked loudly in case he was, by some miracle, still asleep, despite her doubts. With a shiver, she waited, standing on the porch outside his room with no coat.

She knocked again, harder. Charlie didn't answer, so she pulled out her phone and called again, but it went straight to voicemail. Starting to really worry now, Scarlett pounded as powerfully as she could with her fist. "Charlie! It's Scarlett! Open the door." Sharpening her hearing, she held her breath to home in on any sound that might give her some inkling as to what was going on, but the only sound was the faint rush of water down the mountain. She hurried back to the kitchen and to Gran.

"Where's the universal key?" she asked, out of breath, her nose numb from cold.

Gran eyed her questioningly.

"Charlie hasn't opened his door all night and I can't get him to open it now. He isn't answering his phone… I'm concerned about him."

"It isn't policy to allow you to use the universal key when a guest is in residence," Gran warned.

"I'll blame it entirely on myself. But something isn't right. We need to check on him."

Gran stood in front of her with her lips pursed and her hands clasped together, her deliberation making Scarlett feel panicky. She had to have that key… Her uneasiness about Charlie's silence was too great not to go in and make sure everything was okay. Gran's words about complicated men came sailing back to Scarlett but she pushed the thought away.

"All right," Gran finally said. "I'll get it."

"Thank you."

After she had the key in hand, Scarlett sprinted back down the icy porch, trying to move quickly without slipping. She got to Charlie's door and knocked one more time to no answer. "I'm coming in!" she called, sliding the key in the lock. Slowly, she turned it and cracked open the door. "Charlie?"

No answer.

Scarlett pushed the door wider and looked around. The bed was made. The lights were all off. The bathroom empty. "Charlie?" she called again, more out of disbelief, hoping he'd pop out from somewhere. She walked around the bed, which was slightly disheveled but with the covers pulled up, and peered into the bathroom once more. She yanked open the shower curtain. He wasn't there.

He didn't have a car at White Oaks. Anywhere he could've gone, he'd have had to travel on foot. In the snow? He'd have frozen, surely. The terrain was too hilly to get anywhere in this weather without a vehicle. Trepidation crawled up her spine. Her mind started to move to terrible thoughts—possibly due to the accident last night. It had put her on edge. She ran around to view the back lot. Thank God, her dad had gotten the truck out of the snow. She needed to look for Charlie.

Without a word to anyone, her heart beating wildly, she ran back into the main house, grabbed her coat and boots, and got her dad's keys.

When she started the engine, Christmas music poured from the speakers. She cut it off. The silent minutes seemed to stretch indefinitely long as she waited for the engine to warm up enough to drive. The temperature gauge sat at "cold," as if the needle were weighted and couldn't be lifted. Scarlett tried Charlie's cell once more, but service was spotty again. Frustrated, she tossed her phone onto the seat. When the gauge of the old truck had barely cleared the cold mark, she threw it into reverse and hit the gas, the tires grinding against the powdery snow.

Driving down the road, Scarlett surveyed the ditches, the edges of the mountain, all the clearings, praying she didn't see anything. The snow was falling again, covering whatever had fallen last night. She put her wipers on to clear the windshield.

When she'd reached town, Scarlett pulled the truck to a stop outside The Bar and went inside.

"Hey, Cap," she said, moving toward him with purpose. "Have you seen Charlie?"

"Not since last night," he said. "Why, is everything okay?"

"I hope so. Thanks. I can't stay… I need to find him."

"Anything I can do to help?"

"Call me if you hear from him?"

"Okay. Good luck."

She checked the bakery, the coffee shop, and the general store—no sign of Charlie. As she was walking briskly back to the truck, her breath short from fear, she ran into Loretta.

"You look like a storm cloud," Loretta said. "Is everything all right with the woman and her son?"

"Yes," she said, Loretta's question slowing down her racing mind for a moment. "Uncle Joe is taking her to get some final tests done to make sure she's completely out of the woods."

"Oh, good." The skin between Loretta's eyes wrinkled as she took in Scarlett's demeanor, clearly trying to make sense of it.

"Have you seen Charlie, by chance?"

"I saw work trucks at Amos's on my way into town. Could he be there?"

"The roof! Loretta! You are an angel!" Scarlett threw her arms around Loretta and squeezed her tightly, relief settling over her with the hope that Charlie was okay and just directing the contractors on the roof repair. She'd forgotten that he'd organized someone to come out quickly. Maybe they'd picked him up…

Loretta offered a knowing smile and tightened the wool scarf around her neck before folding her arms, clearly trying to combat the icy temperatures. "You sure seemed worried about his where-abouts."

"It's more than that," Scarlett said, not bothering to deny that she was feeling something for him this time. "And it's...complicated."

"It always is."

"I need to run," Scarlett said, getting into the truck and starting it up. "I'll catch up with you later, okay?"

"Definitely!"

Scarlett put the truck in gear and headed straight for Amos's.

Chapter Fifteen

Scarlett marched through the snow to Amos's and rang the old buzzer at Charlie's door, to the inquiring glances of the workmen on the roof. Their loud hammering subsided briefly in response to her presence, but then resumed. She wondered how they could even work in these temperatures.

She exhaled in complete relief when he answered, feeling as though she'd been holding her breath the whole time. She hadn't expected it, but she felt a rush of caution at seeing him, an unforeseen need to shield him from his own perception of himself. Perhaps it was his childhood, and the kind of guilt he carried that she'd never experienced, but she wasn't even upset that he'd come to Amos's without telling anyone. After all, he was free to go as he pleased. She only wanted to make sure he was okay.

He hadn't shaved and he looked exhausted, his eyes red. "I can't talk right now, Scarlett," he said gently, but it was clear that he'd closed right back up again—his usual coping method.

A wood saw squealed loudly, the sound moving between them, making it nearly impossible for him to hear her when she asked why.

When it lulled for a second, he said, "You should go."

She shook her head, defiant. He wasn't getting off that easily. She'd let him in, trusted him, given him a place to stay, and while her motives certainly had begun as a means to impress him with the inn, that wasn't her entire intention anymore. She liked him. She liked how he felt comfortable enough with her to tell her things that were important to him—he trusted her with those feelings. She liked the way his smile made a flutter in the pit of her stomach. She couldn't deny it.

The saw whined again, piercing her ears. She ignored it, walking past him, shrugging off her coat, and sitting on the sofa he'd pushed to the side of the room. "I'll wait," she called over the ruckus.

Charlie seemed to be flustered by her presence. He marched over to her, openly exasperated but clearly keeping himself in check, and took a seat beside her. The kindness she'd seen was slowly fading from his eyes, replaced by a manic sort of hurry. It was clear that he wanted her to go, and nothing they'd shared prior to this moment was present in his mind as he sat there beside her.

She was just bothered enough by the situation that her emotions got the best of her. "You don't like facing things," she decided loudly.

What if she had stars in her eyes and she was missing the bigger picture, a picture Gran was able to see, being a bystander to the situation. If he was really the kind of person Gran had thought he was, then maybe he needed to hear that. He'd been vulnerable about his own feelings, but when she thought about it now, other than monetary donations, last night was the first time she'd seen him think about others. Could it be because he didn't do that very often?

"What?" he asked sharply, evidently taken aback by her observation.

"You don't face anything," she repeated. "I know you miss your dad. But you came back here *after* Amos was already gone. Why didn't you come before, when he was aching to see you? And something went on with you and Janie, but when it came to facing that, you ran again."

Charlie took her by the arm lightly and pulled her into his bedroom, shutting the door, muffling the noise a bit.

"You don't know anything," he said, frustrated, standing so close to her that she could smell the clean scent of his shirt.

His breathing was slightly harried but steady, his eyes boring into her, and she realized once they were alone that he wasn't angry. She'd hurt him with her assessment. It wasn't that he wouldn't face things; it was that he was wounded. Even the most aggressive wild animals often sought out solitude when they were hurt. As she took him in right then, she could see remnants of the commanding presence he must have had in business, but something had caused him to flee, to find refuge in the only place he'd ever found love.

"Then tell me," she said tenderly. "There isn't anything that can't be fixed, Charlie."

"That's not true." He hadn't let down his guard yet. He was still clearly stung by what she'd said. Remorse rose in her throat, and she realized in that moment that she hadn't trusted her gut like she'd told Heidi to do. Instead, she'd let someone else decide how she should feel, and that wasn't like her.

"I came back to see my father," he said, his lips pursing with emotion. He moved so close to her that she could feel the warmth of his breath, the intensity and longing in his eyes making her want to put her arms around him to calm him down, but he continued. "I came back to find him and he'd died, and no one told me. I was a horrible son, but I deserved to know. I didn't run from a thing. I came back because I needed to tell him what an awful son I'd been, to tell him that I love him, and that I'm so sorry for all the years we didn't have together. Janie was the person who made me see what I'd done."

His admission stunned Scarlett. And she was even angrier with herself for letting others change her opinion of him. His behavior was just so confusing that she couldn't get a hold on what he was thinking or who he was. She was still making sense of his actions. "Janie thinks you're a terrible person," Scarlett said in a whisper, confused, wondering how they knew each other.

Charlie nodded. "Yes. She would think that. In a lot of ways I am, Scarlett."

"I don't believe it." She put her hands on his face and looked into his eyes, needing him to trust her. She'd never doubt her own conclusions again. She could barely stand to see the pain in his heart and she wanted him to know that if he needed her, she would be there for him.

"You don't want to believe it." He pulled away from her. "You want me to be that boy you met so many years ago, but I'm not. I'm broken."

Scarlett winced at that word. She could feel herself moving toward feelings she didn't want to have for him. She didn't need him to be broken. She couldn't go down that road again. Was she only attracted to his brokenness? *Old habits die hard*, she thought to herself.

"I don't want you to be anything," she said. But that was a lie. She wanted him to be strong. His authoritative presence told her that he could be, had his life been different. She had to focus on the issue at hand. "Janie came all the way to Silver Falls to see you. And you disappeared. That's why I came over today. She clearly has some unfinished business with you, and I just want to make sure that whatever it is she needs is taken care of."

"I disappeared because the last person she needed to see after such a traumatic night was me. I ruined her life. And I don't know why she's come to find me, except maybe to yell at me some more. But I can't help her." He ran his fingers through his disheveled hair in frustration. "I came here to try to move forward, but I've made such a wreck of things that I can't escape it."

"Why don't you at least talk to her?"

He started to turn away in uncertainty, but she grabbed his hand, sending his gaze back to hers.

"I'll be there with you." And as she looked at Charlie, it occurred to her... She felt something different between them than she'd had with others. She'd only grasped it just now, in this very moment. She wouldn't be there to be his strength, but rather his supporter. He didn't need someone to fix him. He needed someone to be in his corner when he felt alone.

Charlie didn't answer. While he hadn't yet agreed to meet Janie, something had shifted in Scarlett and she knew that they could do this together.

"She's pregnant—did you know that?" Scarlett took Charlie's hand and wound her fingers around his, openly showing her affection for him to let him know she'd be right there when he needed her. He didn't pull away. "She's gone to have a few tests to be sure she and the baby are all right."

Charlie blew air through his lips, his shoulders tensing. "My God." The news seemed to surprise him. "How is Trevor today?" he asked, suddenly concerned.

"He's just fine."

"A baby...?" He looked into the distance, obviously stunned.

"I know. She said she didn't have money for the hospital co-pay. And her car is totaled. Trevor doesn't have a Christmas... I want to help her."

He nodded, thinking. "I can at least give them a Christmas," he said. "Could you help me wrap some gifts up for her and Trevor? I'd like to do it anonymously. She may not want any of it if it's from me."

"Of course." While she didn't understand what was going on yet, Scarlett had faith that Charlie could handle this on his own. She didn't doubt it anymore. And Scarlett would do whatever she could do to encourage him.

"I know the town closes down on Christmas Eve. Are any of the shops open at all tonight?"

"People will unlock their shops for us—for this. I'll make some calls and explain what's going on. Janie and Trevor both need clothes. She's about my size and even fits my shirts, but she'll need some maternity clothes as she gets bigger, I'd imagine. Trevor could do with some new shoes as well."

"No problem. I'll get them whatever they need."

"Should I call Cheryl who owns the clothing shop in town and tell her we're on our way?"

"Yes." He opened the door and grabbed his coat from the hook in the hallway, then retrieved hers from the sofa.

"I'll call the toy shop too."

"Of course."

On their way out, Charlie told the roofers to use whatever they needed in his house, that he'd leave it open for them. Then, as he led the way, he placed his hand affectionately on Scarlett's back to help her through the snow. She looked up at him and, in that moment, they were unified in their effort to help Janie and Trevor.

"You say you're broken," she said to him, "but it's in your kindness that you're whole. You're so kind, Charlie. You just need to let more people see it."

He stopped, facing her as the snow fell lightly around them. She stared at him, not even attempting to hide how she felt about him, and she knew that he could sense it, but it didn't bother her.

His lips parted and he shifted slightly toward her, tipping his head down to line up with hers as she looked up at him. She didn't feel the cold or hear the construction anymore. She was lost in the silent, unspoken thoughts between them. She'd not seen this moment coming, and she hadn't prepared for it. She believed in him, and she understood now that he found strength in her belief. Unsure of why, she wanted him to take her hand or kiss her lips. It wasn't choreographed under a bunch of mistletoe or beside the fire. It was real and honest, and just between the two of them.

But then he took in a breath of icy air and stepped back. "We need to work fast," he said. "We only have a few hours to find the gifts, wrap them, and get them under the tree."

The change in direction jarred her and she scrambled to refocus while simultaneously processing the shift in his dark eyes. But then she realized that he was right. They had a lot to do and not much time to do it.

Scarlett texted Uncle Joe just before going into the shop to find clothes for Janie. She'd explained quickly what was going on and told her uncle to secretly find out a few things that Trevor liked, along with their clothing and shoe sizes.

Cheryl, the owner of the clothing shop, let them in, locking the door behind them and turning on the overhead lights. "Take all the time you need," she said, with concern on her youthful face. She'd always looked younger than her age. She was about as old as Scarlett's father, but her sandy brown hair had never grayed, and the only lines on her face were the ones that creased when she laughed, which she did quite a bit. She pointed them to the women's section of the shop. "I have gift wrap. As you find things you want to buy, bring them up, and I'll start wrapping."

"Oh, you're so wonderful, Cheryl," Scarlett said.

They started looking. Scarlett feverishly flipped through the racks of clothes, Cheryl standing by to take items to the counter. Charlie helped get things down that were hanging up high, and he searched for accessories like belts and socks. It didn't take them long to have a nice-sized pile at the register, Cheryl speedily unfolding gift boxes, stuffing them with the items, and wrapping as fast as her fingers would go, each gift disguised in shiny red paper with gold oval seals from the shop holding the ribbon in place.

Scarlett's phone pinged with a text from Uncle Joe, giving her everything she needed to finish their shopping.

"I need shoes in a size ten for kids. Do you have anything?" she asked Cheryl.

Cheryl hurried over to the wall of shoes and pulled down an armful. "Which ones do you want?"

"All of them," Charlie said. "Do we know Ms. Farmer's shoe size?" he asked.

"Janie?" Scarlett looked at her phone. "Yes, she said. My dad was able to peek at them by the door. He says Janie wears a size six."

"Perfect. Get her whatever you think she needs."

They got everything wrapped and paid for at the counter, then carried the armloads of gifts to the truck, squeezing them behind the front seats and in the floor of the vehicle—anywhere they'd fit. Then she and Charlie thanked Cheryl and headed off to Toy Land, the small shop owned by Ato's brother Waya. His name meant "wolf" in Cherokee, which was a fitting name for a man with a thick, long crop of gray hair and a beard to match, his almond eyes consuming his other features. He'd have been intimidating were it not for the warmest smile that spread across his face the minute he saw a friend and the guffaws of laughter that escaped from the very bottom of his broad belly whenever he told a joke, which was all the time.

During Scarlett's phone conversation with Waya earlier, he'd offered to donate a few extra gifts for little Trevor. When they arrived at the shop, he was waiting for them outside, towering above them in his fur-lined boots and thick down coat.

"I'd heard the child is looking for Santa Claus," he said, his umber eyes creased at the edges. "I'll do my best to make sure he finds him." He opened the door wide to allow them to enter the shop.

Scarlett led Charlie over to the train sets, Waya following along behind them. She checked the price tag on a large one with sixteen individual train cars and a village to go with it. Entirely too expensive for only the first gift. She dropped the tag and turned toward a smaller set.

"What's wrong with this one?" Charlie asked, pointing to the larger set.

"It's a lot of money. It might be better to spread out the cost over lots of gifts since we don't know exactly what he likes."

"I can drop the price a little," Waya offered.

"You don't have to do that," Charlie cut in. "If you think he'd like the big one, then get it. Cost is no problem."

"That's very kind," Scarlett told him. "But it might not be practical anyway. How would we get it to White Oaks?"

Charlie fell silent as he considered this. Then, he regarded Waya. "Wait," he said, the word coming out slowly as he solidified the thought. "Trevor is looking for Santa Claus…" He and Waya shared a look of understanding that was lost on Scarlett for a moment, and then she realized what they were both thinking. "Do you know where we can get a Santa suit in about four hours, Waya?" Charlie asked.

"I've got an idea," he said, before bobbing up and down with a belly laugh. "Leave it to me."

They continued choosing toys, Waya dismantling the displays and piling boxes onto the counter. Charlie handed him a credit card and refused to let Waya pay for any of it, despite his offer to contribute.

With the shopping finished, they left the toys in Waya's care and headed back to the truck to return to the inn, so they could get the rest of the presents under the tree.

"We have a minute to grab a coffee," Charlie said to Scarlett as they noticed that Love and Coffee was still open. "Maybe this time I can drink it all." He grinned at her, giving her the fluttery feeling that was becoming the norm whenever she was with him.

"I'd love to," she said.

Once they'd gotten settled at a table inside the coffee shop, their cold hands wrapped around warm mugs, Scarlett relaxed. The atmosphere and his kind eyes calmed her. She leaned back in the chair, letting her shoulders unwind, the twinkling of the Christmas tree in the corner and her view of all the gifts through the window, outside in the truck, making her feel festive. Then something occurred to her. She asked Charlie, "If you didn't go home when you were in school, what did you do for Christmas?" She was genuinely curious. Her Christmases were so full of family, so many memories made, that she couldn't imagine what it must have been like for Charlie on his own. "Did you get a tree?"

He shook his head. "I just didn't celebrate it. I have magical memories of it when I was little, and sometimes I wonder what it would've been like to continue to have those moments, but they were lost along with the rest of my childhood."

"You should have Christmas with us," she offered. Gran probably wouldn't like the idea of it too much, but Scarlett couldn't stand the thought that he'd be alone yet another year during the most wonderful time for family and friends.

"No, I really shouldn't."

"Why?"

"Well, for one, Ms. Farmer and her son, Trevor, will be there, and I'd rather not ruin their Christmas. They deserve it more than I do. And I wouldn't want to impose on your family."

"You're not just sitting in your room at White Oaks, and you definitely shouldn't be all the way out at Amos's. I couldn't enjoy my Christmas knowing that."

"The roof should be patched by the end of the evening. Don't worry about me. I'll start a fire, make myself a whiskey on ice, and read a book I've been wanting to start." He drummed his fingers on the table casually.

She wanted to make a gesture to let him know that she cared for him, so Scarlett reached over and put her hand on his, stilling his fingers. Without saying a word, he seemed to understand her intent, consideration flooding his face. She wound her fingers over his knuckles, yearning for him to reciprocate. Every time they'd had the possibility to move into that different realm, he'd pulled back. She begged him with her eyes not to this time. Slowly, he turned his hand over under hers, locking their fingers. He caressed the palm of her hand with his thumb, making her swallow, suddenly feeling like a schoolgirl across from her first crush.

His jaw clenched, as he seemed to be looking for the right words. He took a quiet breath, and Scarlett waited eagerly to hear what was on his mind. Their hands still linked, he said, "I'm not prepared to begin anything like this."

The chance she felt they had slid away, but she understood his hesitation. When she'd first started to feel something for Charlie, she'd experienced a similar sense of caution, having experienced heartbreak in her past relationships. She didn't feel that way now, but at the time, no one could've convinced her otherwise. This was something Charlie had to work through, and Scarlett had no idea how long that might take him, if he came around at all.

He let go of her grasp and pulled his hand back.

"Why not?" she pressed, trying to keep the disappointment from showing. "I wouldn't ask anything of you that you aren't ready to give."

He leaned back in his chair. "I've spent most of my adult life making a mess of things. I need to learn how to be the person I want to be in life before I can be trusted with someone's heart." He tipped his head to the side, regret flooding his face, clearly aware of the fact that he was causing her sadness. She wasn't able to hide it anymore. "I couldn't bear it if I hurt you," he admitted.

"How do you know you will?"

"I don't know that I won't, and until I can figure everything out, I can't risk it."

"You sure you can't at least come for Christmas?"

"I'm sorry, I can't." He gave her a sad smile. "But you'll have to tell me all about the looks on Ms. Farmer's and Trevor's faces when they see the gifts, okay?"

She nodded, her heart aching for him.

*

"I'm so relieved Janie had a clean bill of health," Gran said, as she held on to Scarlett's arm on their way into the living room. "I can't believe what you've done for them. They're going to be overjoyed, I'm certain."

"It wasn't me, Gran. It was Charlie. But he refuses to take credit for it."

Gran's eyebrows rose in thought, but she didn't say anything.

Scarlett had sent a quick text to Waya to let him know they were all there. Then she'd told everyone what they'd planned. Riley and Mason were already asleep, still tired from the party the night before, so tonight was just for little Trevor and his mother. They'd all gathered in the grand living room and told Janie they had a Christmas surprise for her. When Scarlett and Gran walked into the room, Trevor was sitting eagerly on the sofa, to his mother's side.

Once they were all comfortable, Aunt Beth passed out hot chocolate with peppermint sticks and marshmallows, the tree glistening, the presents now spilling out from under it.

A loud knock came from the front entryway. "I'll get it," Scarlett said, taking her hot chocolate with her. When she opened the door, her eyes grew along with the laughter that threatened to escape from her lips, but she held it back. Waya was wearing a Santa hat, his gray hair curled into ringlets around it, his beard styled the same way. He had on his black boots, red velvet trousers with enormous white fur cuffs, and a matching red fur coat that hung loosely without the traditional belt, a Hawaiian shirt peeking out from underneath it.

He caught her looking at it. "I'm a bit tan for the part," he said. "Been delivering to the kids in the islands." He winked at her.

They both had a good laugh.

Sitting beside his feet in the snow was an enormous burlap bag full of all the toys they'd picked out. "Showtime," he said, picking it up and slinging it over his shoulder. "Ho ho ho!" he called deeply, as he walked past her and into the living room.

"Is that Trevor Farmer over there on the sofa?" he asked, lobbing the bag onto the floor. A small motor from one of the toy cars growled inside and Trevor's eyes lit up.

"Yes, sir," he said, breathless. As Waya moved closer, Trevor's little brows pulled together, showing his confusion. "You don't look like the pictures, Santa," he said.

"Nah, they never get it right," Waya said. "And I'm not very photogenic... Plus, I don't set them straight as to what I really look like because it helps to keep my identity a secret." He pulled the bag over to Trevor. "I heard you were looking for me. Want to know another secret?" He leaned in closer. "Your mom actually found where I live when I'm not at the North Pole." He whispered, "She was right. Always trust her." He winked at Janie, whose eyes were already glistening with emotion. "You see, I have a toy store in town, and I go by a pretend name so no one will know it's really me."

"What is the name you go by?" Trevor asked in awe.

"Waya."

The little boy gasped.

"So you'll have to keep the secret, okay?"

"Yes, sir."

Waya opened his bag and pulled out the toy truck, handing it to Trevor. "What do you think of this?"

"It's the best present ever! Thank you," he said, alternating between hugging it and inspecting all the buttons. "You have a lot of other toys to deliver to the kids..." Trevor looked at Waya's bag.

"Well, I do, but their bags are in my sleigh. This is your bag."

Trevor's eyes doubled in size, his cheeks flushing. "Mine?"

"Every single toy."

Gran handed a box of tissues to Janie, her cheeks streaked with tears. She looked around at everyone, clearly trying to figure out who was responsible for all this.

Waya began pulling out the toys, one by one, setting them up for Trevor, taking them out of the boxes, and showing him how they all worked. There were drawing kits and puzzles, science experiments, a microscope, a toy movie projector, the giant train set, an entire town's worth of cars and trucks with a mat that had a road painted on it, modeling clay, and even an archeology kit with plastic bones hidden in blocks of sand, to name a few.

"I don't know how to thank you," Janie said to Waya through her fingers.

"You don't have to thank me," he said. "I'm just the messenger. You'll have to talk to my elves." He grinned at her and she looked around the room. Gran pointed to Scarlett.

"I'd like to talk later," Janie said quietly to Scarlett.

"Of course."

"We'd love you two to join us for our family's Christmas morning tomorrow," Gran said to Janie. "You both have quite a few gifts under the tree."

"This is like a dream," Janie said, her voice breaking. "After what we've been through, it gives me hope that things can get better."

"Things can always get better," Gran said. "As long as we're here to help each other. That's all we need."

"May I take a few photos of you and Trevor tonight?" Scarlett asked.

She wanted to have something to show Charlie. She'd already decided that she wasn't going to let him spend tomorrow alone. After everyone had opened their presents, she planned to visit him, and she wanted to bring him photos so he could see how Janie reacted to his generosity.

"Of course," Janie said.

Scarlett started snapping away: Janie's sniffly laughter, a balled tissue in her hands, Trevor on his knees, pushing his truck across the floor. Waya in that hilarious Santa outfit… This Christmas was turning out to be one of Scarlett's favorites.

Chapter Sixteen

Time had slipped away from Scarlett as she lay in her bed, letting the events over the holiday settle in her mind. The smell of Christmas morning casseroles and the hum of her family whirled around outside her bedroom door, but her thoughts hadn't caught up to the festivities just yet. This Christmas had turned out to be such a wonderful surprise, and the last thing Scarlett wanted was for the trouble with the inn to ruin everything. Tomorrow, they'd all tell Gran that they were selling White Oaks, and Scarlett had nothing to offer yet in terms of options. She hadn't been able to even come close to broaching the subject with Charlie.

This morning, the joy that surrounded her once she was with her family would be bittersweet. She'd try not to linger on the fact that this was the last time they'd all be together for the holiday, the final moments in a history at the inn that spanned her entire lifetime. They'd have no say regarding what happened to the inn. Would it sit in disrepair until someone bought it? Would it be leveled for something more modern—centuries of stories evaporating into the air as the boards crashed down into a pile of rubble? Scarlett shuddered.

She got up, drew her brush through her hair, and padded into the en suite bathroom to wash her face and brush her teeth. Then she put on her red and green Christmas sweater and a pair of jeans and headed out to see her family.

Riley and Mason ran over to her, both talking at the same time, showing her what they'd gotten from Santa last night.

"Neither of them believe that Trevor actually met Santa Claus," Aunt Alice said, as she stood in her Christmas tree leggings and poinsettia sweater, her hands wrapped around a cup of Christmas spice tea. "But I hear he was, in fact, in town."

"That's true," Uncle Joe joined in from behind his reading glasses. He held the instructions for some sort of toy in his hand and had been diligently scanning the steps for setting it up. "I've heard of others who have seen him in this area. They say he's always around."

"He was on vacation but now he's here," Trevor said, as if it were totally regular information, not even looking up from his toy truck.

Later that night, Waya had told Trevor that he'd been resting up for the big night in the Bahamas, and that was how he'd gotten his tan, as well as his souvenir shirt that stood out loudly from under his fur coat. He'd said he'd nearly gotten his gray hair braided in cornrows, but he was worried the reindeer wouldn't recognize him. That was when Scarlett had cut him off—before the story got so outlandish that if Trevor ever told his friends, they would think he'd dreamed it all.

"While the whole family is in one place," Gran said, using her hands to steady herself as she stood up from her chair, Stitches hopping down from her lap, disturbing Archie who'd curled up by her feet, "I have something for each of you." She pointed under the tree at a pile of silver packages. "Scarlett, dear, would you pass those out? Hand one to everyone—they're all the same."

Janie crawled out of the room beside Trevor as he pushed his new car across the floor, and Scarlett grabbed a couple of the silver gifts, each one tied with white and silver ribbons. She handed one to her dad before kissing him good morning on the cheek. Then she gave one to Aunt Beth and another to Aunt Alice. As she continued, Gran went to the middle of the room to address them.

"Remember in the storm last summer when we lost the old oak tree in the back garden?"

"Oh, I was devastated," Aunt Beth said, putting her hand to her chest, the gift balancing on her knees. "It had to have been at least three hundred years old."

"At least." Gran nodded in agreement. "It held the baby swing that Scarlett used as a toddler, and later the rope swing all my grandkids adored climbing, and then finally the porch swing that overlooked the valley. I used to sit out there for hours as the sun went down behind the mountain."

"I loved to prop my feet up on the pillows you had out there," Scarlett reminisced. "I'd tip my head back and read all the messages that couples had carved into it. The trunk was full of whittled hearts and initials." She could still see the pattern of it if she closed her eyes.

"Yes, dear. I remember. All messages of love." Gran took stock of the family. "Does everyone have their gift?" Once she determined that they'd all gotten one, she said, "Open them now and I'll explain."

Scarlett untied the ribbons and tore the paper from her gift, revealing a beautifully crafted wooden picture frame. She ran her hand along the grains of wood that were encased in the high gloss of the frame.

When the others had opened theirs, Gran said, "Each of these frames was made from the oak tree. When you all get home, I'd like you to fill the frame with a photograph of your best family memory at White Oaks, and I'd like to hang them as a gallery in the main hallway."

She picked up her own frame that had been leaning beside her chair and turned it around, revealing a black-and-white photograph of her and Pappy on their wedding day in the back garden. She was in his arms, her white gauzy dress draped down to the grass below in a frozen swirl, her head thrown back in laughter, her arms outstretched as he spun her around.

"This is my memory." She made eye contact with each of them before continuing. "I've saved both the company address of the frame maker and piles of the wood in the back shed, so if your children would like frames, they can have them when they're ready. There are so many little remnants of lives past in this house that I thought we should put our mark on the place."

It was only obvious because Scarlett knew about the possible sale of White Oaks, but she could feel the rise in tension in the air as the family's eyes discreetly shifted between one another beneath their happy smiles and the buzz of conversation, as they all talked among themselves about the thoughtful gift Gran had gotten them.

"You might not have your memory yet, and that's okay," Gran said. "We can make them now. And over time, we'll fill the wall. There's no hurry."

But there was a hurry. In fact, they were out of time. Unless Scarlett could make something happen right now. She needed to see Charlie. He was their only hope.

While the living room would be closed to guests for the remainder of Christmas Day, the fires were going in the parlor for the visitors who wanted a Christmas morning common area with views of the mountains. The living room was reserved for family, and it had certainly seen its share of great moments today. The floor was littered with Christmas paper and the stockings were lumped on the hearth, the little prizes they concealed long gone. Mugs of cocoa were scattered on tables… The place was a festive Christmas mess.

Scarlett wanted to freeze time right then, with the remainder of the afternoon stretched out lazily in front of them. Her family was sprawled across sofas, Janie and her aunts laughing at something. The twins and Trevor were playing with their toys, Stitches was pawing at the loose ribbon on the floor, and Archie could be found in the corner behind the Christmas tree, trying to bury his new holiday bone in the mass of balled-up wrapping paper.

Scarlett didn't want to leave that beautiful scene, but she buttoned up her coat and slipped on her boots, headed for Charlie's. While she'd promised herself she wouldn't let him have Christmas alone, she also knew that it was time to find out for certain if he could help them with White Oaks in any way. She asked her dad for the truck keys and he didn't even question where she was going. She could sense that he felt the squeeze of time just like she did. All Scarlett could think about was the betrayal Gran would feel when they all sat her down to tell her the news, her brilliant idea of framed memories crashing to the floor, and her realization that they'd all known while they were thanking her for such a thoughtful gift. The whole thing soured in Scarlett's stomach.

She'd been careful not to tread on Charlie's emotions over the holiday, dancing around the subject of his work, but she'd reached that moment where she had to face the music. She was going to ask him outright—the inn's future depended on it. She'd texted him to let him know she was coming, and she hadn't asked; she'd simply stated that she needed to talk to him.

When Scarlett arrived, he was already standing at the door waiting for her under the patch of new shingles on the roof. The workmen had gone and the cottage was back to normal. Charlie locked eyes with her as she went inside, as if he knew the discussion would be a heavy one. She slipped off her coat and boots.

"How was your morning?" she asked, sitting down on the sofa across from the fire. A book was open, facedown, on the coffee table next to a near-empty glass of orange juice.

"Good." Charlie sat slowly beside her, his eyes wary, clearly sensing her tension as she tried to find a way into the conversation. He could read her easily.

"Okay," she said nervously, preparing herself for the big question. "I'm going to get right to it," she said. "What's going on with your work? Why won't you talk about it?"

She waited for the backlash, for the frustrated look or the loud exhale as he avoided an answer, but he just sat there, quiet, pursing his lips in thought as if he were trying to formulate the most efficient answer.

When he didn't say anything, she decided that she'd have to just be honest with him. "Cappy gave me your business card when I arrived last week. He said you're looking for a property to acquire in Silver Falls." She swallowed, her hands trembling. "White Oaks is for sale."

He remained silent, the information obviously settling in.

"That's why I came to see you the day I got stuck in the snow. I want you to buy it, Charlie."

Suddenly, he stood up, running his fingers through his hair in frustration. He looked back at her and then away, visibly upset with himself or the situation—she couldn't figure it out.

"So all the time we spent together—that was so you could sell me the inn?" He nodded to himself. "That's why you were so quick to offer me a room and why you wanted me involved in the festivities… You're good, Miss Bailey." He peered down at her, his eyes like daggers.

"No," she said hurriedly. "No, that's not it at all!" She'd worried this might happen, but she'd been so concerned with Gran tomorrow that she hadn't planned out the right way to explain it all to Charlie.

He picked up her coat in his fist and thrust it onto the sofa next to her, then opened the door. "I'm not in the market anymore." He looked away. "You can leave now."

Scarlett left her coat where it had landed and ran over to him, pushing herself between him and the open doorway, the icy air slithering down her spine. "Charlie."

With a deep breath, he pulled back, but she wouldn't allow it, taking his hands with her own. A tiny fizzle of hope fluttered around inside her when he didn't let go.

She pushed her face up toward his, forcing eye contact, and she saw the hurt again that he was working to conceal. She squeezed his hands affectionately. "That's what brought me to you originally," she said, "but it isn't what made me stay. *You* were what made me stay. And whether or not you buy the inn, I'll still be here. For *you*."

The anger in his eyes lingered while he pondered her admission. He pulled away from her and turned toward the door, and her heart dropped. Panic rose in her throat as she saw the pain she'd caused him. His wounds were still too fresh to believe her with confidence. Scarlett held her breath, fear coursing through her. When she'd hurt him, she could feel that pain. Right then, it hit her that she didn't want to spend another day without seeing him. No matter what happened with White Oaks. He grabbed the doorknob and paused. But then he closed it, sealing them back into the warmth inside.

"I'll tell you about Ms. Farmer," he said, picking her coat up gently this time, shaking it out and hanging it on the hook by the door.

Still shaken by the misunderstanding, Scarlett sat on the edge of the sofa, her whole body trembling. It was then that she realized how important it was to her that he believe her, because she was completely falling for him. When she turned toward him to listen, he was searching her face.

"I'm sorry I upset you," he said, taking her shaking hand into his warm grip, stilling it. "That's what I mean about needing time. I still feel like an awful person, so I immediately jump to conclusions, forgetting that you don't know about me."

"I only know what you've let me learn, and… I adore that person." His gentler presence was calming her already. "Why don't you tell me everything and then let me decide my opinion of you?"

"I was afraid to tell you because I worried it would rob me of that look in your eyes when you listen to me. You make me feel like I can do anything."

She squeezed his hand. "I'm not here to judge you on your past. I'll stay by your side with or without the knowledge of it," she said. "But it would be nice to understand what you went through."

He regarded her fondly. Finally, he said, "I'm only going to tell it once because I prefer not to relive it."

"That's all it takes. I won't ask again. Nor will anyone else, certainly."

He sat back, undoubtedly preparing himself. Then he began. "In my twenties, I found success as a developer," he said. "Once I'd built myself up enough to have my own company, I worked out of a penthouse office in New York, building resorts across the U.S., and it all came very easily for me. I never saw any of my properties—they were numbers on spreadsheets; it was all a figures game, each one a trick of management and organization, a skill on which I thrived.

"I'd heard rumblings of complaints from small businesses in different towns here and there where I'd developed, but that was to be expected, and the success of the resorts in those areas spoke for itself. So whenever someone contacted me about a grievance, I sent him or her to my director of public relations who 'handled' the situation. How he handled it was up to him, as long as it wasn't on my desk..." He shifted tensely on the sofa, the memory clearly getting to him. "Would you like a drink? Maybe a glass of wine?"

Charlie stood up abruptly without waiting for an answer and went into the kitchen, returning a minute later with two glasses of white wine, handing her one. She'd never said she'd have one, but she didn't mind. This was clearly difficult for him to tell, and he needed the moment to regroup.

"When I first arrived at boarding school, I cried every night, missing my father. A young teacher by the name of Mrs. Beasley comforted me. She had the kindest smile... I still remember her humming and braiding her hair as we sat together in the common area outside my bedroom. It was sort of a way of filling the time for me, and taking the pressure off of the situation. She'd ask me questions about my artwork and sports to keep me company, and eventually I associated calmness with her.

"Years later, I finally decided to scope out the locations myself because I was touring areas of Tennessee for my newest venture, and I wanted a firsthand look at the options. It was just after leaving my card with Cappy. Ms. Farmer must have gotten wind of the resort

I was visiting, and as I sat in the boardroom, she burst through the doors to the horror of my administrative assistant, who was fielding questions outside.

"The woman bursting through reminded me of Mrs. Beasley and I remember smiling at her at first, but then realizing how upset she was. She started screaming at me, telling me she'd used the very last of her money for gas to get there, to tell me what an awful person I was and how I'd ruined her life. She wanted her shop back." He shook his head at the memory.

"Her eyes were red from crying—I could see it through her anger. She said she'd worked as a puppeteer in a children's shop. I remembered it from the spec research; it wasn't profitable, had barely been hanging on financially for years... She said she'd worked there her entire adult life, and it had been the best job she could imagine, but I'd bought out the owner and leveled the place. She had to waitress to pay the bills, but the hours weren't working for her because she had a son to take care of. She'd been through three jobs and they'd fired her for taking off too much time, but it was because of the hours they'd given her. So with limited options, no one would hire her because she was now known as someone who didn't show up for work." Charlie cleared his throat, emotion welling up, but he pushed through.

"She got in my face and shouted at me. She said, 'I'll bet you've never awakened in the middle of the night to find that your only parent wasn't there because she was at work and the worthless sitter—the only one I could afford—had never shown up! And the reason you woke was because your tummy was so hungry that you couldn't sleep, because the free preschool food program didn't include dinner, and your mom had to choose between keeping the heating on in freezing temperatures or feeding you.'" With tears filling his eyes, he said,

"She fell onto my chest and sobbed before pushing me away in anger. She said her son had been having terrible asthma attacks recently due to their living conditions, and the medical bills had piled up." Charlie searched Scarlett's face. "Trevor. It's Trevor."

"That's heartbreaking," Scarlett said, barely able to get the words out through her emotion.

"Ms. Farmer reached into her bag, grabbed a stack of papers, tossed them onto the table where I was working, and then walked out." He took in a jagged breath. "I thought about those nights without my parents at school and I ached for little Trevor. She'd had to leave him alone to go to work, with no other options." He tipped his head up at the ceiling, the pain etched across his forehead. "When I gathered up the papers she'd left, they were all articles of others who had the same sort of experience. They said terrible things about me: I was heartless. An unemotional tycoon. They debated the benefits of the rise in tourism my resorts created versus allowing someone like me to invade their towns. My director of PR had done a bang-up job—I had no inkling at all that people thought these things of me. I honestly had no idea of the impact my business decisions were making on their lives.

"After that, every time I lay in bed at night, I was haunted by the woman's red eyes. I tried to find her to help her, but she hadn't left her name. I had no idea who she was. I tried to track down the owner of the shop where she'd worked, but when he passed away the inheritance went to his children in another state, and they didn't know who he'd employed. He didn't have any documentation of employment in his records. I hired a lawyer to try to track down tax documents, but that information was confidential."

"None of it is your fault if you didn't know it was happening."

"Yes, it *is* my fault. I should've known." His jaw clenched tightly in frustration and emotion. "It was *my* company. I was out of touch at my own doing." He dragged his fingers down his face and squinted his eyes shut, shaking his head. In a whisper, he said from behind his hands, "When I dropped off my business card that day, I was on my way out of town to catch a flight, and I didn't even stop to see my father." He looked up at her. "He was already gone, but I should've stopped then. I hadn't spoken to him in so long that it seemed odd to pop by when I only had a few minutes. I figured I'd rather catch him when I had time to talk… What kind of person does that? Not a very good one.

"My father had been silent, and quietly fell away from my life without ever confronting me with the hurt I'd caused him. But Ms. Farmer changed me that day. She let me have it; she showed me how I'd hurt her. I wanted to find her and make things better, and I couldn't. That made me realize how important it is to act in the present, and not to wait until later to set things straight. I've been working as hard as I can to do the right thing ever since.

"I gave everyone at the office generous severance packages, found them each alternative employment opportunities, and provided my endorsement whenever needed. Once everyone was well taken care of, I tied up all the loose ends with the resorts, and closed the company. Then, after many long months of notifying creditors, filing articles of dissolution and tax paperwork, and completing everything I had to do to dissolve Crestwood Development, I did what I should've done long ago: I went to find my father."

"And he wasn't here," she said, the pieces all fitting together now. "I'm so sorry."

He shrugged helplessly, his pain still very clearly with him. "I wanted to be as far away from that life as possible, so even once I got here and realized my father was gone, I decided to stay. This house was left to his sister, my aunt. She let me buy it from her.

"After purchasing the house, I'd planned to save back some money to renovate the home and then donate the rest of what I'd made to charities. I didn't even want the money in my bank account; not when I'd acquired it the way that I had. I wanted to make sure the money went toward some good, so I researched different charities and donated as much as I could."

"And you bought all those gifts for Janie and Trevor…"

"They need it more than I do."

"Would you see her? Perhaps you can make things better for her somehow."

"If you think it wouldn't hurt her any further, then I'd be happy to talk to her. If there's anything more I can do…"

"I definitely think you should. She'll easily see your kindness, Charlie. All you have to do is show her."

He looked at her thoughtfully, and it was clear that her support meant a lot to him.

Then something occurred to her and the blood rushed away from her face, her hands feeling clammy with the realization, dread settling upon her. Charlie probably had neither the kind of funds required to buy the inn, nor his company, so he couldn't put an offer in on White Oaks. She pushed the thought away. Right now, she needed to focus on Janie.

At the back of the inn there was a glass room that overlooked the rounded edges of the Smoky Mountains. On a summer's evening, the sky would turn pink and orange, the hills and valleys a deep purple. It had originally been a covered porch, but Gran had enclosed it with giant glass-paned doors that opened up onto little balconies, to allow them to be shut so that the views could be enjoyed all year round. At the end of the room was a double-access stone fireplace with openings to the glass room as well as a formal sitting room on the other side, in the interior of the main house. Gran had the mantel draped in fresh greenery for Christmas, the spruce color complementing the gray stones.

With a roaring fire and the views of the snow-capped mountains to keep everyone relaxed, Scarlett thought it would be a perfect spot for Janie and Charlie to have their discussion. She'd asked if they'd like her to leave them alone to talk, but both had assured her that they'd prefer her to be present. They'd all settled on the wicker furniture.

"Before you say what you've come to Silver Falls to tell me," Charlie began gently, as if he were trying to mend what she'd been through already, "I just want you to know how sorry I am. *Truly.*"

Janie's lips were set in a straight line, her hands gripped together nervously in her lap, uncertainty in her eyes. "You hurt us," she said, her voice hoarse. She leaned forward, her forearms on her knees, creases forming between her eyes. "Look, I know the shop wouldn't have been around forever, but it would've been good to have some warning. You swooped in and in a matter of days, I was out of a job. As a single mother, that's not easy. I spent so many days in fear of how we'd survive... I went back to Trevor's father. He said he'd take care of us, which I should've known was a lie since he never had before. I wanted to believe him, to believe that there was good in this world. He's gone again, and I'm expecting his second child." Her lip wobbled. "That's my fault. But now, more than ever, I have to figure out how to feed two mouths and clothe two children." Her gaze fell to the floor, her cheeks flushing. "I came to Silver Falls to ask you for money."

"I'll give you everything that I have left," he said quickly. "I've given most of my fortune to charity." He waited until she looked up so that he could speak directly to her. "Your story changed me. I left my entire life behind after hearing it."

Charlie's admission brought Janie's tears to the surface.

"I should've known what was going on, but I didn't. I'm not trying to excuse it, because there is no excuse for treating anyone badly, but I'm not the same person anymore. That's because of you."

"I'm sorry I yelled at you," she said.

He smiled. "It's fine. And I'll do whatever I can to help you. I'll get you whatever you need."

"I need a job," she said, but then she dropped her head into her hands and started to sob. "And reliable childcare." She sniffled. "And I've ruined my car…" Her chest heaved as she covered her face.

"We'll figure it out," Charlie said.

But Scarlett wasn't so sure how they would. Would anyone in Janie's town do any favors for Charlie? Scarlett could ask around for job opportunities in Silver Falls, but Janie didn't live there, and that still wouldn't give her the childcare or the car she needed. Scarlett certainly didn't have that kind of money either. Did Charlie have enough left for all of that, plus what would be needed for a new baby?

"I'm sorry I'm so emotional," Janie said. "I really don't want to be a charity case. I'm just out of options."

Scarlett patted Janie's shoulder to comfort her. "I think the most important thing is that you now have people around you to help, and we won't let you down."

"Including me," Charlie said.

Chapter Seventeen

Scarlett immediately zeroed in on the new fixture in the kitchen when she came in for breakfast. A massive Christmas bouquet sat in the center of the kitchen table—white and red roses among sprigs of holly and evergreen. It brought a romantic flair to the secretive heaviness in the air among Scarlett's family that hit her as soon as she'd seen their faces. Tonight was the night they'd all decided to tell Gran about selling White Oaks. Scarlett had all day for the elephant in the room to sit on her shoulders, knowing that unloading it wouldn't make things any better.

She kept her attention on the flowers in an attempt to save herself from the underwater feeling she got when she thought about telling Gran. "These are pretty," she said, holding one of the roses in her hand to take in the scent of it.

"They're from Sean," Aunt Beth said, doting as she leaned over them and breathed in their fragrance. "He sent them to say that he really enjoyed meeting me and he can't wait to see me again."

Gran handed Scarlett a freshly made white chocolate eggnog and sat down at the table. Scarlett thanked her, grabbing a spoon from the napkin at her place and stirring it to mix it once more before taking a sip.

"Loretta would like me to fill out some paperwork and settle her bill since our match was promising. I'm meeting her at the coffee shop in an hour."

"May I go with you?" Scarlett asked. "I'd love to get one of Sue's chocolate croissants." She really wanted to do anything other than sit at the table with Gran, because all she wished she could do was hug her grandmother and panic over tonight's conversation.

"Of course!" Aunt Beth said, throwing her arm around Scarlett. "I'd love to have a treat with my lovely niece." Her eyebrows rose in excitement, and Scarlett wondered if she was just as happy to avoid the situation as Scarlett. "We could go early and chat for a while. Are you up for it?"

"Absolutely."

"Hey, Preston!" Scarlett called across the street to Preston, who was carrying his guitar into The Bar.

He waved back to Scarlett and Aunt Beth. "I'm playing a few new songs today if you get bored," he said.

"We should go there first," Aunt Beth suggested. "I love hearing Preston play."

"Fine by me."

They crossed the street and went inside.

"Cappy's letting me write in here today," Preston said to them as they took a seat near the spot where he'd set up. He'd leaned his guitar against a chair and was spreading out notebooks on the small table in front of him. "I've started a couple of tracks and I'm trying to figure out which one is the strongest so I can cut a demo."

"Any slow ones?" Aunt Beth asked. "You have such a lovely voice when you sing ballads."

He picked up one of the notebooks and turned a few pages, rotating them around the spiral to the back of the pad and revealing his scratchy handwriting. "I've just started this one," he said, handing it to Beth.

She read the words aloud:

"The sun always shines on your face
I can't find a thing to take your place..."

Preston began strumming the tune quietly as she continued reading.

"When you think there's no one in this space
When silence pleads its hopeless case
I'm here."

Softly, Preston started to sing the melody with the lyrics behind Beth as she read, the notes sailing underneath his fingers while he played his guitar.

"In the shadows and in the light
While you leave, and in plain sight
I let you go without a fight
Every night."

"That's beautiful," Scarlett said, moved by his poetry.

"It's not finished quite yet, obviously. I have a few more lines to get down. The words just came to me after the party the other night."

Scarlett leaned over to his table and picked up the notebook, reading the words again. "Who's this song written about?" she asked. Beth looked on, interested.

Preston stared at her, clearly not wanting to admit his subject, but Scarlett already knew. He'd written it about Loretta. "Why do you let her go every night without telling her how you feel?" Scarlett asked.

"Who?" Beth asked, turning her head from right to left and left to right again as she attempted to follow the conversation.

Preston was locked into the conversation with Scarlett and must not have even registered Beth's question because he went straight into his answer to Scarlett's. "Because she's always trying to set me up with someone. I must not be her type." Out of nowhere, Preston nearly jumped out of his skin, hastily grabbing the notebook and closing it.

"Oh, hey, everyone!" Loretta said, walking over with a file folder under her arm. "Hi, Preston," she said with a big smile.

Aunt Beth gasped and quickly hopped up to cover the revelation she'd had. "Coffee?" she asked to no answer. "Great. I'll get us all some."

Preston nodded his greeting reticently at Loretta.

"I guess we all had the same idea." Loretta plopped down in the seat next to Aunt Beth's empty chair, dropped the folder onto the table, and shrugged off her coat. She leaned over to view one of Preston's open notebooks, but he grabbed it quickly, stacking them all up and pushing the pile out of Loretta's reach.

Beth came back and sat down slowly, this new information settling over her. "Cappy's making a pot of coffee for us."

"I'm happy to finish the paperwork here if you want, Beth." She held up the folder. "I've got it with me."

"Sit with us," Beth offered, sending a discreet wink in Preston's direction. He turned around and started fiddling with his guitar.

"Sue's gonna stop talking to me for taking all her business from the coffee shop," Cappy said, coming over with a handful of paper napkins. He set one at everyone's place. "I've got regular coffee, juice, or water. If you want anything other than that, you'll have to have it off the tap."

"We all want coffees, yes?" Beth asked, to their collective nods.

"Excellent," Cappy said. "How about you, Preston? Pick your poison."

"Water and an orange juice," Preston answered without making eye contact, busying himself with rearranging his guitar case.

"Done." Cappy went over to the bar to fulfill their orders.

"So what are you going to play for us, Preston?" Loretta asked, turning her chair around toward his corner of the room.

"Yes," Beth added. "What *are* you going to play?" She gave him a knowing look, catching on to the tension that washed over him in Loretta's presence.

Preston slid the notebook with Loretta's song into his backpack and grabbed another of his papers.

"I love your music, Preston," Beth said. "I could stay here and listen to you until you've played every song in those notebooks of yours."

"Me too. I thought I saw your car outside, so I came in. I was wondering if you were playing right now—it's earlier than your usual time," Loretta said. "But I agree with Beth. Early is fine by me. I could sit here all day…"

Preston shifted his guitar off his shoulder, setting it against the table, freeing his hands so he could come out from behind the microphone and focus on Loretta. A small smile formed at his lips, and the affection he had when he looked at her was undeniable.

"But I can't this time. I took your advice from the party," Loretta told him. "I'm meeting someone here tonight—a date."

The blood drained from Preston's face, and his whole body seemed to stiffen. It was clear that he didn't like that idea one bit. In all the years that they'd known each other, as far as Scarlett was aware, Loretta had never made him face the prospect of her dating another man right in front of him. The strangest thing was that Loretta seemed to be imploring him to intervene. It was as if she were willing him to tell her not to go through with it. When he didn't say anything, she looked down at the paperwork she'd brought. He jammed his fists in his pockets.

Come on, Preston. Do something, Scarlett pleaded silently.

What if Loretta started dating this person seriously? She was great at making matches and there was a real possibility that if Preston didn't make a move right now, he'd miss his chance. He swayed forward as if he were going to take a step toward Loretta and, taking his hands from their rigid position in his pockets, he was about to reach for her to get her attention. But before he could say anything, Cappy had returned with their coffees, redirecting Loretta's focus and ending the moment. Loretta pulled out the forms for Beth as Cappy set a mug in front of each of them.

"Normally I get this consent first," Loretta said, sliding a contract over to Beth. "But you're like family. I've highlighted the important parts. If you could just sign—"

Loretta didn't have a chance to finish because Preston interrupted, pulling her up by her hands, his gaze more intense than Scarlett had ever seen it.

"I didn't make myself clear the other night," he said, grabbing Loretta's waist tenderly to pull her closer.

She peered up at him like a smitten schoolgirl.

He held her gaze for a second as if he'd waited for years to have the opportunity that was in front of him right now. He pulled Loretta even closer, embracing her. Scarlett had never seen him so openly affectionate, nor had she ever witnessed him putting his heart on the line like this. "When I said you should go out with someone, I meant that someone should be me." He stared at her, waiting for her response.

"But you've never..." Loretta whispered, only now seemingly collecting all the moments they'd had together. She put her hands around his neck, everything appearing to finally make sense for her. "I've been in love with you for ages," she confessed. "But you never gave me reason to think my feelings were more than one-sided."

"Okay," Preston said, "how about I give you reason to think so right now?" He put his hands on her face and leaned in, pressing his lips to hers, completely oblivious to the ogling eyes of everyone around them. Loretta hugged him tighter and kissed him back. Beth put her hand on her heart, her head turned to the side, and Cappy raised his eyebrows at Scarlett from across the bar, making her laugh quietly so as not to attract attention from the happy couple.

Preston finally pulled back and said, "Cancel that date. I've got a few million songs I'd like to play for you."

When Scarlett and Beth arrived back at the inn, Gran greeted them looking like a storm cloud. "Meeting in the kitchen. Now," she barked before rushing out of the entryway.

Heidi rushed up to them, tears streaking her face. "I accidentally let it slip to Gran that we were selling," she said. "We were talking about next year, and Gran said she worries every year if all of us will get together. I told her not to worry, that even if we don't have the inn, we'll figure out a way to have Christmas together. She caught it and asked if Charlie was trying to buy the inn. I told her I didn't know who was going to buy it. I feel like I can't do anything right these days... If I haven't disappointed Dad enough with my college choice, I've surely done it now." She was trembling with guilt.

"Oh, Heidi, don't beat yourself up about it," Scarlett said. "We were going to tell her tonight anyway. She just heard it a little earlier than expected, that's all."

The moment was upon Scarlett. This was the point that she'd dreaded the entire trip. And she had nothing to lessen the blow, nothing to make Gran feel any better. On her way into the kitchen, her phone buzzed in her pocket. It was Charlie. She didn't have time to talk at the moment so she sent him a quick text: *Gran knows we want to sell. Heading into a family meeting now. Will keep you posted.*

Then she clicked off her phone and slid it into her back pocket, preparing to face this head on.

"How dare you all meet about this without me," Gran snapped at Scarlett and Heidi, as they took the last two seats at the table.

"We worried you'd be too emotionally attached to make a clear decision," Blue said evenly.

"You're damn right I'm emotionally attached!" Gran slammed her fist on the table. Her weathered hands shook as she took in quick breaths, clearly attempting to calm down. "But what you all forget is that this house belongs to *me*. The inn is mine. It's not your decision. I won't sell!"

"You're losing money, Mom," Blue said. "Hemorrhaging money, actually. If you don't sell, you won't have a penny to retire on."

Gran's eyes filled with tears, clouding the defiance in them. She sank into her chair in defeat. "I can't let go of the inn," she said more quietly.

"This is just as difficult for us, Gran," Scarlett said, feeling helpless. "I've lost sleep many nights over it. And I was concerned you'd think we were ganging up on you, but we're not. We just want the best for you, and we want to make sure that you're taken care of."

"I've spent over half my life here," she said. "This isn't just a home; it's my identity. Who am I if I'm not the innkeeper?"

"You're down to a skeleton staff, Mom," Blue said. "Even if you could turn a profit by cutting back, you can't keep up with all the tasks yourself. And people simply want more these days. More than we have to offer."

"Selling is our only option, Gran," Scarlett said, the words hitting her like a punch in the gut.

Gran turned to her. "When your pappy was barely able to hear me, lying in that hospital bed at the end of his life, I promised him I could do this. I told him not to worry about me. I am strong enough to do it all. The moment I said that, he smiled and then he left me." She pursed her lips to keep them from wobbling with emotion. When she'd regained enough composure to speak, she said, "He trusted that I would be true to my word."

"And you have been," Uncle Joe cut in. "These circumstances are beyond your control. Even if Pappy were here, you'd be forced to close. He would understand."

"What do we need—a pool?" Gran scrambled for some kind of answer.

Uncle Joe placed his hand on top of hers. "That would be a start, but we don't have the kind of money it takes to install a pool the size that we'd need. Just hiring someone to blast the rock on this mountain and level it would bleed us all dry financially. And there's upkeep and staff—lifeguards, furniture, cabanas. We'd do all that and patrons would still go elsewhere because a pool is just the tip of the iceberg. To keep up, at the minimum, we'd need a fitness facility, tour guides, story time and in-house nannies for the children, boat and canoe rentals, upgraded bedrooms with entertainment centers, conference rooms with state-of-the-art presentation equipment, and a chef on staff with a twenty-four-hour dining room. Gran, the project is out of our league."

Gran fought back tears and Scarlett's heart was breaking. Scarlett attempted to comfort her by suggesting, "Maybe we can sell quietly— only share the news by word of mouth and find the right person to take over the inn, someone who will run it the way we want it run." But she knew her offer wasn't any consolation to Gran, and there was no way Scarlett would allow Christmas to end like this.

Chapter Eighteen

The door to Heidi's room was open to the hallway so Scarlett went inside.

"Want to talk?" Scarlett asked her younger cousin, as Heidi sulked on the bed.

"Do you ever feel like you're in a low point all around?" Heidi asked, removing her AirPods and sitting up cross-legged, pulling a pillow into her lap.

Scarlett sat down beside her. "Definitely."

Heidi fiddled with the edge of the pillowcase. "I ended things with Michael and he didn't take it very well; I didn't really break the news about college very well to Dad either; and then I messed up by telling Gran before we were all ready for her to hear. Nothing has gone right for me this Christmas."

"We all go through things like that in life, and the good news, at least from what I've found, is that after the lows you notice the highs, and when you're up there, it feels so good. Just hang on. It's coming."

"I guess…"

"Have you talked to your dad any more about your decision to go to college somewhere else?"

She shook her head.

"The one thing I know about Uncle Joe is that he's really consider-ate of other people. I'm sure he understands that you aren't the same person as he is and you might want something different. I think he just hoped you'd go to his alma mater. All you have to do is pull him aside and tell him how you feel."

"I know. I just wish I could've done what he wanted me to do. He's already put a deposit down on an apartment for me on the outskirts of campus at Johns Hopkins. I didn't know he'd done that. It was going to be a surprise." She sank down against the pillows miserably.

"But you can't choose a university because your dad might lose a deposit. I'm sure he'd agree. Perhaps he, too, has to learn how to navi-gate things as they change—it's all new for him as well. Maybe he'll decide that he needs to check with you before making big decisions on your behalf. You're a young adult now; you'll be making your own choices. He's probably not used to that."

"She's absolutely right." Uncle Joe's voice sailed in from the hall-way. He walked into the room and sat down next to Scarlett. "Scarlett couldn't have said it better. Yes, I'd have loved for you to go to my uni-versity, and I looked forward to reliving my good ol' days through you, but that doesn't mean that I'm disappointed about your choice. Only that I won't get to eat the chocolate chip cookies at that little eatery off campus. I was really looking forward to that." He grinned at her.

Heidi leaned across Scarlett to give her father a hug. "Thank you, Dad," she said. "And I'm so sorry about Gran."

"It's all right. We shouldn't have kept it from her anyway. It was terrible timing with the holiday, and we only wanted her to have a nice Christmas at White Oaks so she'd have good memories to take with her."

"What's gonna happen to White Oaks, Dad?" Heidi asked.

"I don't know, honey. I really don't know."

"Has Gran relaxed at all?" Scarlett asked her uncle. Her grandmother had still been pretty wound up when she'd asked to be alone for a little while. They'd all given her the silent time she'd wanted, every one of them wishing they could give her more.

"She's been in her room," he said.

"Do you think I could talk to her? Or should I let her be?"

"I think we overwhelmed her. It's a lot to take in. She'd probably really like it if she could have someone to bounce her thoughts off of, now that she's had a bit of time to process it."

"I'll go check on her," Scarlett said, getting up.

"Hey," Heidi said, stopping Scarlett. "Thank you for listening."

"Anytime."

Scarlett went down to Gran's room and knocked on the door.

"Come in." Gran's voice sounded small from the other side.

Scarlett opened the door and found Gran peering at the snow-covered back garden through the window, as she sat in the wingback chair in the corner with a box of tissues in her lap.

"This was the view that made the decision for us," she said, without greeting Scarlett. "Your pappy and I fell in love with this place, but as we walked the grounds and then the house itself, it wasn't until we stood at this window that we knew." She set the tissue box on the side table with trembling hands and rose, her back to Scarlett and her face to the view. "We imagined our children playing in this yard. Beth, Joe, and your dad hadn't even been born yet, but when I looked out here, I saw two boys and a girl. Then, over the years, as we had our children, and they fit the image I'd created that day, we knew this was right. It was a good place to raise our children because they had the benefits of a small town with the advantage of meeting people from all over the world. I couldn't have asked for a better place to be a mother."

Scarlett walked up beside Gran and put her hand on her grandmother's shoulder, the story creating new perspective. "One thing I hadn't considered before now," Scarlett said, "was that maybe this house is ready for another family. What if there's another mother who needs this view?"

Gran turned toward her, considering the idea. "How can we be sure?"

Scarlett shrugged, helplessness taking over again, but she had to be strong for Gran. "We aren't ever sure about anything in life, are we? But it all seems to work out." The truth was that Scarlett had no idea if it would actually work out, and she feared the worst, but the only way to get through it was to hold on to the hope that something magnificent would happen. If she let that go, she might not recover.

Scarlett received a text from Charlie, asking her to meet him in town at the lookout by the bakery. She had no idea what he was up to, but after talking with Gran, she'd spent the rest of the day fighting the complete panic that rose in her chest every time she faced anyone at White Oaks. She'd sat by the fire with her dad, which was a totally regular thing to do, but all she could think about was how this would be the last time she'd ever smell those particular embers mixed with Gran's vanilla candles, the last time she'd sit in that chair in that very room. And then she'd gone to see how Heidi was doing. Her cousin had been in the library, thumbing through antique design books, when Scarlett nearly broke down in tears. Who would acquire this library? It was original to the house and had been added to by its owners over the centuries.

So when Charlie texted, Scarlett nearly bolted from the house.

She pulled up to the lookout in Blue's truck, and saw Charlie standing next to an old car she didn't recognize. She got out and walked over to the silver 1990 Mitsubishi Mirage. It was in good condition, given its age.

"What do you think?" he asked, when she met him on the sidewalk next to the car. He opened the door to allow her to peer inside.

"About?" she asked, confused.

"Have a seat." He gestured toward the passenger seat.

Scarlett got into the car. It smelled like her old school bus from elementary school mixed with orange spice. Charlie walked around to the driver's side, closing himself in.

"Surprisingly, it only has 103,000 miles on it. I drove it around town for the last hour or so and it runs really well."

The complete confusion the situation caused her made her laugh. What were they doing in this car? "What is this?" she asked.

"It's Janie Farmer's new car." He put his hands on the wheel and straightened his back. Then he turned to her. "I bought it at the used dealership down the road. It was the best they had on the lot. The maintenance check came back clean, and the engine's in good condition. She could get another fifty to a hundred thousand miles out of this."

"You bought her a car?" Scarlett said, not hiding her delight.

"Anything I can do to help." Then he pointed to the backseat. "I got a new car seat for Trevor. I swung by the police department and explained what I was doing. They told me what to get and helped me install it. While they weren't really supposed to let me take anything out of the car, they'd already checked the vehicle, so they let me have the stuffed animal they'd found inside."

"She's going to be so happy," Scarlett said.

"I wish I could do more. All I have left is the renovation money, but I'd use it to help her if I knew the best way. Without a job, she'll run through it and then be in the same situation she's in now."

"Maybe we could ask her how she'd use the money," Scarlett suggested. "Although that would leave you without funds to renovate Amos's cottage, and I've seen the work it needs. The roof is fixed now, but what will come next? You'll need something to manage the upkeep."

"I'll figure it out. Right now, Janie needs it more than I do." He started the engine. "Could I ask you a favor?"

"Of course."

"Would you follow me to the inn in your father's truck? I'll drop the car off for Ms. Farmer, and then you can take me back to the dealership to get my car."

"Yes," she said, still thrilled with the gesture. "I can't wait to see her face when she gets this. I'll text Dad to tell her to wait at the back door to the private lot for us."

Scarlett texted Blue and then got out of the car and into her own. She followed Charlie down the winding road leading to White Oaks, pulling up behind him at the back of the main house. "Shall I go get her?" she asked, once they'd parked and gotten out of their vehicles.

"Okay," he said. "I'll wait here."

On her way to the door, Janie stepped onto the porch. "What's going on?" she asked, looking over Scarlett's shoulder at the old car.

Charlie stepped up the stairs to join them. "I left the engine running for you in case you'd like to take it for a spin." He moved to the side to give her a clear view. "It's the best I could do for now, but this car is yours. Consider it a late Christmas present."

Janie clapped a hand over her mouth.

"It's in great condition and gets pretty good gas mileage. I filled it up for you and put Trevor's seat in the back."

Janie stared at Charlie, her eyes filling with tears of gratitude. "I'm so thankful," she said. But there was something more lurking there.

"Are you okay?" Scarlett asked.

Janie nodded but didn't look any more convincing.

"Tell me, is something wrong? Is it anything to do with the car?"

Janie shook her head, more tears surfacing. She dragged her fingers under her eyes as tears spilled over them.

"You've been wonderful," she said, and then turned to Charlie. "And I'd have never thought you were capable of something this amazing." She sniffled. "I can't thank you enough… But the problem is…" She couldn't finish her sentence, emotion overcoming her.

Scarlett and Charlie both waited quietly for her sobs to subside. Scarlett put her hand on Janie's arm to soothe her.

Finally, Janie said, "The thing is, I have this great car, but I don't have anywhere to go." Janie closed her eyes, more tears sliding down her cheeks. She folded her arms around herself and then looked at them both vulnerably. "I can't go back to waitressing," she said, shaking her head and squeezing her eyes shut again. "I should be thankful for any job, but it's so hard on me. I can't be the mother Trevor needs when I'm working such sporadic hours, and when I do come home, I'm so exhausted. But even if I could manage it, no one will hire me in my town. We were staying with a friend on her sofa, but I can't do that forever…"

"Is there anything I can do to help you with that?" Charlie asked, visibly concerned. "Where do you live? Can I help you get a different job? Perhaps I can fund a nanny…"

"I was evicted from my apartment. I don't have a place to live."

"You can stay here as long as you need to," Scarlett offered. She'd at least be able to give Janie a room while they prepared the inn for sale. After that, they'd have to work out another arrangement, but there was no sense in upsetting Janie with that now. At this minute, she just wanted Janie to feel safe and cared for.

Janie wiped her eyes.

"We'll find a solution," Charlie promised, although Scarlett had no idea how. They could certainly help, but they couldn't work miracles. "Have a look at the car," Charlie urged her.

Charlie walked beside Janie as she moved through the snow to the car, making sure she didn't slip on the icy walk. He opened the driver's-side door and slowly, Janie lowered herself inside. She put her hands on the wheel, amazement visibly washing over her. She ran her hand down the center console admiringly. The car was clearly a younger model than the one she'd had before, and she seemed overwhelmed that something like this now belonged to her.

While Janie was sitting in the driver's seat, Aunt Beth came out all dressed up in heels, wearing her dangly earrings that she always saved for parties and weddings. "Oh! What are you two doing out here?" she asked.

"Giving Janie a new car," Scarlett said, nodding toward the Mirage. "Charlie got it for her."

"That's fantastic!" she said, putting her hand over her heart. "Hey, when you get a chance, will you go in and help Gran? She wouldn't let me help her because I'm going to meet Sean. She's trying to get the party dishes put away and she can't reach the top shelf. She's on the step stool but it's still quite a stretch for her, and Blue and Joe have taken Heidi and your aunt Alice to go shopping at the mall a few towns over. Heidi's overjoyed at the prospect of free Wi-Fi."

Scarlett laughed. "We'll go in right now," she said, waving to Janie, who now had the car door shut and had put the window down to hear her. "We're heading in!" Scarlett called.

"All right! I'll be there in a few more minutes. Trevor is napping and I need to check on him. I just want to enjoy a car that has working heating for a little while longer."

When Scarlett and Charlie got to the kitchen, Gran was standing beside a stack of dishes on the counter, the cabinet doors open wide.

"I can't get these plates up there," she said, frustrated. "I've always put them away by myself, but this year they're just too heavy for me to lift over my head."

Charlie picked up the stack and placed them onto the shelf above Gran while she eyed him guardedly.

When all the dishes were put away, Gran sat down in one of the chairs around the table, looking exhausted. "I'm not sure how to break the news to your father and uncle," she said to Scarlett, as she and Charlie joined her at the table, "but I've decided I'm not selling White Oaks. Like the captain of a cruise liner, if I have to, I'm going down with the ship."

It wasn't surprising that Gran would dig her heels in. On top of her emotional stake in the inn, she was stubborn as a mule when she wanted to be. "That's no way to gamble with your future, Gran."

Gran straightened the already-straight place mat. "For me, giving up the inn would be more of a gamble."

Scarlett turned to Charlie, powerless. "Do you know anyone who would be interested in the inn—someone who would keep it the same?"

"I don't care if he does!" Gran said. "I'm not selling. I'll drain my savings if that's what it takes to keep it running. And I'm sorry, Charles, but I don't want your help."

"I wish I could buy it, but I'm not in the position to do so anymore," he said kindly, despite Gran's abrasive comment. "And I could ask around with area developers, but I don't know any offhand that are looking specifically for historical property. I'd worry that they'd buy to acquire the land only."

"With all due respect, Mr. Bryant, I don't want to have anything to do with people in your circles," Gran said, her shoulders rising with tension. "When it comes to White Oaks, I make the decisions. No one else."

Scarlett didn't voice her thought that it was Gran's decisions that were running it into the ground.

"Ms. Bailey," Charlie said carefully, that familiar hint of vulnerability in his look, "I don't operate the same way that I used to. I'd never steer you toward anyone who would undermine your vision for White Oaks. I'd love to help in some way, even if only to lend my experience—"

"Thank you, Mr. Bryant," she interjected, cutting him off. "But I've gotten this far by listening to my intuition, and right now, it's telling me that I should work this out on my own."

"Charlie might have insight that we don't have, Gran," Scarlett said.

"I have plenty of years under my belt to handle this," Gran returned, standing up. "Now, if you'll excuse me, I have to finish putting dishes away." And just like that, the conversation was over.

Charlie eyed Scarlett and quietly he mouthed, "I've got an idea." Then he nodded toward the hallway leading to the front entrance. "Walk me out?" he asked.

"Do you need me, Gran?" Scarlett asked.

"No, thank you. I've got it on my own," she answered, her thoughts clearly heavy.

Then the two of them left Gran in the kitchen.

"Let's drive into town to get my car, and then I'd like you to come back to my cottage..." he said quietly, once they were in the hallway. He seemed as though he were distracted by something. "I need to put some things together, but I have an idea that might help White Oaks. Will you come with me?"

"Of course." Scarlett felt hope surge in her veins like rocket fuel. She was almost afraid to trust it, but she knew Charlie wouldn't let her down. If he had an idea, it would definitely be worth listening to.

Chapter Nineteen

Charlie unwrapped the cheeseburgers they'd grabbed from the tavern in town on the way back to his cottage and put them on plates, along with a few fries. "I've got beer or milk," he said, peering into his refrigerator. "I probably should've thought that one through while we were picking up dinner…"

"Beer is fine," Scarlett said from the sofa, where Charlie had placed a stack of papers in file folders. He'd gotten them and then made a fire in the old stone hearth before digging into the takeout bags that held their dinner.

He popped the tops off of two beers and brought one over to her with her plate of food, setting it down next to the folders. Then he returned with his own.

"Cheers," he said, holding up his bottle.

She clinked hers to his. "What are we toasting?"

"The thought that I might be able to use my expertise for something good." He took a long swig from his bottle and then picked up the first folder. "When I moved into this cottage, I never thought I'd open one of these files again. In fact, my receptionist insisted I print it all out before I deleted it from my laptop. Even though I'd told her that it wasn't necessary, she did it anyway and packed it with the rest of my things when I closed the business. I had it beside my pile of kindling, to burn if my woodpile outside got wet in the snow." He ran his hand along the outside of the folder and then opened it. "This is a breakdown of every amenity at my resorts, along with survey results data regarding the public opinion of those amenities. I had a team study the surveys as well as the connection to revenue at the highest performing resorts. They included everything from analyzing consumers' bar tabs to which toilet paper brand we put in our bathrooms.

"Basically, that's a long way of saying that I have a very good idea of exactly what people want from their mountain vacation experience." He reached over and grabbed a fry, popping it into his mouth as if it were totally normal to have this level of expertise in their niche.

Scarlett held her burger still in both hands. "You mean to tell me that you can, in essence, prescribe what the inn would need to make it profitable?"

He grinned. "Yep."

"But there's one issue," she said, taking a bite and then sitting back on the sofa, feeling a little deflated. Once she swallowed, she continued. "Gran doesn't have the money to invest in any upgrades. Especially not the ones that are probably in that file."

"I don't have that kind of cash anymore either, or I'd help her out," he said. "But." He held up a finger. "Your grandmother said she had savings, right?"

"Well, yes, but those savings are her retirement. She can't use them all up or she'll have nothing to live on."

"She won't use them all up. She'll invest them in something that will pay her back tenfold."

"How can you be so sure?"

"I've got about thirty-five top-selling resorts to prove it." He tipped his beer up and took another drink. "If you would trust me with the financial records for White Oaks, as well as the company files so I can get a feel for the place, and let me know what we're looking at in terms of her savings, I could draw up a plan to make the inn profitable again."

"What would you charge to do this for us?" Scarlett asked.

"Absolutely nothing. It would be my pleasure to do it."

"Charlie, that would be amazing." Just as she said it, a blob of ketchup fell from her burger onto her shirt. "Oh! No…" she said, dabbing the spot with a napkin from the little pile that Charlie had brought over with their burgers.

Charlie hopped up. "Here, come to the sink and we'll put some water on to dilute it. I've got some laundry spray I can put on after."

"You got me so excited about White Oaks that I squeezed my burger too hard," she teased, making light of the fact that she had an enormous spot on her shirt as she went with him into the kitchen area.

They both stood at the sink and Scarlett turned the water on, before Charlie bent down under the sink to grab a rag so Scarlett could wipe the spot.

"Oh!" Scarlett squealed again, this time for an entirely different reason. "Charlie!" By the time Charlie stood up, she was already drenched. The tap had broken, and the water was fanning out across the kitchen and dousing the two of them. Scarlett dropped the metal piece of it that was still in her hand and tried to cover the spray. Charlie tried to put his hand over the end as well, only succeeding in changing the direction of the water. Scarlett attempted to help by putting her hands on top of his to create a larger barrier, but they were no match for the water.

"Can you turn it off?" she asked, squinting through the spraying water.

"The lever to stop it is on the part that broke off." He took off one hand to point to the piece of plumbing lying on the counter that Scarlett had dropped, the water streaming harder without his hand in place.

Charlie pulled her over to the fire, leaving the geyser still gushing in the kitchen. "Warm up here for a sec. I'll go shut off the main line." Then he disappeared out the back door.

Scarlett stood by the fire, sopping wet and dripping onto the wood floor, the fountain still spurting like crazy. She shivered in the heat of the fire. How different things were now from the first time she'd stood here. The water in the kitchen gurgled and spat out one last time before it was silenced.

Charlie returned with a folded towel, a button-down shirt, flannel pajama bottoms, and a big pair of wooly socks. He wrapped her with the towel and his proximity made her heart patter. "They're all going to be huge on you," he said, holding out the clothes, "but at least the pajamas are drawstring. Why don't we get changed, and I'll dry your clothes and get us a few blankets?"

Scarlett tried not to feel delighted that the tap had broken, causing the two of them to have no choice but to snuggle together under blankets to keep warm. She didn't want to smile at the thought, but her grin emerged anyway. When she looked at Charlie, the expression on his face caused hope to rise from the pit of her stomach, as she wondered if he was thinking the same thing.

Scarlett took the pile of clothing into the bathroom where she toweled off and changed, lumping her wet clothes over the sink. She stopped to breathe in the scent of him from the garments she had on, noting how safe and calm it made her feel. Then she wrapped her hair in the towel like a turban and went out to find Charlie. He grinned when he saw her.

"Do you have a comb for my hair?" she asked, bringing her clothes in from the bathroom and spreading them out along the hearth to dry.

His gaze lingered on her before he spoke. "Yeah, let me get you one," he said.

He went into the back bedroom and returned with a comb and a large quilt. "Can I ask you something?" he said, while she took the towel down and combed through her wet strands of hair. Charlie set the blanket on the sofa and grabbed a piece of twine from the empty mantel. He tied it to two hooks at either end of the fireplace, hanging her clothes over it.

She flushed when he arranged her unmentionables, although it didn't seem to faze him one bit. She refocused on him to hear his question.

The corner of his mouth turned upward, the humor in his face puzzling her. "Why is it that every time you come see me, something major breaks?"

She laughed, his teasing surprising her. "It's my electric person-ality," she said on a quick comeback. "It vibrates the very bones of the house." She kept her eyes on him to avoid the fact that her lacy undergarments were hanging up beside them for the world to see. At least she'd chosen the nice ones this morning.

They shared a moment of amusement and then he grabbed their beers, handing Scarlett's to her. "I'll heat up your burger if you're still hungry."

"No, it's fine." All she could think about was the fact that her laundry was on display and she was freezing. "Do you have a dryer we could put my clothes in?"

"It broke yesterday," he said, before bursting into a loud laugh, making her chuckle along with him.

When they'd sobered from the moment, she asked, "Shouldn't we clean up the kitchen?"

They stared at the mess in silence, as if they were both too overwhelmed by the size of it to move. Water was everywhere—it had drenched everything on the counter, piles of papers and mail were sopping, a heap of clean laundry on the small table nearby was saturated, and the kitchen floor was under an inch of water with puddles on everything in the vicinity of the sink.

Scarlett sat down on the warm stones of the hearth where her clothes had been, the fire having lost its force. Only an occasional pop and sizzle alerted them that the flame was still present at all, the small blue flicker hiding beneath the charred logs.

Charlie took a long drink from his bottle and then grabbed a piece of kindling from the pile beside Scarlett, tossing it into the fire. The flame protested, sending embers rising into the air like little rockets.

"How many towels do you have?" she teased, peering over at the chaos. "Seriously, where's your mop? If we don't get that water off the floor, the wood will warp, and right now, it looks like a lot of it just needs to be refinished."

"You don't need to clean up my house," he said.

Scarlett gestured to her outfit, the pajama bottoms dragging under her feet and the sleeves swallowing her hands. "I don't think I'll be going anywhere for a while, and we'll both go crazy if we don't do something while my clothes dry."

"True. But come get warm first. What will it hurt if the kitchen stays soaked a couple of minutes longer?" He picked up the blanket and shook out the folds. Then he plopped down on the sofa and patted the cushion beside him while covering up.

Scarlett complied, Charlie draping the blanket over her and cocooning them in warmth, making her shiver. Under the blanket, he took her hands, startling her. She smiled nervously, happy for his gesture.

"You're freezing," he said, rubbing his warm hands over hers.

Scarlett scooted in closer. She noticed his change in breathing first, and wondered if he too could feel the chemistry rushing between them like a wild current.

But he let go of her hands. "All warm?" he asked sweetly.

Scarlett nodded, wishing he'd stay next to her. Just the tiny space he'd now created between them seemed like too much. She wanted his arms around her. But he stood up. "I'll get the mops," he said, something lingering in his eyes that he was fighting. He went into the back room and came out with two old mops and a bucket. "This is all I've got."

Scarlett stood up and draped the blanket over the arm of the sofa. "Judging by the size of those mops, we'll be here a while," she said. She didn't mind at all if it took longer than it should… "Okay, hand me one." He held one out to her. Scarlett took it and went into the kitchen, Charlie following.

"Be careful," he said. "This floor has some sort of old varnish on it and it gets really slippery in places when it's wet."

"I'll be fine," she said, barely getting the words out before she lost her balance and caught herself by grabbing on to the counter, only making them both laugh again.

"What's your action plan for this?" he said, surveying the water on the floor. It was too big a job for the small mops they had.

"I think we should absorb most of the water with the mops and wring it into the bucket over and over, until the water is low enough that we can sop it up with a towel."

"Whatever you say, boss," he said, clearly unable to hide his affection for her anymore. The sparkle in his eyes gave it away.

Scarlett liked this new side of him. He'd finally relaxed around her, and she enjoyed being with him. Even if it was mopping floors. She ran the mop around the hardwoods, getting all the fibers saturated. Then she lifted it over the bucket and Charlie squeezed it out. They continued to do this from one side of the kitchen to the other. Feeling confident now, Scarlett took a quick step but slipped, suddenly falling, unable to catch herself. She dropped the mop in an attempt to regain balance, but she was unsuccessful. Suddenly, Charlie's arms were around her, both of them dropping to the floor, his body cushioning her fall.

He rolled her onto her back and was hovering over her, trying to catch his breath. "I told you," he said, looking down at her, his lips set in a smile that knotted her stomach. Uncertainty swam around his face, but she grabbed on to his belt loops, keeping him right where he was and in the moment. His expression softened as he allowed his true emotion to emerge fully, and his gaze swallowed her. Right then, she knew without a doubt the affection he'd felt for her but wouldn't allow himself to show. He'd caused himself a whole lot of hurt over the years, and she knew that he didn't trust himself, but she wanted to show him he'd come through that, and if he just permitted himself to try, he might find a kind of happiness that was greater than anything he'd known.

"What am I doing?" he whispered softly, locked in her stare.

"Feeling," she said, hoping he'd relax into the present again and finally let his guard down. If he made a move, she'd let him.

He allowed a half-smile and then said, "That's for sure." He tore his eyes away from her and stood up, reaching a hand down to help her stand, the moment gone. Perhaps it was for the best, but Scarlett couldn't shake the idea that they might have something wonderful if he'd just let her in.

Chapter Twenty

"Absolutely not," Gran said, as she held her bowl of oatmeal with a trembling hand. She'd been late getting breakfast after working the front desk this morning. All the family had been taking turns to help her so she didn't have to work every morning *and* evening. "It's not even an option."

Scarlett had waited to bring up Charlie's idea until breakfast, holding off eating until Gran was in the kitchen. She'd been so excited coming home last night after being with him. When Amos's kitchen was clean and her clothes were finally dry, Charlie had jotted down a quick couple of points to share with Gran in order to get her on board. But they hadn't worked.

"Why won't you consider Charlie's plan?" Scarlett asked, completely baffled. "He wants to help you keep the inn. That's the best option I've heard yet."

Gran narrowed her eyes. "You've told him we're considering selling. He wants to view my finances. Didn't it dawn on you that he might not have good intentions at all?"

"What do you mean, Gran?"

"He wants insider information because then he can offer to buy us out at a lowball price, knowing exactly what we can afford to pay."

"No, that's not true. He doesn't even have the money to buy us out anymore."

"That's what he's told you, dear. Given his reputation, I have to wonder if he's taking you for a ride. And you're falling for it."

Gran had always been the voice of reason for Scarlett, a wise instructor on life, but when it came to Charlie, she had it all wrong. Scarlett had allowed Gran to lead her away from her own thoughts about Charlie before, but this time she wasn't going to do that.

"Gran." Scarlett moved her own empty plate aside and folded her arms on the table in front of her. "He is good. And I trust him. If you believe in me, then you'll believe him too."

"What's going on?" Blue said, coming in and moving straight over to the coffee maker. His hair was still sticking up a little at the back where he'd slept on it.

Gran stood up to address him. "Scarlett would like to disclose my entire personal and business finances to Charles Bryant. All so he can tell me how to run my own inn. I think I have a pretty good understanding of how to do that by now." She pursed her lips.

The coffee maker whirred to life.

"What, Scarlett?" Blue's face crumpled in concern and confusion as the machine gurgled. When it finished, he poured himself a cup.

Hopefully, her dad would be a bit more open-minded about the situation.

"Dad," she said, getting up herself from the table and walking over to him, handing him the bottle of cream. "Charlie has some really great data that, along with his insight, could help steer our investments in the right direction to make the inn profitable again."

"We don't have any wiggle room for investments. I thought we'd talked about that." Blue took his cup of coffee over to the table, Scarlett following him and taking a seat.

"What Charlie is proposing is to use Gran's savings to upgrade the inn, based on his research as to what specific changes will help it to be profitable again, and if it works, Gran could make a fortune. It's a risk but a calculated one. He's got a ton of success in this and I think he might be able to really change our lives. It *will* work."

"And if it doesn't?" Blue asked. He didn't let her answer. "If it doesn't, we're out of both the inn and Gran's savings." He peered over his coffee mug at Scarlett. "The truth of the matter is that Gran will have to retire at some point, and we'd have to sell then anyway. None of us can take on the massive responsibility of running an inn. And if Charlie's ideas do work, it would be a busy inn, which would require a whole lot of us. We don't have the manpower. The inn that Gran and Pappy ran isn't viable anymore. It's time to let it go."

"I don't believe that," Gran said. "I have no such plans to retire."

Blue shifted in his chair to face her. "What? So you *do* want to hear Charlie out?"

"No." Gran shook her head defiantly. "It's just a low patch. There are still people who want the White Oaks experience. Once the newness of those resorts wears off, they'll all be back. I'll make enough money to hire a staff and I won't have to lift a finger. I'm not selling."

"Mom, you don't have enough funds to keep yourself afloat until they come back. And I can't say they will."

"I'll stay open until I'm out of money."

"That's ridiculous," Blue said.

"I'm sure that things will turn around."

Gran was living in a dream world if she thought things would get better. Scarlett had looked at the information Charlie had collected. He'd implemented new amenities to be brought in in phases over time based on the needs and wants of the consumer, and from what she'd seen, never had he gone backward in terms of what he provided. Yet Gran seemed to believe that people would magically want the old at some point.

"You're dealing with a different generation now, Gran. Charlie has the understanding of this business that you need to move forward, but you're going to have to trust him."

"And that, my dear, is where we are at an impasse." Suddenly, Gran stopped and took a closer look at Scarlett. "There was something in your face just now…" She squinted her eyes as if she were trying to see whatever it was. Then, abruptly, her mouth snapped shut and there was recognition. What she'd seen, Scarlett had no idea. "There's more to this than what's on the surface," she stated.

"What are you talking about?" Scarlett said. Gran was speaking in riddles, it seemed.

"I see it," she said. "That mother hen look you get when you want to protect those that you love. You've been adamant that Charlie's intentions are honorable, and I know he's shown moments of greatness lately, but there are so many other things from his past that make me mistrust him. I'm worried that your affection for him is clouding your judgment. You're head over heels."

"No, Gran… He's a changed man."

"Aren't they all," Gran said, skeptical.

"Then tell me what he's done in the present to make you mistrust him?" Scarlett challenged. "Nothing. He's been the picture of generosity. Because that's who he is. I've seen him shed tears over Amos and how he treated him. He feels an incredible burden for what his resorts have done to people. And now, he just wants to use what he knows and what he has for good. I need you to see that. Not only for the inn's sake, but for mine as well. I *am* falling for him, and I would love your blessing."

Gran tapped the table, thinking.

"I'm sorry to interrupt," Janie said, coming in with Trevor. "But I caught a bit of your conversation—I'm so sorry. I wasn't trying to eavesdrop." She squatted down to get on eye level with Gran. "I hated him," Janie said. "I would've never thought I'd ever want to be in his presence. But he bought me a car." Her astonishment was clear in her tone. "He even went on his own to get a new seat for Trevor, *and* he went to the location where my car had been towed to get Trevor's favorite stuffed animal. People without hearts don't do those sorts of things. And I have no ties to this inn. He doesn't need to impress me. But after everything, I believe he didn't mean to hurt anyone, and he has a kind heart."

Janie took in a sharp breath and let it out. "I don't know where I'll go next or what I'll do," she said. "I don't have a job or a home to go back to. But I would trust Charlie to help me find my way."

Gran looked thoughtful for a long pause. Then she smiled to herself and nodded as if she'd made some sort of decision. She stirred her oatmeal, scooping a bite onto the spoon, but then set it back down while Scarlett waited to see what she was thinking. "How are your managerial skills?" Gran asked. "I need a front desk person. You could live here at the inn and work for me."

Janie lit up with interest, but Blue interjected, "Mom, we don't have enough to pay her. That's why we let Esther go."

Gran covered her lips with her frail fingers, looking out at them with caution. "Well, Charles swears he can make us enough money, right?"

"You'll do it?" Scarlett said, jumping up, throwing her arms around Gran, and making her grandmother giggle. "You won't be sorry, I promise," Scarlett said, giddy with excitement. Then she hugged

Janie, making Janie laugh in surprise. "Thank you for believing in him," Scarlett said to her. She looked over at her dad, who hadn't said anything yet. He had a lighthearted disbelief in his eyes.

"I can't believe I'm allowing this," he said. "Let me state now that I'm very worried about using all Gran's money, but from what she says, she'll use it anyway if we don't. I'll run it by Beth and Joe just to be sure they're on board, and then you can call Charlie. You might just have found the answer we all needed."

Beth and Joe had been overjoyed at Charlie's idea, and they all called him together on speakerphone. Charlie said he'd draw up a formal plan after he saw the funds and the family could give him their thoughts. So, later, when Scarlett found Aunt Beth sitting on the sofa across from the fire chewing her nail when she came into the living room, she couldn't imagine why her aunt's manner had changed so drastically.

"Is everything okay?" Scarlett asked.

"I'm a little nervous," Beth admitted. She patted the cushion next to her and Scarlett sat down. "Sean told me on the phone just now that he has a daughter."

"Oh?" Scarlett crossed her legs and leaned back, waiting to hear why exactly Aunt Beth was nervous about that.

"Her name is Amanda, and she's twenty-one." She folded her hands, squeezing them together. "What if this goes further? I can't be a stepmom—have you heard all the stories about horrible stepmothers? Just look at Cinderella. She'll hate me."

Scarlett found her worry so preposterous that it was funny. "I doubt that. You'll win her over with your alcoholic snow cream recipe."

Aunt Beth laughed despite herself.

One year, they'd been out of ingredients for eggnog, and the roads were so bad that they weren't able to run into town. Desperate for a Christmas drink, Aunt Beth combined rum, cinnamon, cloves, cream, and vanilla with the snow outside. The twins had been so impressed by her presentation in a candy cane–striped flute that they wanted some too, and Aunt Beth had to make non-alcoholic ones for them. Gran hadn't believed that it could possibly be any good, but when she tried a sip, she insisted on making one. Before they knew it, the whole family was drinking snow rum slushies.

"Aunt Beth, you're really great, and it would be impossible for Sean's daughter not to love you."

"That's very sweet," she said, and her fingers, which had been fiddling with her hoop earring, now stilled in her lap. "Thank you for making me feel better."

"You're welcome."

"You looked like you were heading toward the front door. Where are you off to?" Aunt Beth asked.

"Well, I've got the numbers from Gran for how much money we'll be able to spend. I'm going to run them by Charlie so he can get started right away making a plan for some of the upgrades he thinks we need."

"That's the best news I've heard all year."

"I can't wait to hear what Charlie has in mind," Scarlett said, her heart full.

Scarlett sat quietly while Charlie pored over the information she had brought to his cottage once more. She'd rattled everything off at a hundred miles an hour, telling him how excited she was, and how Gran had already offered Janie a place to live and a job. Before Scarlett arrived, Charlie had done some preliminary work, looking into the layout of the property, zoning ordinances, and historical features of the structure and surrounding grounds that had to be maintained. Scarlett waited beside him on the sofa while he scratched down lists, opened and closed files, and checked and rechecked numbers.

"You weren't kidding when you said your grandmother had lost money," he finally said, setting the stack of papers he was holding on top of another pile of documents on the table. "She's gone through almost her entire savings already."

Anxiety swelled in Scarlett's stomach. She hung on every word, waiting for the verdict. Charlie had been silently focused for hours, and she hadn't wanted to distract him with any questions, but now that he'd finally emerged from his planning, his expression didn't look optimistic.

"She barely has enough to cover the bills for the next year."

His assessment was like a kick in the gut. They didn't have any way to fix the fact that there wasn't enough money. At the end of the day, the changes would require funds, and they didn't seem to have what they needed. "What can we do?" she asked, feeling helpless.

"She could take out a business loan to cover the cost of the upgrades. I can do an analysis for her, to set out the options."

"She'll never agree to that."

"She'll make it all back and then some—I'm sure of it," he said. "In fact, I'm so sure that I'll put my own money on it. All my savings."

"What?"

"My investment would help your family to keep the inn, Ms. Farmer and Trevor would have a place to live, and Ms. Farmer would be able to have a job."

Scarlett wanted to be thrilled about this, but she was considering what would happen if his plan *didn't* work, and all those things didn't happen as a result. This was a major investment for him, and he seemed certain of himself, but what if something went wrong?

"If she'll trust me to do so," he continued, "I'll invest with a payout rate that's comfortable for her, but she'll have to give me the authority to make every decision, since it's my money on the line, and if I lose it, I have to live with a fireplace clothesline and a kitchen with no running water," he said playfully.

Scarlett didn't laugh, the anxiety of the situation getting the better of her.

"What's the matter?" he asked.

"I trust you," she said, stopping to chew on the inside of her lip as she considered how to voice her concerns. "But have you worked with historical property before? You know the restrictions to development?"

"No and yes," he said, clearly smiling to put her at ease. "I haven't worked under the constraints of historical properties, but when it comes to making long-term decisions to create accommodations that are profitable and desirable, I'm your guy."

"But what if it doesn't work?" she finally worried aloud.

"That's not an option." He leaned in close, their faces inches apart, and grinned at her. "You can count on me. I've got this."

Scarlett couldn't help but smile. Charlie was going to help them turn things around; she just knew it. "I'm so thankful for you, Charlie," she said, and she meant it. "I can't wait to see what you can do."

*

Scarlett joined the others in the kitchen for a family meeting to discuss the plan for the inn. Gran had asked Janie to come too, since she'd be part of the White Oaks family soon enough.

Once everyone was assembled, they all looked to Scarlett, eager to hear what she and Charlie had drawn up. "There's good news and bad news," Scarlett said. "Which do you want first?"

"Bad news," Gran decided. "That way we can end on a good note."

"All right. The bad news is that we don't have enough money to fund the number of renovations and upgrades required to drastically increase guest numbers at White Oaks."

There was a collective groan followed by looks of bewilderment.

"But," Scarlett continued, silencing everyone with that single word. "I have good news. Charlie is willing to loan us the money. We just have to pay him back."

There was a rumble of chatter all at once, but Scarlett interjected. "And…" She waited for their attention. "There's one more thing." Scarlett avoided Gran's anxious stare. "If Charlie funds it, he said he needs to be involved in all the decisions."

Gran huffed. "I knew there was a catch," she said. "What if he wants to take control of the inn, and we're falling right into it, Scarlett? I just don't know if I trust him to make decisions that I can live with. Have you seen the look of his resorts? They're so flashy…" She shook her head. "I don't want that."

"He's done research on the property, and he'll work within the historical constraints," Scarlett explained. "I don't think he'll do anything we don't agree with, but because he's investing the only money he has left, he needs to have the final say."

"What other options do we have at this point?" Blue said. "We could put it on the market, but Charlie is offering up his own money and we'll get to see what the changes could do for us."

"But what happens when Mom retires?" Uncle Joe said. "None of us are prepared to take over the business."

"We were facing that before we decided to sell," Aunt Beth returned. "I think we should take our chances and see what happens. What do we have to lose?"

"How about we do a vote?" Gran suggested.

They all looked back and forth between each other.

Gran said, "All for renovating and allowing Charlie to decide the fate of our inn? Janie, I'd like you to vote as well." She counted: "Beth, Scarlett, Blue, and Janie. All opposed? Alice, Joe, Heidi, and myself. It's split right down the middle."

"Would it help if I had him share the specifics of his plan with everyone, so we can decide if his vision works with our own?" Scarlett said.

"Given the opposing views, I think it would be helpful, yes," Gran said.

"Okay, I'll let him know," Scarlett said, wondering if this would actually work. But she had to try.

Chapter Twenty-One

After she texted Charlie the news, Scarlett needed to clear her head and at least attempt to defuse the edginess pulsing through her after the family meeting.

If Charlie didn't come through for them, the blame could all fall on her shoulders. She was sticking her neck out by supporting his claims, going on blind faith, which was unlike her. She didn't make big decisions lightly, and she worried that she was grabbing at anything that provided the tiniest bit of hope, out of desperation. To make matters worse, something this big could divide her family, and if that happened she'd never forgive herself. Scarlett wanted to take a step back from it all tonight, so she went to Love and Coffee to digest everything and have a little quiet time.

"Oh, Scarlett, you walked in like a ray of sunshine," Loretta said from the table near the register. She sat by herself behind a cup of coffee and an empty plate, the crumbs hinting at a blueberry muffin, while Sue wiped down the counter with an interested eye. "Get a drink and join me."

Happy for the diversion, Scarlett asked Sue for the seasonal latte and a cinnamon roll, and joined Loretta.

"I never thought I'd hear myself say this," Loretta said when Scarlett sat down with her pastry, the espresso machine hissing behind the counter. "I need advice for what to do with Preston."

"What do you mean?" Scarlett asked, scraping her fork through the cinnamon roll.

Loretta stirred the remnants of her latte with a silver spoon. "I'm sort of terrified." She lifted the mug to her mouth and took a sip before continuing. "I'm an expert at finding the right people to match, but my work ends there. What do I do now that I have that match? What if I fail miserably?" She set her mug down with emphasis. "I don't want to fail with him, Scarlett."

"You won't," Scarlett insisted. "Just be yourself. You're the person he fell in love with, so as long as you stay true to yourself, you'll have the best shot at being the right person for Preston."

Sue set Scarlett's latte down in front of her in a white mug with a heart drawn in the foam artistically.

"What if it still doesn't work out when I really want it to?" Loretta worried.

Scarlett immediately thought about Charlie. "Sometimes two people just aren't in the same place, and while they could be perfect for each other, their puzzle pieces don't line up because they're working on two different pictures."

Loretta's eyes grew round. "Do you think Preston has a different picture?"

Scarlett snapped out of her reverie. "Oh," she scrambled, realizing she'd moved off topic. "No. It's just that *some* people have that issue… What I meant to say was that you and Preston are in the same place in life. He really likes you and you feel the same way about him. There's nothing coming between you, so if you and Preston have the same idea of what you want in life and your timing is right, there's no reason things shouldn't work out." She picked up her mug, holding the warm porcelain in both hands, thinking again about Charlie.

"I've been going over the percentages of my couples who end up having lasting relationships and I've got a long-term match rate of sixty-eight percent. Given the fifty percent divorce rate, I'm above average for finding people who are suitable for each other." Loretta's gaze dropped down to her nearly empty mug. "But that percentage won't help me. Because I didn't even see this coming. I was with Preston on so many occasions and I never once realized how he felt. I didn't match us. How did I miss it?"

"Not everything is planned. When you find someone by chance, nothing is certain but that first meeting, Loretta. After that, it's up to the two of you to write your story. You both have to give it a hundred percent and then see what happens. You can't live your life trying to avoid a broken heart or you might miss out on the one person who'd never break it."

Scarlett heard her own words as well, and the truth of the matter was that Charlie wasn't ready to give his hundred percent, and maybe he never would be. If only things could've been different...

After finishing her latte and reading the first four chapters of a novel from the take-a-book-leave-a-book shelf at Love and Coffee, Scarlett got a text from Charlie. He had a preliminary rough timeline for the changes to the inn along with estimated itemized costs, and he asked if he could run it by her before taking it to Gran. She was beginning to get hungry for lunch, so she asked him to meet her at The Bar for a light bite to eat.

"I created a plan as if I were acquiring the inn for my own company. I started with the regular amenities and renovations, and then scaled it back based on our budget," he said as they sat down.

Cappy handed them each a menu and took their drink orders.

Charlie opened his laptop and slid it between them. He hit a button and an enormous grid came into view. Scarlett could hardly understand everything that was on it, but Charlie broke it down for her. "So, there are different phases to the renovations. We would start with a few major changes, see how the numbers perform, and then, once we'd assessed revenue, we'd move on to other modifications based on the numbers—all the while using the collective data from my previous resorts to guide each phase. Every location is different, though. They sort of take on their own personalities."

"So how long before we begin to see an upswing in revenue?" she asked.

"I'd say, factoring in my investment, within a year or two after modifications are made and marketing is in place."

"And how long will it take to make the changes?"

Charlie highlighted a column on his chart. "Well," he said, "let's look at Phase One." He scrolled down. "I think to get the most bang for our buck, we'll need to begin with an overhaul of the rooms. They're chopped up. We need to take out walls and make them upscale suites with all new décor and updated features. Nowadays, people want to have the comfort of home, but they could get White Oaks' accommodations in a regular hotel, which would be considerably cheaper than what your grandmother is currently charging.

That's why numbers have dwindled. People want more. We need to give them something better than what they can already get."

"Many of the rooms are original to the first renovation of the main house," Scarlett said, voicing the concerns she knew Gran would have. "Knocking down walls would be losing history."

"We can be respectful of the house's past—we *want* to be. But any time you make these kinds of changes, some of it will be lost. What you have to ask yourself is, 'Are the elements you'll be losing to renovations important enough to risk the inn's future if you keep them?' Most of the time, it's worth it to let it go, because the end result will be so much better. My suggestion is to keep the historical appeal of the *original* structure only—otherwise you'll drive yourself crazy."

Scarlett digested this, knowing Gran would have difficulty parting with anything.

Cappy brought their drinks and set them on napkins. "Do y'all know what you want to eat?"

Scarlett ordered the first thing she saw on the menu, having not even taken a second to think about her food choices. Charlie seemed to do the same.

Not having a clue what Gran would say to this, she moved on. "What else would you change in Phase One?"

"We'd also add things like fine dining; we'd expand and upgrade to a restaurant-quality kitchen, and we'd have chefs brought in. The dining room that you all currently use for catered events will also be renovated to accommodate regular guests, and people from outside can come just for the restaurant, even if they aren't staying the night. That will bring in revenue—and ambience—that you hadn't had before, using very little of the budget to make the changeover. The sitting room at the back would also be renovated into a world-class gym, and we'd hire a couple of trainers, install a sauna... We'd expand along the back of the inn because we can get the square footage from the parking area at the rear."

Her heart sank. This was going to be much more difficult than she thought. "That sitting room is my gran's favorite space in the summers. All the windows give it such a gorgeous view—she won't want to lose that."

"I've already considered the view. When we renovate the rooms to suites, all of them will have oversized rear-facing windows that will give them that view." He moved his drink so he could tap his computer, opening a second screen with a mock-up of the remodeled White Oaks. "The way it's positioned now, it wraps around the mountain, with the available land at the rear of it on the eastern side currently used up by a parking lot and that one little outlook spot that you get in the sitting room. But if we open up the inn at the back with floor-to-ceiling windows in every suite..." He clicked a button with a mock-up of the new spaces. "Every visitor will wake up to that view."

"What about Gran? Where will she get to see it?"

He offered a sympathetic look. "Scarlett, what's more important to an inn—the manager's view or the view of the occupants who are paying for it?"

"Could you go back to the whole picture?" she said, pointing to the laptop.

Charlie clicked back, showing the image of the original White Oaks.

She tapped the screen. "This is my gran's room. The view from that window is also her favorite. Could we keep that view?"

"Yes, of course... Although the grounds *in* the view might change."

Her stomach felt like it was full of lead. "She's not going to go for all this, Charlie," Scarlett said, unable to hide her disappointment.

"It's tough all around—I know it has to be difficult for her. But if she wants to compete with her competitors, you'll have to convince her to give a little."

That was easier said than done.

"I see what you're doing here," Gran said calmly to Charlie, as they sat in the sitting room that would be a gym if Charlie had his way. "I fear you're using the tactic that built your reputation: make money at any cost."

Charlie visibly flinched, and Scarlett leaned closer to him protectively.

"You're misinterpreting my intentions," he said, regaining composure. "I want to have a conversation about what you love about White Oaks—what you just can't bear to part with—so that you feel comfortable with the renovations. But in order to bring in the large numbers that I'm projecting, you have to give up some things as well. In the hotel industry, it's all about forward movement and giving people that next thing that they haven't had yet to bring them to your door."

"Look at this furniture you've put into the suites," Gran said with a grimace. "It isn't representative of White Oaks at all." Gran's frustration came through in her words. "It's far too modern."

Charlie nodded, listening, taking in everything Gran was saying. "If you have a vision for what you'd like instead, then we could take a look at other options once we finalize the actual budget."

"What's wrong with the furniture that's in there now? It's quaint."

"It won't hold up with the level of traffic this place is going to have. And it's a bit outdated."

"Outdated? It's perfectly in line with the atmosphere at White Oaks."

"Right," he said, "but White Oaks is about to *change* its atmosphere. It will maintain its elegance, but within a twenty-first-century framework. Old meets new."

Suddenly, Gran's frustration gave way to tears, her eyes glistening. She wrung her hands, her brows pulling down with her frown. "This is all too much," she said before clearing her throat. "It isn't what I want at all, or what my husband and I envisioned when we bought it. I might as well sell it." She stood up. "Do you want it, Charlie? If you do, then just take it. I can't be a part of this." She walked over to the wall of windows and looked out at the snowy landscape.

Charlie eyed Scarlett helplessly. She got up and walked over to Gran. The bright light reflecting into the room off the snow outside made her grandmother appear even more tired than she was.

"We're proposing some pretty drastic modifications, and I know that it's a lot of change all at once. I also know that you haven't been thrilled with any of this, but you have to relax into the change." She put her hand on Gran's shoulder. "Remember when you had Pappy bulldoze all the brush to get the flower garden back to its original state? It was a massive undertaking and he told you that you were crazy. He didn't think it would turn out well at all, but he trusted your idea."

Gran turned toward her, considering.

"Charlie just wants a bigger garden, that's all."

Gran looked back out the window.

"Charlie's here to listen, Gran. Don't be intimidated by all these changes. We'll take them a little at a time, and you can talk to Charlie all the way through it."

"What if he ruins my inn and we still lose money when he's done?" Gran worried.

"I won't let that happen," Charlie said from the sofa behind them. Gran went back over to him and he stood up to face her.

"We'll go through each item," he said. "You tell me your honest opinion. And then I'll tell you mine. But in the end, it's going to take trust on both our parts to get this done the best way. If you'll work with me, I think you'll be very surprised at what I can deliver."

Gran stood silently for a long pause. Then she finally spoke. "I think we need to get Beth, Blue, and Joe in here, and Janie can come too," she said. "I want their opinions. We have to all be on board."

Gran wasn't saying no. It was a start.

Chapter Twenty-Two

"Where's Blue?" Gran asked Joe, after they'd gathered in the sitting room with Charlie.

"He ran into town to get a load of firewood. We're running low."

"All right then," Gran said. "We'll wait for him."

Just as she said that, there was a pop and the lights went out, plunging them into the gray light of dusk.

"What's happened?" Joe asked.

At first, Scarlett worried that the electric bill hadn't been paid, but then she wondered if the storm had knocked out the electricity. "Could ice have broken the power lines?"

"I'll call Cappy and see if the lights are on in town," Joe said, pulling out his phone. He dialed the number and put it to his ear. "We're on the same power grid, so he'll be out too."

"I need to check on the guests," Gran said, heading to the door with purpose. "Scarlett, keep your phone on so I can reach you if I need you, and light the candles in the main rooms. Beth, you and Janie take the front desk. Will Trevor be okay up there for a little while?" Janie nodded, taking Trevor's hand. "Joe," Gran continued, "can you get the generator going so we'll have lights once the darkness hits?"

"It wasn't working last time we tried it," Joe said, clearly concerned.

"Great." Gran huffed. "Have a look at it and see if you can get it working. Will someone text Blue to ask if he can get a whole truckload of wood? We'll want to keep the fires going to preserve the heating while we work on the generator. We might have to pull the guests into the main rooms until power is restored."

"How many guests do we have?" Beth asked.

Gran turned to Beth, her expression intense. "Fifteen." Then she snapped her fingers. "Let's go."

Charlie followed Scarlett as she rushed through the main house to light candles. She opened a small drawer at the front desk and grabbed two packs of matches, tossing one to Charlie while walking to the living room.

She began lighting the candelabras on the mantel. While scratching the match on the side of the box to ignite it, she voiced her concern. "I wonder how long it will be before we get power again? With the terrain up here in the mountains, it could be a while." The Christmas tree was dark, its shadowy presence illustrative of her mood.

"The generator's not working?" Charlie questioned. "How come?"

"Gran did mention to my dad that it was on the fritz a while ago, but we had to manage where we put our funds, and there were more pressing needs. I wonder if that's why she seems overly upset at times. She's a great inn manager, but she's limited by the lack of resources and personnel. If it had been up to Gran, the generator would've been fixed right when it had started acting up—my pappy would've been able to repair it—and we'd have power right now. I know she feels a sense of duty to the guests, and it puts more stress on her that she can't provide them with the perfect mountain experience."

Charlie's stillness caused Scarlett to stop talking.

"What?" she asked, wondering why he was standing motionless, his gaze somewhere in the distance.

"The *perfect* mountain experience…" He looked around the room. "Your grandparents ran this themselves?"

"Yes, but they did have a small staff. Gran's had to let some people go."

"And your family pitches in?"

"Of course. We're always there for each other."

Thoughts were evident on his face, his forehead creased, his mouth turned down, his eyes darting around the room. "It's about family…"

"What are you talking about?" she asked, turning around to face him with a candle in one hand and an unlit match in the other. He wasn't making any sense at all.

"I can't go through with the renovations—I'm so sorry," he said, still clearly lost in his own thoughts. "That's why your grandmother was in tears…"

Scarlett set the items she'd been holding down on a side table, freeing her hands, and walked over to Charlie, putting her face in his line of vision. "What. Are. You. Talking about? You're speaking in riddles."

"It just hit me. I can't provide your grandmother with a plan that works because I don't know a thing about family, and family is at the center of her world. *That's* what she wants for the inn—a family feeling—and I can't envision it for her. I can think up a great resort, but I can't help you with *this* inn." He shook his head. "You should find your grandmother someone who shares her vision. She'd be happier. I'm not your guy, Scarlett."

"Yes, you are! Let her guide you," Scarlett said. "You have the expertise and she has the family vision for White Oaks. I'll get her to come around."

He shook his head and gazed deeply into her eyes, and she knew that whatever he was about to say, he was going to mean it. He had her full attention. "Scarlett, I've wrecked my life and a lot of other people's lives. I will not put myself in the position again where I am the cause of pain or sadness for another human being. Yet here I am, trying to convince your grandmother, while she's in tears, that stripping her inn of what she loves is the *right* way to go. 'Make money at any cost,' she said. She's exactly right. This instance is no different than what I used to do to people. I was just kinder about it this time around. I can't be involved in this." He ran his hand along his forehead, bewildered. "And I've already ruined things, because if I can't take on the project, I can't invest my money. Oh my God, I'm so sorry, Scarlett…" Charlie paced across the room, obviously upset with himself. "I'll have to find another way to help your grandmother with the money…"

All the breath in Scarlett's lungs left her, and she struggled to get enough air to speak. This couldn't be how her last Christmas at White Oaks ended. She'd been so close to having a resolution, and she'd really felt it was the right one, but Charlie was causing her doubt. She had complete faith in Charlie. She didn't trust anyone else to take over the inn. Not to mention that they'd have to sell it outright, which would mean no more Christmases in Silver Falls, no more summer holidays in the only place they had that was big enough to accommodate their entire family. Scarlett wanted to get married one day, have children… They'd never know the serenity and grandeur of White Oaks. They wouldn't get to catch lightning bugs down by the stream or swim in the fresh mountain water. They'd never have Gran's lemonade on the hottest day of the year or her apple cider on the coldest. Scarlett could feel the opportunity to hold on to all that literally slipping through her fingers.

"Charlie," she said, still breathless. She counted to three and steadied herself. She didn't want to appear desperate, but she had to get this off her chest. "Another buyer may not have our interests in mind. If you think you're off base, it could be nothing compared to someone else's vision. You're allowing my gran a chance to keep the inn! Nobody else will provide that for her."

"I don't know what to give her, Scarlett," he said, exasperated.

She moved closer to him and took his hands, looking up at him with no agenda other than to have complete transparency. "If you don't want to invest in White Oaks, then that's fine—it's your money. But don't allow the only thing stopping you to be the fact that you don't have experience with being in a traditional family. We'll work it out together," she said. "That's what being a family is. That's really *all* it is."

"You're oversimplifying it."

"*You're* making too much of it. Family is about being there for the people we care about and showing each other every day how much we love one another. I am confident you can make the inn accommodating in that respect, and I can help you along the way."

"I know what to do to make accommodations successful for the masses, but if your grandmother wants something specifically matching her view of what family is and how they operate within the walls of this inn, I'll come up short. There's a difference between the two, Scarlett. I won't do it. I'm just sorry I got your hopes up." He pulled away from her gently, moving over to one of the candles next to the sofa and lighting it. "Let's get these candles lit for your grandmother. It's getting dark."

"Beth got in touch with your dad." Gran's voice cut through the heaviness, as she came into the room with resolve, apparently unaware of the tension between Charlie and Scarlett. She seemed un-ruffled now, busy, in work-mode, clearly energized by her interactions with the guests.

Scarlett wished Charlie could see how great her grandmother was with the visitors at the inn. She stopped whatever she was doing to help them, talk with them—anything they needed. Sometimes, she'd make them a cup of coffee and just chat about the area's history, her children growing up here, things to do... The guests called her by her first name, Georgia—she insisted on it. What with the weather and the holiday, along with the duties she'd had to assume after letting staff go, Gran hadn't had much chance to show off how personable she was.

"He's bringing more wood for all the fireplaces. We'll need some-thing to keep the guests busy, and to take their minds off of the power issue. Your Uncle Joe is getting the gas lanterns from the storage area and wiping them down. They'll provide enough light." She reposi-tioned one of the candelabras on the mantel so it reflected off the mirror, sending a glow across the room. "We have two small solar power sources that Pappy used on fishing trips, but they don't have enough power to run a heater or anything. However, I'm going to get Joe to use one for the Christmas lights in here and another for the coffeepot. I told the guests we'd offer candlelight coffee at seven o'clock—that's in fifteen minutes. Any chance we could get you to play piano, Charles?"

"Charlie," he said with an uncertain grin. "Please. Call me Charlie."

"All right," she said, looking him over with a content glance, mak-ing Scarlett wonder if Gran was warming to him. "*Charlie*, could I impose upon your evening and ask you to play for us? I can pay you in glasses of wine."

"It wouldn't be imposing. I'd be happy to."

Blue came bursting into the room with an armful of wood and Loretta and Preston in tow, bringing a draft of icy air with them. The fire in the fireplace danced wildly in protest. "Power's on in town," he said, stacking the wood neatly on the hearth beside the fire. "I ran into these two while I was out." He pointed to Loretta and Preston.

"I've got my portable generator in the truck outside," Preston said. "Maybe we can use it for something."

"Thank you, Preston," Gran said. "If we could get a few more of the kitchen appliances running on it, I might be able to provide some light food. Perhaps I can warm up a pie or some cider."

"I can help you," Loretta said. "I can make sure the guests are comfortable and serve food if you need me." She shivered, pulling her coat tighter despite the fact they were inside.

"Thank you, dear. You are lovely."

Blue threw more logs on the fire, poking it until it was raging in the fireplace. "I'm not sure what's going on, but once I get the rest of the fires loaded, I'll inspect the grounds. It could be something on our lines specifically. Or maybe it's just a breaker, and we can be back in business shortly."

"I'll help you check." Joe came in with the small power source and hooked it up to the Christmas tree. The lights came alive, twinkling like stars in the night sky, glimmering off the shiny black piano top.

Charlie took a seat at the piano. "Do you have any sheet music, by chance? If not, I can improvise," he said.

"There's a book of Christmas carols in the drawer over there, Scarlett." Gran pointed to the antique sideboard on the opposite wall.

"Perfect," Charlie said, as Scarlett retrieved it and handed it to him. He opened it to a page in the middle and placed his fingers on the keys.

"I'll put together a platter of cookies for now and brew some coffee," Gran said, rushing out of the room.

Loretta and Preston followed her out to assist with any further tasks, while Blue and Joe went to the other rooms to load up the fireplaces with wood, leaving Scarlett and Charlie alone. The candles flickered around them, an overwhelming scent of vanilla and cinnamon filling the air. Charlie began to move his fingers along the instrument, playing effortlessly, his hands touching the ivory keys as if he were caressing them. Scarlett rubbed the goosebumps on her arms as she imagined those fingers moving along her skin. This time, she didn't push the thought away or try to rationalize anything. Her affection for him was real, and she allowed herself to feel it.

"I'd forgotten how much I love to play piano," he said, the melody dancing around them as he spoke.

She didn't recognize the song.

He continued to play as he stole a glance at her, not missing a beat. "It's relaxing."

"Reading does that for me," Scarlett said as she sat down next to him.

"I love reading too." Charlie turned the page and continued. "I'd gotten so consumed with work that I didn't get to do a whole lot to unwind. In fact, now that I think about it, I haven't relaxed in about ten years."

"And how does it feel to relax?"

"Weird." He laughed. "And nice." He sobered as his hands stilled, the song coming to an end. His eyes were sympathetic as they found hers. "I'm so sorry I can't help you with the inn. I wish I could've had the answers for you."

"You really don't think you can do it?"

He shook his head. "I don't think so."

The last thing Scarlett wanted to do was to push Charlie back into that world. It was very clear to her that he wasn't the person he had been when he'd built all those resorts. He'd changed, and forcing him back into it wouldn't be good for him. He needed to find his balance, as Ato would say. What would be that new thing that got him out of bed every morning with a smile on his face?

"We should let Gran know," she said, coming to terms with the situation. This was out of her hands now. Whatever happened to White Oaks would have nothing to do with her, and she'd just have to wait and see how things worked out.

"Let her get through the power outage before you throw something else at her," Charlie said.

A couple of guests filtered in with Gran and Loretta right behind them, carrying the most gorgeous platter of confections. They set it down on the coffee table and offered the visitors some before getting their coffee orders. Scarlett noticed Charlie watching the interaction with interest as he played the next song. Gran and Loretta continued bringing in a few more platters, setting them around the room. Gran placed a coffeepot and holiday cups and saucers on the sideboard with cloth napkins, while Joe set up the lanterns he'd brought in.

Preston, who'd been in the kitchen helping Gran with her appliances, came into the room and took the cookie tray from Loretta, setting it in front of a group of women who were visiting on a girls' trip. Scarlett knew that fact because they'd arrived wearing matching T-shirts with "Ladies' Week" and the date printed on the front of them. Preston took Loretta's hands and twirled her around the open space on the floor, the ladies swooning over him as he did. He pulled her close and kissed her lips.

"I didn't know you could dance like that, Preston," Gran said, settling back into one of the chairs by the fire once everyone had what they needed.

"Ah, I just never had such a wonderful partner before." He gave Loretta another spin.

"You two look like you've been dancing together for years," one of the ladies said.

"He learns quickly," Loretta told them. "And the minute I first danced with him it felt like we'd been dancing our whole lives together. But everything with him feels like that." The women all fell into lovesick grins.

The room was so festive that a bystander would think it was any other holiday evening at White Oaks.

Aunt Alice came in with the twins and an armful of board games, setting one of them up on the floor by the fire, while the other guests drifted in. Blue had finished stoking the fires and settled on the chair by Aunt Beth, who'd been talking to a couple in the corner. Joe joined in on their conversation. Gran, clearly energized by the atmosphere, had gotten back up and was fluttering around, laughing and talking with people, patting them on the back, smiling.

Scarlett paid attention to Gran. She made tonight look effortless, and to her it probably was. Being with people was her strength. As Charlie looked on, Scarlett wondered if the scene in front of him made him feel even more unsure than he had before, since he'd said he'd never really been around family.

Scarlett's dad motioned for her to join him.

"Be right back," she said into Charlie's ear as he started another song. Then she headed over to Blue. "What's up?" she asked him when she got to his chair.

"It's difficult to tell, because I'm not an electrician, but it looks like the old power lines have weakened in the elements outside."

"Weakened?"

"Yep." He let out a huff. "A portion of our grid was exposed to the elements, because the insulation had deteriorated and nobody noticed."

Scarlett bit her lip. Pappy would've noticed. The thought occurred to her that even if Charlie could've restored the inn, Gran would need a lot of help to run it without Pappy. Pappy had been a jack-of-all-trades, and those sorts of maintenance items came easily for him. Gran would've required a grounds staff as part of Phase One, to keep up with all the things that Pappy used to do. Not to mention, what would they come across when the renovations started? What else had deteriorated? Had Gran and Pappy ever had anyone check the electrical lines to be sure they'd been installed correctly? The insulation? The plumbing? Projects on older structures seemed to unearth all kinds of problems. Had Charlie been ready for that possibility? It didn't matter anyway.

"What are we going to do?" she asked.

"I don't know who to call for this type of work. It's an old system. Charlie has collaborated with electricians in his line of work, I'm sure. Will you ask him if he has any connections to an electrician who might have a specific knowledge of historical properties to fix it? We need someone who we can trust to give us a very reasonable price because we don't have a lot of money to work with for the repairs."

"Of course," she said. "I'll ask him now."

"Thank you." As she got up, he stopped her. "And, Scarlett?"

Scarlett turned back to her dad.

"Since it's on our end, it can't be fixed unless we take care of it, and without any power, our guests won't stay for long. Time is of the essence."

Scarlett hurried over to Charlie to tell him what her father had found.

"I can call around," Charlie said, concerned. "We'd have to go back to my house to get my laptop. Should we do it now or do you want me to keep playing?"

"I think we should move as quickly as possible."

"All right." Charlie finished the song he was playing and stood up. "Thank you for listening, folks," he called to the group who'd now assembled in the living room. "I'm going to take a break to give you all time to talk. Have a wonderful evening." As Scarlett followed Charlie toward the door, she saw Blue explaining to Gran. She just hoped Gran wouldn't worry too much.

When they'd left, Scarlett noticed the White Oaks living room getting drafty, the cold seeping in despite the fire. It was even clearer when they arrived at Charlie's, the heat so warm inside that it gave her a shiver.

"We never got our wine that your grandmother promised," he said with a wink in her direction. Charlie, still in his coat, leaned down on the hearth and started the fire with a few of the logs stacked beside it. "I bought a bottle after I had nothing to offer you last time." He righted himself and went over to the sink, which still appeared to be broken, and took a bottle from the fridge. He removed the cork, a hollow pop echoing in the room. "I'll get us each a glass so we can settle in and start calling my contractors." He pulled two glasses from the cabinet and filled them. "Will you grab my laptop from the table over there?"

Scarlett shrugged off her coat and hung it on the hook by the door. Then she grabbed the computer, holding it against her chest with both arms around it like she used to hold her notebooks when she walked to class in high school.

"You look really tense," Charlie said as they went over to the sofa, eyeing her arms crossed over her chest.

"Sorry," she said, loosening her grip and setting the laptop onto the table.

Charlie handed her the glass of wine. "Drink this," he said. "It'll help."

His suggestion was cheerful, but she noticed the thoughts in his face as he looked down into his wine glass before drinking it. Scarlett wasn't going to try to convince him to save the inn, if that was what he was worried about. Yes, tonight had made her tense, but Charlie needed time to find his place in this new life he was creating for himself, and she wasn't about to force him to do anything he didn't want to do right now. What she did wonder, however, was whether he had any idea what kind of new life he was after.

Scarlett took a drink of her wine and Charlie opened up his laptop, his documents popping into view as he clicked them open. "I think I'll start with Five Star Electric. They've done some work for me on demolitions before—sort of unwiring things in old buildings and preserving the connections, replacing old wires, that sort of thing."

"How much will they charge?"

He took a sip of his wine and then crossed his feet on the coffee table, leaning back with the computer in his lap. "That depends on the size of the problem. But I'll take care of it," he said, looking over at her with those dark eyes.

She leaned away from him to make eye contact, concerned. "You can't continue to just give away money. At some point, you'll need some to live on."

"Let me worry about that," he said contentedly.

"Charlie, despite the things you aren't happy about having done, you have accomplished a lot of wonderful things. You used your intelligence to be productive, you learned from your experiences, and you made the choice to follow your conscience. You can't keep holding yourself responsible for things that are in the past."

"Where is all this coming from?" he asked.

"You're doing so much for others that you haven't done anything for yourself. You didn't allow yourself a Christmas, you're living in a cottage that needs more work than White Oaks, and you continuously give away money you need to repair it. You keep giving and giving, and while that is admirable and wonderful, it will run you dry as well. All the giving in the world won't erase the guilt you feel. Only living can do that."

Charlie quietly absorbed her words. "Let me worry about me," he said, but his words weren't blasé anymore. "I'll be okay." He sat up and pulled his computer toward him. "Let's get back to the task at hand. I can probably get someone to come out and assess the damage and give us a quote, so we know how much it will cost to repair the lines. Then we can shop around for the best price."

"We don't have that kind of time," Scarlett fretted. "The guests are going to start to get cold and go home. We'll lose business and have to refund bookings, which we really can't afford to do…"

He nodded, clearly thinking. "Getting someone out now, at this time of night, will be costly, and without daylight, chances are slim that they'll be able to fix this. Especially if it's due to weather damage. I'm not an expert, and perhaps someone will prove me wrong. I'm just giving you my honest opinion."

White Oaks couldn't continue on much longer like this. Scarlett was beginning to understand the urgency that her father must have already seen, which was why he'd called the meeting to sell in the first place. What would happen if the guests discovered that the outage was due to negligence on the inn's side rather than an act of nature on the town power source? She didn't even want to think about it, but they might have to close White Oaks for good, buyer or no buyer. There was no way she could let that happen.

Chapter Twenty-Three

Scarlett hadn't slept well at all. When she'd gotten home from Charlie's, she'd decided to brave the cold and spend the night in her room instead of staying in the living room by the fire like many of the others had done. She was completely under her sheet, duvet, and fleece blanket, and the cold still managed to seep below it, wrapping around her until her skin was numb. What must the guests feel like?

After Charlie had left a few messages with electricians last night, he'd offered to take Scarlett home, promising her he'd let her know as soon as he heard something. So when she saw his text waiting on her phone on the nightstand, she nearly catapulted herself onto the frigid hardwood floor to view it. Grasping her phone, she read his text: *Come downstairs.*

What? she thought. Scarlett checked the number again to make sure she hadn't misread the sender through the fog of no sleep and chilliness. It was definitely Charlie. Then she noticed the time. She'd slept until after eight o'clock! Scarlett never slept that late. She padded into the bathroom in her fuzzy socks and slippers to brush her teeth. When she finished, she ran her fingers through her hair and went to the door of her room, headed downstairs.

When she opened the door, she nearly fell backward, shrieking in fright before she regained her composure. There stood Charlie. His hand, which was raised to knock on the door, fell to his side, amusement on his face.

"Good morning," he said, his gaze moving down her pajamas to her sock feet.

Normally, she'd be mortified by someone other than family witnessing her appearance first thing in the morning, but an unusual calm settled over her as if he'd seen her like that a hundred times before. Perhaps it was the fact that she felt totally herself with him, or that she was so thrilled to see him right then that she didn't care what she looked like.

"Want to hear some good news?" he asked. But he didn't get what he wanted to say out in time and instead, he pointed upward toward a quiet shushing sound that suddenly began above them. It was coming from the heating vents.

"Heat!" she said, her excitement making him laugh.

"I had a guy here by five this morning. The kitchen and guest rooms have had electricity for over an hour now."

That was when she noticed the hallway lights were on. Impulsively, and out of utter relief, Scarlett threw her arms around Charlie in gratitude. And just as she realized she had, she felt his arms around her too. He held her affectionately and she was surprised he hadn't pulled away. "Thank you," she said into his chest, happy that he hadn't.

"You're welcome," he returned.

Scarlett pulled away from him at last. "How much did it set us back?" she asked, afraid to hear the cost of the repairs.

"I took care of it," he said happily.

"Charlie, remember what I told you last night?"

"Yes," he said, stopping her with one finger on her lips, taking her breath away with the tenderness of his touch. He looked her in the eyes. "And you're exactly right." He turned around, headed toward the stairs. "When you're ready, we've got breakfast waiting."

We've?

The first thing Scarlett noticed when she entered the kitchen was the presence of Loretta and Preston at the table. They were sitting next to one another, holding hands and talking with Gran as she listened beside Charlie. Janie was cutting a pancake for Trevor. He looked so happy in his chair, still propped on cushions. Everyone else in the family was there as well, their plates empty, half-finished mugs of coffee and glasses of orange juice littering their places. Even Heidi was there, smiling strangely at Scarlett, her phone nowhere in sight. The whole picture was a bit of a jolt first thing in the morning, and Scarlett struggled to make sense of it.

"Mornin', sunshine!" Blue called, grinning like a Cheshire cat.

"Morning…" Scarlett said, walking past everyone to make herself a cup of coffee while eyeing them as if they were all crazy, which, given the situation, seemed entirely possible. Perhaps once she got some caffeine in her and woke up, she'd realize she'd been sleepwalking and this was some sort of bizarre dream. She got a mug from the cabinet and Charlie said something quietly to Gran, making her laugh. *Charlie made Gran laugh?* He hadn't made her laugh before. Ever.

"Charlie took care of the wiring problem for us, Scarlett. Isn't that nice?" Gran said, getting up and fixing a plate of eggs and bacon. Gran dropped a biscuit onto the plate and left it by the empty place at the table, apparently for Scarlett. Gran was smiling and strangely agreeable this morning.

"Yes, he told me," Scarlett said hesitantly.

"Which is wonderful because Preston and Loretta have some news!" she said. "Hurry up with your coffee and come over here with us."

Scarlett quickly added sugar and cream and threw a spoon into her mug, interested to hear what was going on. Charlie patted the empty seat on the other side of him and Scarlett sat down, all faces on her, everyone overly excitable like she was in some kind of hidden-camera show.

"Look," Loretta said, holding up her left hand. A beautiful emerald-cut diamond swung around her finger. "Preston popped the question."

Scarlett had to close her gaping mouth. All those years he spent pushing her away… "Congratulations," she said. "I can't believe this!" Scarlett was at a loss for words. She was so delighted for them both, and she was flabbergasted that Preston had finally been impulsive enough to do something about how he felt so swiftly.

"We've already known each other for so long and we didn't want to wait another minute," Loretta explained. "We haven't left each other's sides since he told me how he felt. When I'm around him it feels…" She looked over at Preston. "Perfect."

"I took a gamble," he said, addressing Scarlett before leaning over and kissing Loretta. Loretta snuggled up next to him.

"The funny thing is," Loretta said, "I always had a crush on him. I just didn't think he was interested in me. I wanted him to be happy even if it wasn't with me, so I kept trying to find someone perfect for him."

"Which was impossible to do," Preston added. "Because to be perfect, they'd have had to be her."

"What a wonderful story," Gran said, her face alight with joy. Then she leaned around Charlie to speak to Scarlett. "That's not the only news." Gran clasped her hands together. "No one's heard this yet—that's what they're all waiting for." She scanned everyone at the table dramatically. "Preston and Loretta would like to have their wedding and reception at White Oaks next Christmas."

As Scarlett assessed her family, they were all so relaxed, chatting enthusiastically between each other, congratulating Preston and Loretta… Did anyone realize that White Oaks might not be open in a year? Did they not just come off a major power outage—a direct result of White Oaks' decline due to *lack of revenue*? How would they have enough money to update the inn *and* host a wedding? Scarlett had been involved in weddings at White Oaks. It was a major affair. There was lighting, tables and chairs, flowers to be planted in the gardens, runners, parking attendants and staff to work the reception— all provided by White Oaks. Even contracting some of the services would take money. But no one seemed fazed by it. Wasn't this the same group of people who'd decided to sell the inn because it was losing money?

"What is going on?" Scarlett asked Charlie, unable to sugarcoat her complete confusion. The table fell silent, all eyes on her.

Charlie twisted around to face her. "If we move forward on renovations and get started right away, I project we'll have construction finished in six months. I've put a rush on a couple of the major changes, and I'll have them scheduled by the end of the day."

"What are you talking about? You didn't want to do this…"

He nodded, his gaze nearly consuming her.

"And even if you changed your mind, what about you, Gran?" Scarlett leaned back in her chair to see Gran on the other side of Charlie. "You seem happy about this."

Charlie got up and walked over to the other side of the kitchen, retrieved his laptop, and sat back down, opening it so Scarlett could view the screen. "I deleted my original plan," he said, clicking keys.

"I've revamped the idea completely. We're enlarging the back sun-room, keeping all the windows but using the rear parking to give us room for expansion. And we're changing the furniture." He showed her a simulated image of what it would look like. "We're upgrading the furniture to oversized white wicker, adding quilts and fresh flowers. The back wall will be made of planks of wood salvaged from area farmhouse demolitions..." He scrolled to another mock-up. "I've added a self-guided tour where visitors will travel the grounds, learning its history quietly—nothing flashy. At every stop, there will be different 'attractions,' if you will." He pointed to a photo of the grounds, just behind the flower garden. "We'll have a barn constructed here, where we'll have wine tastings." He moved across the screen. "And over here, we'll hang porch swings from the trees. Each one will be fitted with coordinating cushions and pillows for taking in the view of the valley. I plan to clear just a tiny number of trees on this side because at the moment, they obstruct the most gorgeous view of the waterfalls. All the outside porches leading to the rooms will be extended with lines of paddle fans in the ceiling, rocking chairs, and more flowers. In the summers, we'll have small silver and glass carts with lemonade and iced tea..."

As Charlie clicked through to the next photo to continue his new plan, Scarlett caught a glimpse of Gran. She was smiling, her fingers at her lips, tears of happiness in her eyes. That was when she understood the faces of her family. Charlie had shared this with them already and every single one of them was on board. He'd brought them all together. But Charlie had said he couldn't do this, that he didn't know how. What had changed?

"There will be a café in the current parlor that will run like a coffee shop. Constantine will provide freshly made pastries daily—"

Scarlett stopped Charlie, afraid to believe this was really happening. He couldn't get them all this excited and pull out of the plan for any reason. He had to be committed to this because it was the most wonderful thing she'd ever heard. She hadn't even seen the rest of his plans for the inn, but she already knew that they would be just perfect. "Can I talk to you for a second in the hallway, please?" she asked him, her heart pounding.

"Of course." He stood up, offering his hand.

She took it and they walked out of range of her family.

Scarlett stared at him, feeling the enormity of what was going on and wanting with everything she had to believe it. "What are you doing?" she asked.

"Living." He gave her a knowing look. Charlie gripped her hands. "You're right, Scarlett. I sat around my dad's cottage after you left, and all I could think about was that every time you walked out that door, you took all the light with you. I tried to think of a way that I could show you how I feel about you, and that was when I opened up my laptop and deleted the original plan. I wrote this one for *you*. It was easy," he said, smiling down at her. "I just started making changes that matched the feeling you give me every time I see you. In an old run-down cottage, you are like fresh bouquets; you're like a misty-morning view, a sunrise, a barefoot dance in a field of wildflowers…"

Scarlett blinked away her tears.

He pulled her closer, but didn't lean down to kiss her like she wanted him to do. "I'm staying in Silver Falls," he said. "Without a doubt." He caressed her hand with his thumb, sending a current of happiness through her. "Will you stay here with me?"

"What?"

"White Oaks needs a marketing manager. I haven't shown you that plan yet." He beamed. "Your grandmother gave me full rein to do all the hiring as the primary investor. She told me you're the best around, and if you're willing to leave your new job at Electra, we'd love to have you. You're hired if you want the job. The salary would be small, but the benefits would be great."

Scarlett pulled him to her, pressed herself up onto her tippy toes, and put her arms around his neck.

Charlie leaned down toward her. "Is there any rule about kissing your investor?" he asked.

"You haven't officially hired me yet," she teased. "But even when I say yes, which I will, you can kiss me."

"Good," he said, his lips so close to hers that she could feel his breath. "Because I plan to do it a lot." Charlie leaned in and pressed his lips to hers, and Scarlett had never felt more certain about anything in her life. She knew what he meant about her being his light in the room. She felt the same way about him. His kiss was like air in her lungs, like plunging into the water on a scorching summer day... Never before had she found someone who fit her like he did. It hit her then that her advice to him applied to her as well. She hadn't really taken chances, put herself to the test, and trusted her instincts until she'd met him. She hadn't *lived*. And she couldn't wait to get started.

Epilogue

Scarlett walked forward blindly, Charlie's hands over her eyes. "Don't peek!" Charlie said, leading her over the bumpy terrain.

She was cold, still wearing the cranberry dress from Preston and Loretta's Christmas Eve wedding and Charlie's suit jacket over the top, but she didn't mind as long as she was with Charlie. They'd been inseparable over the last year, and she couldn't imagine her life without him. The more she got to know him, the more she loved him. Every day that she spent with him at White Oaks was a blessing. He'd helped Gran with all the transitions and growth at the inn; he'd watched Trevor when Janie had her baby—a little girl that Janie named Hope; he'd tutored Heidi in a business planning class she had at her design school over video call. She'd pointed all this out to him once, saying, "Don't look now, but you've become an expert at being a family member."

Her balance wobbled from the uneven ground and the three glasses of champagne she'd had. The wedding had gone off without a hitch. The party was still going even after the happy couple left for the airport. Scarlett had made a special request to the resort in the Bahamas to postpone the trip she'd won last Christmas, and she'd given it to Preston and Loretta so that they could have a honeymoon. The minute they'd left, Charlie insisted he had something to show her.

Unable to open her eyes the entire drive, Scarlett had laughed all the way to their location while she fidgeted with her blindfold made from Charlie's tie. When the truck finally stopped, he'd taken it off her as long as she promised to keep her eyes closed. Before he untied it, he surprised her with a kiss.

"Okay," he said. "Open your eyes."

Scarlett gasped at what was in front of her. Amos's cottage had been transformed. It was completely repainted a bright white, the roofline pulled upward with new dormer windows added, and the whole thing was landscaped with dark green foliage lining a stone path, each flat gray stone outlined in moss, which led to the front door. The small stoop of a porch had been altered beyond recognition and now stretched along the entire refaced front of the home, all the windows replaced by glass French doors that opened up to the outside.

Charlie took her hand. "Come with me," he said, excitement clear in his voice.

He opened the beveled glass door into the newly remodeled space. The ceilings were now vaulted—white with natural wood beams like rays of sunshine, reaching down to the walls. The entire place had been professionally decorated in whites and neutrals with pops of red and deep blue. But what caught her eye immediately was the enormous Christmas tree in the corner, full of twinkling white lights, and silver and red ornaments.

"Last year, you mentioned that I needed a tree," he said, grinning fondly at her, his hand at her back. "Jax promised me this one would last the entire season."

Scarlett laughed through her excitement. "This is beautiful," she said, so thrilled for him. "How did you have time to do this with all the changes at the inn?"

He raised his eyebrows, happy. "Are you surprised?" he asked.

"Absolutely. All those nights you insisted on staying here, I thought you were living in the old shack instead of staying at the inn where there was running water…" She snickered. "You said you were fixing things and that it was a disaster zone—that's why I stayed away."

"It *was* a disaster zone," he said. "Just a different kind. And I wouldn't have let you come anyway. I'd have figured out a way to keep this from you so it could be a surprise." He took her hand. "But I have one more thing to show you," he said, leading her to a set of brand-new double doors at the back.

He opened them up to allow her to step back outside. She walked out onto another porch, this one taking her breath away. It had oversized bench swings at either end, both facing a stunning view.

"I cleared the land, and look what I found," he said, pointing his hand toward the sweeping outlook across the valley below—but while the purples and blues of it in the light of dusk were incredibly beautiful on their own, it was the yard full of little lights and candles leading to that view that robbed her of all speech. The backyard looked like a sea of fireflies, all hovering along the ground, pointing to the path that led to the edge of the yard. Charlie took her hand and they walked down that winding path together to a gazebo with cushions to match the interior of the house, more candles and party lights strung above them. The view from it was incredible; it felt as if they were on the edge of the world.

"I wanted to put out enough lights to show you how big my feelings are for you, but I ran out," he said, the corner of his mouth turning upward. "If I could've, I'd have lined all the hills and valleys with them."

Scarlett looked up at him, completely in love with this man. The last year had been trying and fantastic, as they'd gotten the inn renovated and ready for the wedding. Revenue was way up, and all the rooms were filled, with a waiting list to get in. They'd hired the staff they needed, and Gran had been able to stop working so hard, spending her days walking the tour route and telling the stories of her journey at the inn.

By scaling back from his original plan for renovations, Charlie had enough to invest in the inn as well as funds to restore Amos's cottage, where he planned to live, since Gran had insisted he be the manager of White Oaks. He'd pitched in his own efforts to save money, painting, stripping floors, banging on walls with sledgehammers to knock them down. And Scarlett had been by his side the entire time.

They'd spent late nights covered in paint, dirty and exhausted, drinking wine, laughing, and roasting hotdogs around a campfire they'd made in the back garden. When the bedroom furniture she'd so meticulously chosen, the suite she'd had her heart set on and couldn't wait to have in her room, didn't show up because the manufacturer had said there was a mix-up and it had been discontinued, Charlie had taken her to a furniture store in the next town and spent hours with her, making jokes to cheer her up while finding an alternative. There were so many memories from last year filling her mind, and every single one of them was amazing.

"I feel like I'm finally alive," he said.

Scarlett knew exactly what he meant.

"I love this life we've made for ourselves over the last year." There was no hesitation in his voice, his honest eyes upon her. "I never want to lose it. You make me a better person, Scarlett. You see the best in things, and you always have hope that everything will work. And the crazy thing is, somehow it does." He laughed at the thought. "You make me feel like I can do anything as long as you're by my side."

Then, he began to move, kneeling in front of her, his hand going into his pocket. Scarlett's pulse rose, her complete adoration for him nearly more than she could bear.

"Stay with me on this journey," he said, his fingers trembling around the small box in his hand. He opened it up, revealing an enormous solitaire diamond, set in a platinum band. "Marry me."

"I love you," she said, taking his hand and pulling him to a standing position. "Yes," she said, tears of happiness coming to her eyes. "I can't wait to marry you."

Charlie slipped the ring on her finger and there in the middle of a million Christmas lights, he kissed her. She'd never felt safer or more cared for than she did right then. Life could only get better from this moment. But Charlie pulled back sooner than she would've liked.

"I'm not finished," he whispered in her ear, giving her a shiver. "It's cold out here. I need to warm you up." He scooped her into his arms, making her squeal as he carried her back into the house. "You need some warm blankets," he said, kissing her hands as she reached for his face to kiss him again. When they got back up to the door, he set her down. "Follow me." Charlie led her inside and down the hallway to the place where the old bedroom with all the books had been. It had now been expanded into the other room to make one large space, and when she saw what was in it, her mouth dropped open.

"No way," she said, turning to him. "The furniture guy *lied*?!" She clapped her hand over her mouth, unable to stop the laughter that was escaping. Her dream bedroom suite was completely assembled in the room and topped with the most luxurious bedding, masses of throw pillows piled on top. "I gave him a free weekend at any Crestwood resort if he told you that. It only took a few calls to the regional managers of the resorts to ask for a favor."

"I can't believe you!" she scolded him lightheartedly, while spinning around in the room. "It's incredible."

"I figured it would be easier to put the furniture in the room where it was meant to be..." He winked at her and caressed the finger that donned her engagement ring.

"You certainly were sure of yourself," she teased, unable to hide her happiness.

"Nah, it wasn't that. What I *was* sure of was that I didn't want to live a minute more without you. So by making this room, I was manifesting my destiny," he teased back, grabbing her and pulling her to him playfully, but as he looked down at her, he became serious. "And then I just prayed you felt the same way."

In the old house where Amos had lived with unfulfilled wishes, Charlie took his fiancée into his arms and kissed her one more time, the promise of a family filling those walls lingering all around them on that special Christmas Eve.

A Letter from Jenny

Hi there!

Thank you so much for reading *Christmas at Silver Falls*. I really hope you found it to be a festive, heartwarming getaway!

If you'd like me to drop you an email when my next book is out, you can sign up here:

www.ItsJennyHale.com/email/jenny-hale-sign-up

I won't share your email with anyone else, and I'll only email you when a new book is released.

If you did enjoy *Christmas at Silver Falls*, I'd love it if you'd write a review. Getting feedback from readers is amazing, and it also helps to persuade other readers to pick up one of my books for the first time.

If you enjoyed this story and would like a little more Christmas cheer, check out my other winter novels: *Christmas Wishes and Mistletoe Kisses*, *It Started with Christmas*, and *A Christmas to Remember*.

Until next time!

Jenny xo

Acknowledgments

Giant hugs must go to my editor, Natasha Harding, and to the incredible team at Bookouture for all their creative vision and hard work on this novel. There is no other team with which I'd rather work.

Thank you to Oliver Rhodes for his vision and continued guidance. He is incredibly generous with his time and patience, and has helped to point me in the direction of success over and over again. I am still writing today because of his support.

To the Hudson Five—you know who you are! Thank you for a lovely family trip to the Smoky Mountains, where I pulled together the inspiration for this novel. It was a blast!

I am forever grateful to my husband, Justin, who watches the kids, does the laundry, gets groceries—anything I ask, to give me writing time when I'm under deadline. He is my rock, my emotional support, and my time manager, who keeps the house running while I daydream for a living.

About the Author

Jenny Hale is a *USA Today* bestselling author of romantic women's fiction. Her novels *Coming Home for Christmas* and *Christmas Wishes and Mistletoe Kisses* have been adapted for television on the Hallmark Channel. Her stories are chock-full of feel-good romance and over-flowing with warm settings, great friends, and family. Grab a cup of coffee, settle in, and join the fun!